"How Geri begins to drink and what it does to her and sometimes even for her is superbly handled . . . The voice of Geri Peters is an authentic one. I think you should listen to her."
—Eugenia Thornton, *Cleveland Plain Dealer*

"Sandra Scoppettone skillfully 'gets inside' Geri, helping the reader to understand her . . . Geri's funny, touching story will interest readers of all ages."
—*San Francisco Examiner-Chronicle*

"THE LATE GREAT ME is a book which will make us all more aware of a problem that is growing around us. It will help us grow in our own understanding and awareness."
—*Best Sellers*

THE
LATE GREAT
ME

Sandra Scoppettone

BANTAM BOOKS
TORONTO • NEW YORK • LONDON • SYDNEY • AUCKLAND

F
Scop

*This low-priced Bantam Book
has been completely reset in a type face
designed for easy reading, and was printed
from new plates. It contains the complete
text of the original hard-cover edition.*
NOT ONE WORD HAS BEEN OMITTED.

RL 5, IL age 11 and up

THE LATE GREAT ME

*A Bantam Book / published by arrangement with
G. P. Putnam's Sons*

PRINTING HISTORY

Putnam edition published January 1976
Bantam edition / February 1977

2nd printing .. February 1977	7th printing .. February 1980
3rd printing ..... April 1977	8th printing ... October 1980
4th printing .. September 1977	9th printing . September 1981
5th printing .. November 1978	10th printing ... October 1982
6th printing .... August 1979	11th printing ... October 1984

*The writing of this book was made possible through
a grant from the Ludwig Vogelstein Foundation, Inc.*

PRINTED IN THE UNITED STATES OF AMERICA

H   20 19 18 17 16 15 14 13 12 11

3782 HL

For Gloria Safier,
my indefatigable agent

1

"You've got to be *some*body, Geri. You can't be *no*body . . . you've got to be *some*body," my mother was always saying. She was also always saying, "You don't want to be president of a lot of leftover people," which is a line from *The Member of the Wedding,* a play she saw when she was fourteen and obviously never forgot. The other thing she was always saying to the point of driving a person bananas was, "You have to be popular, Geri. If you want to get along in this world you must be popular. A person has to have all-round popularity." Now this "all-round popularity" stuff was something from 1954, which was the year she graduated from high school. Don't ask me why they couldn't say all-*a*round popularity if they had to say it at all! As far as I'm concerned, my mother never got past the year she graduated from high school—emotionally, that is. She was stuck somewhere between 1946 and 1954 and it almost drove me nuts!

I don't want to give the impression that I hate my mother or anything. I definitely don't. Now. I guess I did at one point. I don't guess. I know. I hated her. A lot! Now I've come to understand her a little and I feel sorry for her. I don't mean I pity her—pity is actually contempt. I feel sorry for her because I understand her pain. Besides, she's changed. I guess I even love her.

You probably think, since I've been raving on and on about my mother, that I don't have a father. You probably think I come from a broken home. Isn't that a dumb expression? Broken home! Whenever I hear it I get this mental picture of a house with a zigzag line down the center and tears dripping from an upper window on each side. Of course, maybe that's because I often think of things as cartoons. That's because someday I'd like to be a cartoonist. Anyway, back to dear old dad! They weren't divorced and he wasn't dead. He was THERE. And that was just about it. At least that's the way it was before everything blew up.

My father was the exact opposite of my mother. While my mother practically never stopped talking, my father hardly ever said anything. He was of the school that spoke if he had something important to say but saw no point in idle chitchat. My mother believed that if a story was worth telling once it was worth telling two or three or even four times. My mother said my father had "B.P." That means "bad personality"—another little expression from the fifties! I often wondered why she married anyone with B.P. Of course, maybe he didn't have B.P. when they got married. I can't believe that my mother would deliberately pick someone to marry who had B.P. After all, she had a choice of seven or eight, although by the time she met my father she had, as she said, "given them all the gate!" I once drew that on an anniversary card when I was about ten. I drew a row of seven stick figures of men and a stick figure of a woman holding out to them a gate tied with a red ribbon! Underneath it said "Happy Anniversary." Neither of my parents understood it and I was crushed and cried for hours. Anyway, I guess my father developed B.P. over the years. The really interesting question was, if he didn't have B.P. when she married him, did he get B.P. *because* of her or *in spite* of her? You know what I mean? It's something I could ponder for hours. My father, George, was an engineer and his interests were engineering, baseball, football (as a spectator), reading mystery novels and doing crossword puzzles. My mother, Virginia—better known as Ginger—hated engineering, baseball, football, mystery novels and crossword puzzles. Her interests were movies—the one thing we had in common—music from the fifties, reading best-sellers, living in the past and playing bridge. My father, and this should come as no surprise, hated all of those things. They say that opposites attract, and I guess they do, but what's the point? My parents were complete opposites and they were very unhappy people. If and when I ever get married, or involved, I'm going to make very sure that we have lots of things in common.

The only thing my parents had in common was their children: me and my brother. He's eighteen now and in his freshman year at Harvard. We're fourteen months apart. I'm younger. His name is Jack. I guess you could say he was just about perfect. *You* could say it. I couldn't. My mother certainly said it—over and over and over. And my father looked it, if you know what I mean. Whenever he looked at Jack he sort of lowered his eyelids and nodded to himself at if to say "Ah, yes . . . perfect."

Jack was a football, basketball, baseball and swimming star. He played the guitar, sang with perfect pitch, composed his own songs and was the lead in the senior play. He had an A average, was valedictorian of his graduating class, went steady with Barbara Hagerman, the prettiest and smartest girl in school, but was sensible enough to know that when he went to college it would be the end of his relationship with her. During his senior year he had his own car which he bought with his own money earned working in his spare time as an assistant mechanic at a local garage. He was a great carpenter, wrote poetry and, God knows, he had "all-round popularity." In short, he was perfect and I found him revolting. However, he did have one small failing, if you choose to call it that, and I certainly did. He was a raging hypochondriac! When he watched medical programs on TV, which he managed to find the time to do, he always developed the symptoms of the disease he'd just seen. In his last year at home he was convinced that he had leukemia, myasthenia gravis, leprosy, lupus, and Parkinson's, to mention only a few. Now I happened to think this was very neurotic and made him definitely less than perfect. However, my mother said it was because he was so sensitive he couldn't help identifying. Actually, it was the only thing I liked about him. It made him human.

The last members of the Peters family were Tansy, Max and Sophie, two Yorkshire terriers and a cat. Tansy, the mother of Max, was also called Tan, T, Teetle or Miss Berger. I'm not even going to bother to explain the last. You'll just have to accept it. She was not what you'd call beautiful. In fact, she looked quite insane. Her hair stuck out in all directions and, quite often, the expression on her face was a leer, if you can picture that. My mother thought she was gorgeous. Other people, looking at both dogs, would say, "Oh, what a cute little Yorkie [Max]. And what's this [Tan]?" By that I guess it's clear that Max, whose full name was Maximillian Richard, was really the gorgeous one. He was also quite bright and his mother was not. He was as docile as she was stubborn and as lovable as she was annoying. Sophie was a marmalade cat, part Persian with a tail like a squirrel's. She was magnificent, always distributing kisses and striking incredible poses. She also gave her name to the Sophie Ratings. You've heard of the Neilsen ratings for television programs? Well, in our house, we had the Sophie ratings. If you'd rather watch Sophie for sixty minutes the program really stunk.

So that was the Peters family unit. They could have put us on TV—as a series. We were the all-American family because, at the core, like every other typical American family, there was rot. This past year was the worst year of our lives. I'm going to tell you about it, but first let me fill you in on me.

I turned seventeen in July and am in the second half of my senior year, which is practically a miracle. I'm very short, five feet one and three-quarters, and I weigh one hundred and ten pounds. At one point last year I weighed one hundred and forty-five! I have brown hair, which I wear long and straight. My eyes are also brown. I am not ordinary-looking, but I'm also not unusual-looking. I have dimples, which I dearly love and I'm very fond of my nose, which is straight and the proper size for my face. My mouth is just a mouth, which I do not color red or any other color. I now have one chin. Last summer I had two! I am interested in movies, books, music and most of all, art. I like boys. I used to be very, very shy. Now I'm just shy and learning, day by day, one day at a time, to be less so. I will never, never have "all-round popularity" but I don't care. At least I don't have B.P. I am, I have discovered, many things. I am a young woman, an artist, both considerate and inconsiderate, generous and selfish, funny and sulky, rigid and open, arrogant and humble, and absolutely, definitely, without any doubt a drunk. My name is Geri Peters and I'm an alcoholic and I think you should know about it.

2

"That's what you're going to wear on the first day of school?" my mother asked.

"It's probably what I'm going to wear every day of school," I said. "Or at least something like it."

She slammed a bowl down in front of me. Whatever was in the bowl, some kind of breakfast cereal, hissed and booed at me. Have you noticed that cereals are becoming very aggressive lately? They used to just snap, crackle and pop. Now they do everything but bite back. I have this vision that one day I will sit down to breakfast and two hundred squares of corn or wheat will be giving me the finger!

"When we were in school," my mother was saying, "we *dressed*. Sometimes we even wore stockings . . . with seams."

Mother knew perfectly well that jeans and shirts were the accepted thing to wear. She had seen me go to school in them day after day, year after year. She had this thing of playing dumb, acting as though it was the first time she saw or heard something so she could launch into a reverie about her past.

My father, Jack and I looked at her for a moment until we saw the glaze come over her eyes. Knowing that meant a long speech on the fifties, we dove back into our sneering cereal. Not that it would make any difference. Mother didn't need an attentive audience. Sometimes I wondered if she needed an audience at all. It wouldn't have surprised me if she'd spent her afternoons telling the dining room chairs about the heart-breaking quality of Johnny Ray's songs, and the sofa and coffee table about adorable Teresa Brewer and something called "Music! Music! Music!" I say "something" because that's probably what it is to you. *I* know very well what "Music! Music! Music!" is. Mother kept all of her old 78 records and I've been raised on them. From a person named Frankie Laine to a person named Jo Stafford I am an expert!

Meanwhile, back at the cornflakes shoot-out, Mother was raving on and on about the beauties of cinch belts and peasant blouses or some such thing.

Daddy rose from the table. "I may be home late, Ginger. Meeting."

She nodded and looked me over again as I stood up. "The idea of wearing, dirty, filthy, patched, ugly jeans to school is simply beyond me."

"Ah, don't let it get you down," I said.

"Are you gonna ride with me?" Jack asked.

I told him I was if he didn't mind having a dirty, filthy, patched, ugly-jeaned person in his car.

As we pulled out of the driveway we could hear the first strains of Eileen Barton singing "If I Knew You Were Comin' I'd of Baked a Cake." They had real message songs in the fifties!

For eight blocks I rode in the front seat of Jack's '67 red Volkswagen. He called it "The Red Baron." Sometimes I wondered if there wasn't a lot of Mother in Jack! We stopped in front of the Hagerman house and Jack beeped his horn four times. The reason it was four times, and Jack would have died if he thought I knew, was because each beep stood for a word. The words were: Do you love me? The reason I knew was because I am not a moron. When Barbara got into the car she always said: "Yes, I do," before she said anything else and then they both grinned at each other like two idiots. To them, I suppose, it was a code only the CIA could break. To me it was elementary and sickening. I climbed into the backseat while we waited for Barbara. Finally she came gliding down the walk. Have you ever noticed how beautiful people glide everywhere they go? It's as though they're wearing invisible ice skates. I, on the other hand, move as though I am wearing invisible tin cans. Remember when you were little and you attached strings to tin cans and held the strings and walked on the cans? Well, that is the way I walk all the time.

"Yes, I do," Barbara said as she got in the car.

They grinned.

I groaned.

"Hi, Geri," she said. "All ready to start your junior year?"

"Yes," I said. Yes. That was all I could say. I simply could not talk to people like Barbara Hagerman. In fact, there were not too many people I could talk to. But the Barbara Hagermans of this world were almost impossible. She was the female Jack. Perfect. Glib. Slick. She always knew what to say and when to say it. She could talk small talk. I could not. I mean what can a person say when someone says, "All ready to start your junior year?" You can say yes, or you can say no. What would you say? I had said yes.

And she said, "Good. It's an important year, you know. Much more important than your senior year in a way. If you get a lot of your credits out of the way and make good grades you won't have any problems getting into college. Then you can sail through your senior year. Junior year is for work . . . senior year is for fun."

All that to my yes. What if I had said no? I wished I had just to see what she would have said. Actually, I knew. She would have said almost the same thing but instead of starting with "good" she would have said, "Oh, Geri, that's no attitude to take." The rest would have been the same. The point is there would have been an answer—something for every occasion—the art of small talk. But who needed it? Not me, I told myself. I had other things, like my mind and my art and good books. Barbara, and people like her, were basically shallow while I was deep. They needed the superficial things. I did not.

Barbara and Jack babbled away about the wonderful fun year that lay ahead of them. I thought of the year ahead of me and tried to be honest. Another thrilling year of creeping around the halls trying to be invisible and sharing small secrets with my two friends Carolyn

Rysko and Betty Jean Drumm, better known as B.J. They were perfectly nice girls but, like me, no balls of social fire. I suppose we were attracted to each other by our mutual creepiness.

I realize I'm giving you a terrible impression of myself. Let me clear it up. I am not, in the true sense of the word, a creep. Although it may appear to the naked eye that I am, deep down inside and in my head, I am not. It is just that I am shy or, rather, at the time I am telling you about I was shy—horribly, painfully, grotesquely, twistedly shy. And when people are that shy they often appear to be creeps. So the truth is that I appeared to everyone in Walt Whitman High School in Goose Bay, New York, with the exception of one Carolyn Rysko and one B.J. Drumm, to be a number one, certified creep. Believe me, there are easier things to live with. So you can imagine that the prospect of another year as Head Creep didn't hold great joy for me. If only the world could know the inner me. If only the inner me could become the outer me. I pictured my body turning inside out. Disgusting. Anyway, if the inner me could become the outer me I too could jump into some boy's car and say "Yes, I do!" Is that what I wanted? I didn't have time to answer the question because, at just that moment, we pulled into the parking lot.

The junior class's homeroom this year was the library. Our homeroom teacher was Mr. Kelly, who taught biology and always seemed to look at you with one eye squinting as if he were looking through a microscope. I had had him in my sophomore year and I was not his favorite student. I sat at a table near the back of the room, waiting for Carolyn and B.J. and watching all the other kids greeting each other. They all seemed to be miniatures of Jack and Barbara. Of course, they weren't. There were five groups in school: the jocks, greasers, straights, juicers and freaks. Both boys and girls made up each group. The jocks, of course, were the athletes. Greasers were the car jockeys and their girls. Straights were the perfect people, the beautiful ones like Jack and Barbara. They were often jocks, too. The juicers were the drinkers—big booze parties on Friday and Saturday nights, often in the afternoons, and, I was to learn later, frequently during school hours. The freaks were the hardest to define. They were everybody who didn't fit into any of the other groups, I guess—pot smokers, loners and creeps, to name a few. Yes, you guessed it. I was a freak! Not that that meant I *belonged* to any group. Oh, no. Freaks were so freaky that they didn't even hang around together. It was just that the other four groups, being a product of middle-class America, had the need to label everybody, and so they lumped us all together in the group called freaks. It didn't matter that practically none of us associated with each other. We were still a group by their standards.

Anyway, as I watched them file in and greet each other, they all looked like wonderful, happy, perfect types to me, even though I told myself that this one was dumb, or that one was trash and the next one was immature. I was so lost in putting each one down (I know now I was really lost in envy) that I didn't notice anyone sitting next to me until he spoke.

"Do you like the Stones?" he asked.

"Huh?" I said, one of the clever responses I had at my fingertips.

"The Stones. Do you like them?"

It so happens that I do. "Yes," I said. The wonderful world of *yes* again. But this time I had an excuse —sort of. I mean, it wasn't every day that a handsome boy sat down next to me and then spoke—to me. I was in shock. Obviously, this guy was new to Walt Whitman. I knew everyone in school even if they didn't know me.

"My name is Dave Townsend and I think you should know me." He held out his hand.

I took it. I thought I should know him, too, but I wondered what he'd think when he found out what the score was. I mean, looking the way he looked and coming on the way he did, he was obviously going to be a jock or a straight or both.

"I'm new," he said.

"Yes."

"Aren't you going to tell me your name?"

"Oh, yes, sure. Geri Peters."

"Nice name."

"You think so?"

"Sure . . . don't you?"

"Well, I. . . ."

"I bet you've always hated it," he said.

I had. "How do you know?"

"Psychic," he said, and smiled from one side, a thing to make your very heart melt.

I wanted to ask if he really was psychic, because I definitely believe in that. But just as I was deciding how to ask, Carolyn and B.J. came squealing and shrieking over to our table. I had never, in all my life, hated any two people like I hated my two best friends at that moment.

How should I describe Carolyn and B.J.? Truthfully, I suppose. Well, to begin with, Carolyn looks about forty-five and B.J. about forty! By this I don't mean that they are mature-looking, just old. In Carolyn's case part of it, I think, has to do with the fact that she is enormous—not fat, although it wouldn't hurt her to trim down a little, but huge all over. For example, the Cougars, our football team, could have used her at halfback last season. She is five feet nine and one-half inches and still growing. But most of all she has a very big face—big nose, big eyes, big chin—big face. Nothing looks out of proportion because it is all big, except her mouth which is hardly there at all. This spoils her looks. If she had a mouth that matched the rest of her, Carolyn wouldn't be a bad-looking big person. I mean, there is nothing wrong with being big, and who says that all women must be small and dainty? Actually, everyone says it. But that's wrong. If Carolyn had a little more mouth she would be a very attractive enormous person. Anyway, to me, her personality makes her attractive and I hardly notice her mouth unless I am describing her or drawing her. She is a very kind and generous friend with a good sense of humor. After graduation Carolyn wants to become a mortician. I guess a lot of people would think that's creepy. My mother, for instance, finds it repellent. But, of course, she would. You have to have some kind of maturity to face the idea of death. Carolyn faces it and intends to keep facing it for the rest of her life. She says she has no particular talent and she wants to make money so she can get out of Goose Bay. Most of all, she wants to travel, and if she is a mortician, she says, she can work anywhere, make money, take off for a year traveling, and then settle anywhere she wants for another year. You probably won't believe this, but there is nothing morbid about Carolyn. Her plans are simply practical. Carolyn is a life-lover and the kids in Walt Whitman High would adore her if they could get past her hugeness. Why is everyone so shallow?

B.J. is quite small. She is a quarter of an inch shorter than I am. I can't explain exactly why she looks forty years old. Maybe it's because she is the oldest of nine brothers and sisters and feels as though she has raised them all single-handedly. When you look at B.J. for the first time you think that she is heavily lined. Of course, she isn't, but you feel that because she is so serious. B.J. doesn't have much of a sense of humor but that's often what makes her so funny, if you know what I mean. She works very hard at school because, more than anything, she wants to go to college so she can have a room of her own and some privacy. Her father has promised that if she gets top marks he will pay extra so she can have a room by herself. Another reason B.J. wants to go to school is because she wants to be a veterinarian. She loves animals, sometimes, I think, more than she loves people. Her father and mother have given her part of the barn for a small out-patient clinic. Where we live, animals are always getting hurt by cars or hunters or other animals. When B.J. finds them, she takes them to Dr. Safier, the vet, and after he's fixed them up, she brings them to her clinic and they come and go until they are ready to go permanently. It sounds crazy, doesn't it? I mean that they would come and go? But they do. B.J. has a way with animals. It's as if they know they're in this clinic until they're well enough to go home. Something magical happens in B.J.'s clinic because once she had a cat, a sea gull and a baby raccoon at the same time, and they all got along. She has the touch.

So there they were, shrieking and squealing as they approached us, the mortician and the vet, looking older, bigger and more forbidding than they had ever looked.

"Geri, Geri, guess what?" Carolyn screamed. "He spoke to me . . . he actually, genuinely spoke to me!"

"He really did, Geri . . . honest," B.J. added.

And then they saw him. And he certainly saw them. He didn't look horrified, he just looked stunned. Well, now I knew the jig was up. I mean, the combination of the three of us—there was just no way that Dave could not know we were freaks!

Both B.J. and Carolyn hovered over the table, gawking at Dave.

"Who spoke to you?" he asked.

"Stan Karanewski." Carolyn answered as though she'd been hypnotized.

"Lucky you," Dave said.

"Is he a friend of yours?" B.J. asked.

"Never heard of him."

B.J. furrowed her already old brow. "Then why did you say 'lucky.' . . ."

"A joke, B.J., a joke," I broke in. B.J. is very literal. If you say a thing you must mean it—that is her creed. Sometimes it can be very annoying. "Are you going to sit down or what?"

They sat down, Carolyn next to Dave and B.J. next to me. I introduced them. At that moment Mr. Kelly rapped on his desk.

"All right, animals, let's have a little quiet."

Mr. Kelly believed that all people were animals until they reached the civilized age of thirty. B.J., of course, thought this highly objectionable because she found animals far more civilized than people.

"Animals?" Dave whispered.

"He thinks it's funny," I said.

"A riot."

"Okay, Joey will pass out your schedule cards. Please copy them down because, after you sign them, they'll be collected, never to be returned. So the point is, animals, if you don't copy them down, you won't know where you're supposed to be when. Not that copying them will help most of you."

"Oh, he's a real card," Dave said.

"A thigh slapper," I added.

"What's that, Miss Peters?" Mr. Kelly asked.

All heads turned my way. I could feel the red creeping up my neck toward my cheeks. "Nothing," I said.

"That's what I thought. Okay, do this quickly . . . your first class is in fifteen minutes."

When I got my card I saw that my first class that day would be shop. This was the first year they were letting girls into shop and I wanted to be a pioneer. Anyway, I liked the idea of working with wood and making things. Besides shop, my other subjects would be history (American studies), chemistry (general), English (American novel), French 2, humanities, chorus and gym. Also, of course, I had study hall. There were six periods a day, forty-five minutes for lunch. Naturally, you didn't have every subject every day. I was pleased to see that some days I had study hall twice. I began to copy.

Dave leaned over and looked at my card. I turned to look at him and we were almost nose to nose. It was very embarrassing.

"I just wanted to see if we had any classes together," he said, pulling back slightly.

We examined our cards and found that our schedules were almost identical except, of course, for gym. Also, he was not taking chorus or shop.

"Good," he said, "we've got lots of classes together."

I nodded and tried a quick smile. We went back to copying. Maybe he was nuts! I mean, why did he care if we had classes together? He didn't even know me.

A few minutes later the bell rang. Dave said he'd see me second period and he was off. Carolyn and B.J. looked after him, then back at me. Before they could begin their millions of questions, I said:

"I don't know any more than you do except that he likes the Stones." Then I realized that I didn't even know that. He had asked me if *I* liked them. He never said that he did.

"The Stones?" they said in unison.

"Never mind. Come on, let's move."

We were all going in the same direction though not to the same class.

"He's really neat-looking," Carolyn said.

"Not bad," I said.

"Not bad?"

B.J. grabbed my arm and looked at me very seriously. "Geri, don't get your heart set on him. You know, I know and God knows that by the end of the day Beverly Maher or Joyce Fell or Joan Goldstein will have him wrapped around one of their little fingers. Geri, promise me, don't let this boy break your heart."

"I promise," I said and we parted company at the stairs. You see, that is a perfect example of how seriously B.J. takes everything. I mean, she wasn't fooling when she told me not to let this boy break my heart. She meant it with every fiber of her little body. Of course, it wasn't as though she was talking out of nowhere. There once was a boy who broke my heart. But I was much younger then and very foolish. I could tell you about it but what's the point? When something is over, it's over.

There were eight boys and me in shop class. I was stunned and also disgusted with my sisters that none of them had the courage or interest to break through the sex barrier and join me. I also felt very much alone— and unwanted! Eighteen eyes stared at me—those included Mr. Derrick's, the teacher—as though a walking pestilence had just entered the room. Have you ever felt hate like a thick gooey paste, a huge pot of it that you've just fallen into? Well, that is what the climate of the shop room was like.

Mr. Derrick made a speech about the tools, about the kinds of projects we could do and then went into a safety rap. I have to say, in all honesty, that I don't think I'd ever heard anyone more boring. The things he said weren't boring—I mean, they had to be said and they were informative—but the way he said them was. I suppose it was his rhythm. I believe there are two kinds of people in this world: slow rhythm and fast rhythm. It has nothing to do with intelligence. Some people speak quickly, react quickly, move quickly. Others do

the same things slowly. Usually, fast rhythm people are
attracted to slow rhythm people and it's a mistake.
Eventually, the fast R's get annoyed by the slow R's and
the slow R's begin to feel inadequate around the fast.
R's. Needless to say, I have fast R. Mr. Derrick had slow
R—very slow. He was also very, very white. There is
nothing worse than a very white slow R. He was so
white that he almost looked as though he didn't have
any features. In fact, his face looked very much like a
peeled potato.

When he was finished with his speech he started
asking what each person had in mind for a project. True
to type, he saved me for last.

"And what, eh, what will you, eh, be making? A
doll's house, eh?"

Naturally, guffaws filled the room. Mr. Derrick, as
you can see, was also a great wit.

I wished I could say something cutting to put him
in his piggy place. I knew the perfect response would
come hours later when I played the scene in my
head. It always did. What would you have said? I said,
"I don't know yet."

He grunted and shuffled through some papers. Then
he said since we couldn't begin today we were free to
talk quietly among ourselves for the next ten minutes.
Having no one to talk among, I spent those minutes
thinking about what I would make and about Dave. By
the end of the period I had decided to make a chest for
my art supplies and I had decided that the next time
I talked to Dave I would explain right off the bat that
I was not the kind of girl he wanted to get involved with.
That way I could avoid heartbreak.

Second period was English and Dave took a seat next
to me. Mr. Dolan was the teacher and I was thrilled with
that. He was probably the best teacher in the school. A
large man, very overweight, he had a great smiling face
and a shock of black hair that always hung in his eyes.
He was talking about the American novel and how
it influences our daily lives when a piece of folded white
paper flew onto my desk. A note from Dave. I opened
it on my lap. This is what it said:

Dear Geri,
How would you like to meet me tonight and go
for a drive or something? Since I just moved here
I don't know the places to go or what you guys
do. Maybe you could show me around.

                                                          D.

I couldn't believe my eyes. I read it a second time
to make sure I'd read it right. Dave was asking me for a
date! Immediately I knew this was the time to tell him
where I stood in Walt Whitman High. If I didn't, he'd
be told by someone else. B.J. was right. By the end of
the day Beverly or Joan or another of the jock/straight
girls would be leading him by the nose or finger or
whatever it was. By the last bell he'd be breaking the
date. To avoid heartbreak I composed in my head the
note I knew I should write. This is what it was:

> *Dear D.,*
> *Thank you for asking but there is something you*
> *should know. I am a Freak. You are committing*
> *social suicide by asking me out. If you want to*
> *have any life at all forget you ever met me. Better*
> *you should ask a leper! Have a good life.*
> > *Geri*

That was the note I knew I must write. This is the
note I did write:

Dear D,
Great! Where and when?

                                                          Geri

Heartbreak, here I come!

3

When the last bell rang Dave was walking right be-side me. Obviously, no one had gotten to him. There were a few moments right before lunch when I wondered if maybe I wasn't in some kind of dream world or enchanted cottage. Did you ever see *The Enchanted Cottage* with Dorothy McGuire and Robert (Dr. Welby) Young? It's a very, very old movie, made in the forties, I think. It plays on television a lot. Anyway, it's about these two very ugly people who fall in love and each thinks the other is terrific-looking. In other words it's about the eye of the beholder and all that. Well, it occurred to me that maybe Dave was really funny-looking and I was just seeing him the way I wanted to. Then, as we were walking to the cafeteria, I noticed quite a few girls turning around to look at him. Of course, that really didn't prove anything. They could have been looking at him because he was so ugly. But who could think that black curly hair was ugly? And those deep-brown eyes with the long lashes? And his small but perfectly proportioned nose—could that be considered ugly? Not to mention his full mouth. Put them all together they spelled gorgeous. So how come if he was gorgeous no one had nabbed him by day's end? I got the answer to that by the time we hit the street. We were standing in front of the school making plans for that night while I waited for B.J. and Carolyn.

"Look, Geri," he was saying, "I wish I could pick you up but my wheels are in the shop." He took a mouth spray from his pocket and squirted in into his mouth.

I thought it was kind of an odd thing to do in front of someone and I guess he saw that in my eyes because he smiled that one-sided smile and said, "I'm hooked. I love this stuff. I use about one a week. Ever try it? Open your mouth."

"No, that's okay," I said.

"C'mon, open up."

I opened up and he squirted me with something very wintergreen.

"Terrific, isn't it?"

"Yeah, it's okay."

"I love it." He gave himself one more squirt and then put it back in his pocket. "Anyway, as I was saying. . . ."

And then it started happening. A car pulled up next to us. I looked around and saw that Beverly Maher was driving and next to her was Joyce Fell. In the back were Joan Goldstein and Stan Karanewski.

"Hi, Dave," Beverly said. "Need a ride?"

"No, thanks," he said.

Beverly looked shocked and embarrassed and drove off with a screech of tires.

Of course, I was more shocked than Beverly. "How come?" I asked.

"How come what?"

"How come you didn't go with them?"

"What for?"

I was about to explain just who the four in the car were when two more jock/straights, Rachel Jacobsen and Liz Murray, stopped to talk.

"Hi, Dave," Rachel said. She had been eyeing him during history.

"Hi."

"This is my friend Liz Murray . . . Dave Townsend."

Liz wrinkled up her nose in what she thought was just the most adorable and cute expression and said, "Hi, there."

"Hi," he said coldly. "This is my friend Geri Peters."

"We know each other," Rachel said, looking as if she smelled rotting meat. Then: "Dave, we were wondering, would you like to go down to Ziegler's and have a Coke?"

"No, thanks," he said in a way that made further conversation almost impossible.

"Oh," said Rachel, stunned. She and Liz stood there, unable to say anything and, apparently, unable to move. Dave just stared at them. Then he put his arm lightly around my shoulder and started walking away from them with me. "See you," he said.

We had our backs to them so I couldn't see what they did, but I was sure I heard the word *freak* uttered between them several times before we were out of hearing range.

"Now where were we?" Dave asked.

"Dave, do you know who those girls are?"

"Rachel and Liz," he said.

"And the ones in the car . . . I don't mean their names."

"What *do* you mean?"

"I mean, *who* they are!"

"I don't get it."

"They're just practically the most popular girls in the school."

"So?"

"But. . . ." I was about to go into a long thing about the class system in Walt Whitman and then I realized that he really didn't care. I mean, Dave was no dummy and he had eyes. He probably knew all about it, maybe not our specific system, but he knew. And he didn't care. The reason he hadn't been nabbed by the last bell was that he didn't want to be. And the reason for that was a mystery. At least it was at the time. Now I understand that those girls were much too straight for Dave. And, instinctively, he saw something in me much more to his liking. He knew something about me that I didn't know. Not that I blame Dave for anything that happened. I really don't. It would have happened anyway. The point is, I was exactly what Dave wanted.

"So about tonight . . . could you pick me up?" he asked.

"I don't have a car . . . or a license. I don't even know how to drive."

"Oh. Well, could we meet somewhere?"

In Goose Bay it's almost impossible to get around without a car. I knew I'd have to get someone to drive me and I wasn't sure how I would accomplish it, but I didn't have time then to think it through. "Okay . . . where should we meet?"

"You tell me. It's your town."

"You know where the library is? Well, let's meet in front." Lots of the kids hung out on the library wall and it was a well-known meeting place for kids without cars.

"What time?"

"Seven-thirty."

"Right." he said and started to walk away.

"Hey," I yelled, not wanting him to go quite yet.

He turned.

I had nothing to say so I said the first thing that came into my head "How will I recognize you?" I asked.

He liked that because he smiled slowly and a funny twinkle came into his eyes. "I'll be the one with the carrot sticking out of my left ear." He waved and walked down the street.

Let me say just a few words about the place Dave had called my town. It's one of ten small villages on what is known as the East Shore, which has a population of about seven thousand, but in the summer it swells to about seventeen thousand. The summers are good for small businesses, real estate, and getting a tan. There isn't much to do unless you want to play miniature golf or go to one of the three movie theaters that change their films only once a week. (In the winter, by the way, we have two theaters.) Lately they've been showing these horrible movies with titles like *Bite My Crotch* and *Sisters of Sodom, Guys of Gomorrah*. They are what's known as soft-core pornography and are really boring. Although you're not supposed to be allowed in until you're seventeen, everyone gets in.

Anyway, the summer is better than the winter because it *feels* like there is more to do. There are auctions (boring) and fairs (seen one, seen them all) and yard sales and yard sales and yard sales and yard sales. And there is a summer stock theater of horrible amateurs who put on things like *Arsenic and Old Lace* or *On Borrowed Time* or, if they're feeling very adventurous, *Ten Little Indians*. I can't imagine how they can afford to continue because nobody ever goes. So, as you can see, it's really all an illusion. There isn't anything much to do in the summer either. Why people come here for vacations is beyond me. I suppose it's the water. We stick out right in the middle of the bay. All the frenzy, the swell of people, starts on Memorial Day weekend and ends on Labor Day weekend. Then we go back to normal.

To give you an idea of what normal is like I'll tell you the headlines and front-page stories of one of our two local newspapers. It's called the East Shore *Times* and this front page was from a week in February. The biggest headline: OCEANHEAD TOWN TAKES STEPS IMPLEMENTING SEWER DISTRICT. Another smaller one: GOOSE BAY MAN SNAPS UTILITY POLE. A picture of a cracked-up car appeared above that. Every week there is a picture of a cracked-up car. SOUTH HOLLOW RESIDENTS ATTEND APPEALS BOARD HEARING. FISHERMAN PRAY FOR CHANGE IN THE WEATHER. EASTPORT FIRE DEPARTMENT TO HAVE CHICKEN DINNER. The most prominent picture was of an Irish setter sniffing a flower. The caption read: "Pearly Mae of New Nassau is seen here sniffing an early crocus. The early dog gets the crocus!" That is the East Shore *Times'* idea of humor.

Throughout the paper there is picture after picture of groups of people eating. That is all anyone seems to do here. There are pancake breakfasts, sliced steak dinners, fried chicken luncheons and anything else you can think of. And always, the people eating in these pictures are the fattest people you can imagine. Of course, there are an awful lot of fat people on the East Shore. It doesn't seem to matter what age they are, they are fat. They are also very white. My father says both these conditions exist because this is potato country.

There's no industry on the East Shore so unless you

farm, work in a local store or business or teach you have to commute at least sixty miles one way, if not farther.

Perhaps the most important thing to note here is that in 1972 ninety-five percent of the East Shore population voted for Nixon and if he were to run again ninety-four percent of the population would vote for him again. I really think that tells you everything you have to know about the area.

Anyway, B.J. and Carolyn arrived and we all went over to Carolyn's house which was around the corner from school. Both Carolyn's parents worked so we had privacy there except when Ralph, Carolyn's thirteen-year-old brother, decided to hang around, which wasn't too often, thank God.

We sat around the counter in the kitchen, drinking Cokes and eating ginger snaps.

"Since when can you go out on a date on a school night?" Carolyn asked.

"Since tonight," I said. "I mean, how do I know I can't? It's never come up."

"Well, where will you go? What will you do?" asked B.J.

"How do I know? Anyway, the important question is how will I get back to town by seven-thirty?"

"Can't Jack drive you? Or your father?"

"Why don't you say you're coming over to my house to study and then when whoever drops you off, just walk around the corner to the library."

"Because, Carolyn, even my parents are smart enough to know that there is nothing that requires heavy studying on the first night of school."

"So just say you're coming over to Carolyn's."

It was so simple that it really annoyed us when B.J. came up with it.

"Why don't you go groom a rabbit," Carolyn said.

"Carolyn," B.J. said, her face squished into a frown, "you don't groom rabbits."

"No kidding?"

So that was the plan I had in mind when my mother picked me up at Carolyn's at four-thirty.

4

When I got into the car Mother signaled me to be quiet by putting her finger up to her lips. WNEW, her favorite station, was on and they were playing Tony Bennet singing "Because of You." She wouldn't even start the car until the song was over. She just sat there looking as though Tony were sitting right on the dashboard singing just to her. I wondered who she was thinking about when she listened to the sickening words. Surely it couldn't be my father! And I was pretty sure my mother didn't fool around with anyone. It was probably some guy she had dated during high school, one of the ones who had written in her yearbook: "Dear Ginger—You are Debbie Reynolds, Marilyn Monroe, Jane Russell and Donna Reed all rolled into one. Stay as sweet as you are. Love, Bill." or Bob, or Joe. How anyone could think my mother was anything like any of those actresses, let alone all of them, was beyond me. Maybe whoever had written it was living in an enchanted cottage. The song ended and she started the car.

"Don't you just love him?" she said.

"No," I said. "I think he's goopy."

"What do you know . . . what do you kids of today know about anything? All you know is a lot of screaming and electric music. You don't know anything about real love songs."

I could have answered her, but I decided not to. I didn't want to get in a big hassle about Tony Bennett

24

and ruin my chances of going out that night. It wasn't worth it.

"How was school? Did you make any new friends?"

My mother was always hoping I would make new friends. She thought Carolyn and B.J. were losers and wished I'd find someone else to hang around with.

"Only about twenty or thirty," I said.

"You shouldn't lock yourself in to just two friends ... especially those two. You don't want to be president of a lot of leftover people, you know."

"Please don't start in on them."

"Imagine wanting to be a mortician," she murmured.

Fortunately, Rosemary Clooney began singing "Come on a' My House" at that very moment, so we had silence for the next three minutes. I don't know what my mother would have done without WNEW. Almost every other song they played was something from the past. When the song ended I took the opportunity to ask her about that night.

"I'd like to go back to Carolyn's after dinner," I said.

"Well, you can't."

"Why not? I think it's very bigoted of you to keep me from going there just because she's going to be a mortician. If the radical morticians heard about that they—"

"That's not the reason. Your grandparents are here."

My grandparents, my father's parents, lived about forty-five minutes away from us and when they came to visit about once a month, it was a big occasion. That's because my grandfather was the way he was— you'll see what I mean.

"I didn't know they were coming."

"Neither did I," she said.

"How long are they staying?"

"Just overnight. They'll leave early in the morning, as always."

"Well, I have to go out tonight."

"Why?"

"I just do."

"That's not good enough."

"I thought you wanted me to have all-round popularity."

"What could that possibly have to do with going back to Carolyn's?"

Earlier, I hadn't really known why I didn't want to tell her the truth, but now I knew. It was because she'd make a big deal out of it and drive me nuts.

"Well, she's sort of having a party."

"On a school night?"

We pulled into our driveway. "Not all parents are so sticky about school nights. Some parents are a little more with it than other parents."

"Are you trying to say that I'm fruity?"

In case you don't know, "fruity" or "fruit" was the fifties word for square. "I'm just saying that some people are different from other people."

"Very profound," she said.

We got out of the car and crossed the lawn. "The point is," I said, "you want me to have all-round popularity and meet people and everything and then you don't give me any opportunities to achieve these goals."

She stopped at the door. "Geri, there's no point in going on about it. Your grandparents are here and you'll have to spend the evening with them and that's that." She opened the door and went in.

I stood on the steps a moment thinking over what she'd said. It was true that in the past whenever my grandparents came I'd had to spend time with them. The thing is I knew if I told my mother the truth she'd be so thrilled a boy had finally asked me out, even if it was just to hang out at the library wall, that she'd find a way for me to go. But the price I would pay for that just might not be worth it. Then, of course, there were my grandparents themselves. I'll show you what I mean.

I went in the house and there they were. My grandfather, age sixty-six and behaving as though he were ninety, was sitting in a chair staring. My grandmother, age sixty-nine, looking fifty-nine and behaving like twenty-five, was chattering on and on at him. My mother was banging things around in the kitchen.

"There she is," my grandmother squealed, rising and coming toward me. "There's my sweetheart."

She threw her arms around me and hugged—hard.

Has anyone ever noticed that about grandmothers? No matter how old they are they seem to hug harder than anyone else. My other grandmother used to hug me so hard you could see the breath shoot out of me like a puff of smoke. I've observed it in other grandmothers, too.

Before I could even say hello, she went on. "Look, Ted, doesn't she look beautiful?"

"Too thin," he said from his chair.

I gently extricated myself from my grandmother and walked over to where he was sitting and bent down to kiss him. Now there was absolutely no reason that my grandfather couldn't get up. No real reason, that is. The only reason was in his head. When you're sixty-six and behave like you're ninety and think you're one hundred and ten, you don't get up. As I pulled back from him I saw the tears welling up in his eyes.

"Oh, God, God, God," he mumbled.

"Ted, please, don't start," my grandmother said.

"I can't help it."

"What's wrong?" I asked. I should have known better but it was hard not to fall for it.

"I may never see you again," he snuffled.

"Ted," she said, "you're seeing her *now*."

"I could be dead tomorrow," he said, the tears running down his cheeks.

"We all could be dead," she said, her voice rising.

"You, Alice, will live forever." You couldn't miss the scorn in his voice. "Geri, Geri, let me look at my baby granddaughter . . . let me look at you for these last moments."

"Aren't you feeling well?" I asked stupidly.

"He's feeling fine." She stroked Sophie, who jumped into her lap.

"I'm an old man . . . there isn't much time."

"He's in perfect health."

"I could go like that." He snapped his fingers. "Thank God I have this one last night with you."

I groaned inwardly, guilt stabbing at my heart. I mean, *I* knew this was a routine of his and that he'd probably be around to be a great-grandfather several times over (Jack's children, not mine), but he didn't. Since I was determined to keep my date with Dave that night, I knew I'd have to tell my mother the truth.

"Will you excuse me for a minute, Grandpa? I have to talk to Mother for a minute."

"You make me sick," Grandma was saying to him as I started toward the kitchen. "I'm three years older than you are and I could dance all night. I could do cartwheels, go skiing, swim sixteen laps, run around the block sixty-five times. I could. . . ."

I shut the kitchen door behind me. Mother had her back to me and was stirring something on the stove. "I have to talk to you," I said.

"I'm listening."

"I lied to you. I don't want to go to Carolyn's tonight. I have a date."

If this had been a bad movie or a soap opera there would have been great chords of organ music as my mother slowly turned to face me, dripping tomato sauce from a spoon down her wrist and onto the floor. There would have been the sounds of birds chirping or a thousand violins trilling madly. The expression on her face—well, it was enough to make anyone throw up. Had I been drawing it I would have enlarged her eyes and put hundreds of little stars in them and painted her mouth like an upside-down rainbow. Even her nose seemed to be glowing.

"A date," she said in a syrupy voice, " a date . . . with a boy?"

"Yes."

"Oh, my darling." She remembered the spoon then and put it on the stove, led me over to the table and seated me as though I were forty months pregnant. The tomato sauce was still running down her arm but she didn't seem to notice.

"Tell me . . . tell me everything," she said, sitting across the table from me.

"There's nothing to tell . . . I haven't had the date yet." I could imagine the questions I was going to get *after* the date.

"Who is he? Where did you meet? What does he look like? Where is he taking you? Geri, you don't know . . . this is the moment I've been waiting for . . . a mother's dream come true . . . her daughter's first date . . . a moment of sharing . . . this is what having a daughter is all about. Tell me, tell me, tell me."

I told her.

"At the library wall? I don't understand. I mean, isn't he going to call for you? Aren't we going to meet him? Are you ashamed of him . . . of us?"

"His car's in the shop, Mother. How would he get here?"

"I don't know, but . . . when I was dating I never would have gone out with a boy who didn't call for me."

"Things have changed since you were dating . . . it's perfectly normal to have a date this way. Don't worry about it."

"Well, what are you going to do? Where is he taking you?"

"I don't know . . . we'll probably just hang out."

"Hang out?"

"Mother, I don't see why I have to go through an inquisition. I thought you'd be pleased."

"I am. But why on a school night, Geri? Tonight of all nights . . . your grandfather. . . ."

"I know, I know. That's why you have to clear it for me. I won't be home late or anything and it's really not like a school night. I mean, we don't have any homework or anything."

"All right. I suppose that's true. But you'll have to be home by ten. And, Geri, don't get serious . . . play the field like I did. That's the way to have fun. There was one night I had three different dates all in the same evening. There was Doug at seven and Jim at. . . ."

I'd heard the story many times before. "I hardly know him, Mother, so don't worry about it. I mean how could I be serious about someone I've known for less than twenty-four hours?"

"Stranger things have happened. Nancy Thompson met a sailor one day and married him the next. Of course, they're divorced now. That's what happens if you don't know the person you're marrying."

"I'm not going to marry him . . . I'm just going to hang out with him awhile."

"Hang out," she muttered.

"So I can go then?" I asked, getting up from the table.

She nodded. "Jack will drive you and pick you up. I'll talk to your father when he gets home. He won't be late after all."

"Thanks," I said. Now I knew I had to join my grandparents for a while. If I spent every minute with them until dinner maybe they wouldn't be too upset when I went out. I opened the kitchen door.

". . . walk on my hands crosstown on a hot summer day, play six sets of tennis, wash every window in the house in half an hour . . ." my grandmother was saying.

My grandfather was staring.

I sat down next to him.

He looked at me.

I looked at him.

Grandmother said, "Enjoy life, Geri. Think big, have fun, have a ball."

He said, "Expect the worst and you won't ever be disappointed."

What would you have said?

I said nothing!

At seven o'clock, as we finished dessert, my mother announced that Jack and I were going out. She said proudly that we both had dates. My grandfather began to whimper.

"Grandchildren who have dates. Do you know how old that makes me feel?"

"You *are* old," my grandmother said. "So what?"

"How could she be having a date? Just yesterday she was playing with dolls."

"I never played with dolls," I said. "I played with stuffed animals. I hated dolls."

"My daughter had a Shirley Temple doll," he said, and that memory made him cry.

Aunt Chris, my father's sister, had died three years before. She was really neat and I loved her a lot. Everyone did. She was driving back to New York from her house here when she was killed in a three-car crash. And that was when my grandfather became obsessed with death. Chris was his darling and he never quite got over losing her. Of course, he had always been on the negative side but nothing like he was now. Anyway, he adored his daughter and any reference to her made him really, genuinely sad.

"It's all right, Ted," my grandmother said, reaching out to hold his hand.

"I'm sorry," he said. "I miss her so."

My mother reached out and took his other hand. "We all do," she said and there were tiny tears in the corners of her eyes.

Nobody said anything for a little bit—I think we were all having our private memories of Chris—and then Grandpa cleared his throat, pulled his hands away from Grandma and Mother, and said in a teasing way:

"George, you had a Charlie McCarthy doll, but the thing you wanted most was a Sonja Henie doll! You begged and begged for one."

"Did you get him one?" Jack asked, grinning.

"Had to. Couldn't stand the howling. He slept with her until he was about eight."

Well, that just cracked Jack up and he was practically rolling on the floor when my mother cut off his laughter with a well-directed remark.

"I guess you've forgotten all about Baby-Sue, haven't you, Jack?"

Now I started laughing. Baby-Sue was this hideous rag doll that my mother made Jack when he was a baby. He carried that thing around, smelly and dirty as it was, until he was in the sixth grade—twelve years old.

"What's all this dumb talk anyway?" Jack said. "I thought we were talking about going out tonight."

"Yes," I said proudly. "Jack and I have dates."

"What kind of dates?" Grandpa asked.

"What kind of dates are there?" Grandma said.

"Are you going out with a boy?" Grandpa asked me.

"Yes." Why did they ask that? Did they think maybe I was going out with a goat?

"Just yesterday," he said, "I read in the paper where this nice quiet boy killed his girlfriend. He sang in a choir, was a boy scout, the whole works. Stabbed her seventeen times."

"My date's not a boy scout and he doesn't sing in the choir so I'm safe."

"Just don't let him get funny with you," Grandpa said.

"Papa, please," my father said.

When Mother said Dave wasn't picking me up, there was a whole scene about that. My grandfather said it was important to get a look at him to see if he was a murderer or not. My grandmother said that everyone was a murderer in his eyes. My mother said this was the way things were done now. My father said nothing.

As Jack and I were leaving the house my grandfather pulled me to one side and slipped me ten dollars.

"In case he gets funny with you and you have to take a taxi home. It's called 'mad money.'"

"Jack is going to pick me up," I said, trying to give him the money back, but he refused.

"Thanks for the money," I said and kissed him on the cheek.

As Jack and I drove off I looked back at the house and all four of them were standing on the steps, waving good-bye like we were going to Europe.

Jack and I didn't talk on the ride into town. We had very little to say to each other. I started thinking how awful it would be if Dave didn't show up. I suppose my grandfather's pessimism had gotten to me after all. It hadn't really occurred to me before this, but now that it had I began to feel very nervous. If he didn't show up no one must ever know. I'd make up a whole evening. I knew my mother would want to know every detail. If Jack dropped me off at the library wall and there was no one there he was bound to mention it. Of course I could always say that Dave had been late.

But what if Jack insisted on hanging around until Dave showed up? And he never did?

"You can drop me at Carolyn's house," I said.

"I thought you were meeting this dude at the library wall."

"Well, I have something to pick up at Carolyn's first."

"Okay. I'll wait and take you on," he said.

"*No.* I mean, you don't have to."

"I don't mind."

I knew then that either Jack was nosy at heart or Mother had instructed him to get a look at the boy. Either way, I knew Jack and he wasn't going to leave me until I had met Dave. There was no way out.

"Forget Carolyn's," I said.

By the time we got two blocks from the library I was convinced that Dave was not going to be there. As we neared the library panic overwhelmed me.

"Don't stop," I screamed. "Keep going . . . keep going!"

"What's the matter with you?"

"Just keep going."

He kept going.

"Keep going where?"

"Anywhere."

"Geri, I'm not going to drive you around all night. I have a date too, you know. I'm turning around."

I sank down in the seat. I couldn't look. "Couldn't we drive by once more and you can tell me who's there?"

"All right."

He made a U-turn and we drove slowly up the main street.

"Can you see?" I asked from my position below the window.

"Of course I can see."

"Well?"

"Ahhh . . . there's Willy Kirkham, ahh Jerry Blatt and . . . what the hell is that?"

"What, what?"

"My God."

"What is it?"

"Boy, the freaks are getting freakier all the time . . . there's some character sitting there with a carrot sticking out of his ear."

Smiling, I asked, "Left ear or right?"

5

"I'll get out here," I said. We were about a block past the library.

"You're acting very creepy," Jack said as he stopped the car

"I'm just trying to save you the trouble of turning around again. I certainly can walk one block."

"Okay. Now listen, you're supposed to be home at ten sharp so be at the wall at ten of ten . . . no slipups. You're cutting my night short so just don't goof off."

"I'll be there." Actually, I would have preferred it if he'd taken me home right then. Now that I knew Dave was there I was terrified—much more than if he had stood me up. I wished he had. It would be so much easier to make up a date for my mother than actually having to experience one. I got out of the car wishing it was ten of ten and I was getting back in.

"Just tell me one thing," Jack said. "What do you do with the carrot?" He started laughing and was practically falling over the steering wheel by the time he drove away. Well, it was obvious that he knew the boy with the carrot in his ear was my date. He'd be sure to tell my mother and, I suppose, everyone else. Actually, I didn't give a damn about the other kids in school —I mean, what they thought about a boy with a carrot in his ear. It was my mother I dreaded. I could hear her now.

"A boy with a carrot in his ear? Geri, how could you? In my day a boy would never have had anything in his ear but celery."

35

Oh, well, there was nothing I could do about it now. The wheels were in motion. Frankly, I thought it was hysterically funny that he had put the carrot in his ear. If I hadn't been paralyzed with fear I would have been doubled over with laughter. As it was, I could not even take the first step down the street toward Dave. What would we talk about? There were two hours and twenty minutes to fill. One hundred and forty minutes. Eight thousand four hundred seconds. I couldn't possibly think of anything to say to fill even five minutes of that time. Not even one minute. I should never have said yes. And what was wrong with my mother? It was her duty to keep me home on a school night.

I was just getting into a real hate for my mother and her lax rules when Dave turned his head and spotted me. He waved. I waved back and started walking toward him. What else could I do but put one foot in front of the other? I prayed that a car would come up the street, go out of control, and knock me down on the spot. Or that a mad dog would rush out from someone's yard and attack me. But nothing happened. I kept on walking, getting closer and closer to Dave who just sat there smiling, the carrot hanging out of his ear. Well, at least that was a conversation piece.

"Hi," he said.

I smiled. Some conversation piece. I couldn't think of a thing to say about it. Nothing I thought of seemed witty enough so I chose to ignore it. Willy Kirkham and Jerry Blatt were, thank God, so far down the wall they couldn't hear what we said—which was nothing. I stood in front of Dave, smiling like an idiot, and he smiled back. I guess he was waiting for me to say something about the carrot. When I didn't the smile faded from his face.

"So what do you want to do?" he asked.

I guess he was going to ignore the carrot, too. I wondered how long he would keep it in his ear?"

"I don't know," I said. "There really isn't much to do around here."

"Well, what do you usually do on dates? I mean, if there isn't a party or dance or something."

I couldn't tell him that I'd never had a date before

and I really didn't like to lie so I said, "Well, most of the kids hang out here, or go up to the beach and hang out, or Bohack's parking lot. But you have to have a car for that."

"The beach? That sounds good."

Maybe he *was* going to get "funny" with me!

"Is it far?"

"No . . . just two blocks up."

"Let's go."

He jumped down from the wall, turned around and picked up a brown paper bag that had been hidden behind him. When he grabbed it it took a kind of shape —like a bottle. I figured he'd brought a big bottle of Coke. We started walking toward the beach. I was walking on the inside so I couldn't look at him without the green top of the carrot brushing my forehead. I guessed that he had glued the carrot in his ear or something. Otherwise it couldn't have stayed there even though it was a small, skinny carrot. Now you might think that all the people we passed on the street would have looked oddly at Dave, or pointed, or laughed, or something. But if you knew Goose Bay you would never think that. They would have if it had been high noon or something—but this was seven-thirty at night and even though it was still light out there wasn't another soul on the street. That is the kind of town Goose Bay is. If I were to draw the main street I would draw all the buildings with their shades pulled and big ZZZZzzzzz's coming out of their chimneys. So there was no one to look at the carrot in Dave's ear except for me. We turned the corner.

"This is a really swinging town, isn't it?"

"You noticed," I said.

"A good town is hard to find," he said.

We walked in silence after that. The more we walked, and the more we said nothing, the more I wanted to run away from him. He hadn't been that quiet during the day. I guessed that maybe he was sorry he had asked me to meet him. Then it dawned on me that maybe he was mad that I hadn't said anything about the carrot. I mean, the fact that I hadn't mentioned the carrot forced him to keep it in his ear. It must have been very uncomfortable. But now it was so long after the fact that it was even harder to think of anything to say.

Finally we got to the beach. As usual, it was not empty. There were three cars in the parking lot, one of them Beverly's. The cars were empty which meant that the kids were probably sitting on the beach. I wondered if Dave would take out the carrot now? He did not. We walked through the lot, stopped at the edge of the beach to take off our shoes and went on. No one was in sight.

"Right or left?" Dave asked.

I shrugged.

He looked around a minute and then motioned left. There was a curve in the beach and a high dune so I guess he thought there would be more privacy on the other side of the dune. More privacy for what? As we rounded the dune Beverly and her gang came into view. Surely he would remove the carrot now. He did not. We kept on walking.

"Hey, man," Stan Karanewski yelled, "are you the Vegetable Man or what?"

"Talk about freaks," somebody said.

"Keep on trucking, Carrot Man."

"You better get your act together," said another voice.

Beverly and the other girls just kept laughing.

Dave stopped and bowed very low.

"That dude's flipped out."

I kept walking and Dave soon caught up with me. I could feel that my face was burning red. I hadn't thought I'd care what the other kids thought but I did —particularly when I heard Joyce Fell holler:

"Geri finally has a date and it's with a carrot freak!"

If only she hadn't said *finally* it wouldn't have been so bad.

"Bunch of stupid kids," Dave mumbled.

We rounded another bend and he indicated that we should stop. We sat down, facing the water. I felt his eyes on me, but I didn't dare look at him.

"You shouldn't care so much what other people think," he said.

"I don't," I said, too quickly and a bit too loud.

"Then why are you so red?"

"I'm not red."

"I guess I must be seeing things then," he said.

There was silence for a moment and then I heard him rustling with the paper bag. Suddenly a bottle appeared in front of me. It wasn't Coke. It was a bottle of Annie Greensprings wine. I looked at the bottle and then at Dave.

"Go ahead," he said, "you'll feel better."

"I feel okay."

"No you don't," he said. "You feel like hell. You're embarrassed and you wish the sea would swallow you up."

He couldn't have been more right. "How do you know?"

"I've been there," he said. He waved the bottle in front of me again. "Go ahead. It'll really make you feel better . . . I know. Sorry I don't have a glass."

I took the bottle and looked down into the opening. Strange it as may seem, I had never had a drink. No, that's not quite true. When I was five I finished up the dregs in all the glasses at a party my parents gave and I got drunk. I don't remember it but it's family lore. Apparently, I got very silly for about five minutes, doing somersaults and giggling, and then I started crying, then threw up, then passed out. But this was different.

"Go on," he urged.

I knew I shouldn't have, but something in his voice made me feel it would be all right. More than all right. I *believed* that I would feel better. Slowly I lifted the bottle to my lips and took a small sip. It tasted good —a little bit like very sweet grace juice.

"That's not enough to fill an eyetooth," he said. "Take a good swig."

I did. I felt it go down my throat and hit my stomach. It burned a little but I liked it. He held his hand out for the bottle but I didn't give it back. Instead I took another swig, much bigger this time.

"Hey, hey," he said, "not all at once. Take it easy."

I gave him the bottle.

He took a big swallow, two actually, and a little of

it dribbled down his chin. He wiped it with the sleeve of his shirt.

"Good stuff," he said, and passed the bottle back to me.

I took it, gladly. Another hefty swallow. This time I didn't feel any burning sensation, just a nice kind of warmth. I handed him the bottle and he put it in the sand. Slowly, I turned to face him. There he was, looking at me, an odd expression on his face, a small line of purple in each corner of his mouth, and the carrot sticking out of his ear. I couldn't take my eyes off the carrot. It looked even crazier than it had before. Finally, I looked back into his eyes. He had obviously seen me staring at the carrot and when our eyes met we began to giggle and then roar with laughter. We both fell back on the sand and finally, the carrot fell out of Dave's ear. We kept laughing as we lay there.

"How?" I said through my laughter.

"How to you to," he said.

"No, no. The carrot . . . how'd you keep it in?"

"Trade secret." He sat up and brushed some of the sand out of his hair. "You're pretty cool."

"Cool?"

"Yeah. I mean most girls would've dropped dead walking down the street with me like that. Or they would've asked me to take it out . . . or something. Mentioned it at least. You're a pretty cool customer."

I could have told him the truth—that I *was* a little embarrassed and that the only reason I didn't say anything was because I couldn't think of anything good enough to say—but if he wanted to think I was cool who was I to disillusion him?

"Well, you said you'd have a carrot in your ear, so. . . ." I shrugged. "But, come on, Dave, how'd you keep it in?" I wished he'd offer me some more wine.

"Gum."

I nodded, as if to say: of course. The bottle of wine was between us in the sand and I wondered if it would be all right if I just took it myself. It was his bottle and I decided I'd have to wait until he offered it. As if he had read my mind, he picked up the bottle and handed it to me.

"This is for you," he said.

I took the bottle and looked at him quizzically.

He reached in his back pocket and took out another smaller bottle. A pint (I found out the size later) something clear. Either gin or vodka, I figured. I couldn't see the label because his hand covered it.

"This is for me," he said. "That stuff"—he pointed to the wine—"is for beginners."

"What makes you think I'm a beginner?"

"Aren't you?"

"Yes, but how did you know?"

"I just could tell."

"How did you know I'd want to drink? How come you didn't ask out somebody else . . . somebody who already knows about drinking? Do you want to get me drunk and then try and make me?"

"Listen, you don't have to drink at all. I don't give a damn." He reached for the wine, but I held on to it. He smiled. "I thought you'd like it, that's all."

"But how did you know?"

"I can't explain it . . . just a feeling."

"Could I have been anyone?" I asked, starting to feel like a worm.

"What do you mean?"

"I mean, supposing you'd sat down next to some other girl . . . would you have asked her out tonight? Would you have brought her a bottle of wine?"

He shrugged. "It would depend on the girl. But let's not forget that *I* sat down next to you . . . you didn't sit down next to me. I could have sat other places."

"What made you sit next to me?"

"Oh, wow, you really are something. I need a drink." He unscrewed the cap on the small bottle and took a long swallow. "Ahhh . . . that's the real thing."

"What is it?"

"Vodka." He smiled at me and something about the way he licked his lips after drinking, something about the way he held the bottle in his hands, something about the look in his eyes made me feel slightly uneasy.

"You didn't answer me," I said. "What made you sit next to me?"

He stared at me for a few seconds and then, sort of smiling, he said, "Well, I'll tell you, Geri. . . . I took one look at you and I said to myself: 'Dave, old dude, there sitting at that table is the girl of your dreams. She is obviously a virgin and a nondrinker but' "—he held up a skinny finger—" 'she is also obviously just waiting for the right person to come along and change all that. So tonight you will take her out, pour liquor down her throat, rape her, and she'll thank you in the morning!"

"I don't think rape is funny," I said.

"Who's laughing? Look, Geri . . . what the hell is the big production? I asked you out because you seemed nice. You're nice-looking and I had a feeling you might dig a few drinks. How did I know? I can't answer you . . . it was just a feeling. What difference does it make? You wanna forget the whole thing, we will." He started to stand up.

"No," I said. He was right. What difference did it make? "I'm sorry . . . I didn't mean to hassle you. I just . . . well, sometimes I just get kind of crazy."

"Yeah, me, too."

"Forget it, okay?"

"It's forgotten. Drink up."

There was a moment, just a moment, like a kind of flash, when I think I knew that if I raised that bottle and drank my whole life would change. But maybe that's only hindsight. In any case, I did raise it because, in some way, I had no choice. Not just because I didn't want Dave to think I was chicken or a square, but because I *wanted* to—*had* to. Something inside me wanted to. I liked it. I liked the taste, although it was very sweet. But, especially, I liked the way it made me feel, even though I wasn't feeling that different—yet.

"Here's to good times," Dave said, raising his bottle.

I raised mine and we clinked them against each other.

6

"Okay, whoever throws farther wins," Dave said.

"I don't think this is a flair game," I said.

"Flair? Flair game?" He started giggling.

"Fair . . . fair game."

"Why isn't it a flair game?"

"Because." I had forgotten why. We were standing at the edge of the water, each with our empty bottles, and I couldn't remember why we were there or what we were going to do. All I knew was that I was feeling wonderful. The air smelled great and the spray from the water had never made me feel cleaner—or something.

"Because," I said again.

"Because is no reason. Now, we will throw these dead soldiers into the deep and whichever one throws farther wins."

"Wins what?"

"What difference does that make?"

I shrugged. It didn't make any difference.

"Ready?"

"No." I remembered. "This game is not fair. You got a smaller bottle and a bigger arm and I got a bigger bottle and a smaller arm."

"So we'll trade."

"Trade what?"

"Arms," he said.

Well, that really cracked me up and I fell down laughing and started rolling around. Before I knew it

I had rolled into the water. Then Dave was rolling around with me. It seemed like I was rolling and rolling forever. The only thing I kept thinking was that I had to hold on to my bottle. I don't know why that was so important but it was. And then I rolled into a big rock and I heard the bottle break. It was as though I had broken the most valuable thing in the world and I started screaming.

"I broke it, I broke it . . . oh, God, I broke it."

I could hear Dave laughing and I wanted to kill him. What was so damn funny? Didn't he understand that I'd broken my bottle. *My* bottle. Bottle, bottle, dottle, throttle, nottle—broken, soakin', bro—

"Hey, Geri . . . where are you?"

It was Dave. His voice seemed miles away. I had the neck of my bottle in my hand and I was crying.

"Geri . . . Geri . . ."

"I broke my bottle," I cried.

"Where are you?"

What did he mean, where was I? I was in the water like everybody else. *Everybody* else? Who was everybody? That made me laugh and I was laughing and crying at the same time. Then I decided to get out of the water and I stood up. Glub! The water was over my head and for a moment I panicked. But just for a moment. I was a good swimmer. I floated back up and started swimming toward shore. It was pretty dark—not many stars and the moon was clouded over, but I could tell I was swimming in the right direction because I swam toward the sound of Dave's voice. All I was worried about was losing the neck of my bottle. Finally, I felt myself scraping bottom.

"Geri . . . Jesus! I thought you . . . God. . . ."

Dave reached down and I took his hand with my free one. He pulled hard and dragged me along the stones at the edge of the beach. Then he fell backward and we both lay on the shore. I was out of breath, my heart pounding, and suddenly, without any warning, I felt myself vomiting. It just seemed to spurt out of me. At first I thought it was seawater but then I knew it wasn't. It happened three times and then it was over. Slowly I rolled to the side to get away from it. Now all I wanted was to go to sleep. I felt something tugging at my wet shirt.

"Sleep," I said.

"C'mon, we gotta go." It was Dave.

"Later," I said. I had never felt so awful. Wet, tired and sick. And my head. It was much too big for my body, I knew that for a fact. I would have to go to a head shrinker. Head shrinker! I started giggling. I wanted to tell Dave about my big head and that I would have to go to a head shrinker, but I knew it would take too much energy to get the words out.

"C'mon, Geri . . . don't be a drag. It's after midnight."

"So what?"

Then I felt him grab my hands and heard him yell.

"Oh, shit," he said, "I cut myself. Shit! Oh . . . goddamn it."

He had grabbed the broken neck of the bottle. Somehow his scream got to me and I pulled myself up on all fours. "Dave," I mumbled.

"I'm bleeding all over the goddamn place. . . . I'm gonna bleed to death."

I felt scared. I shook my head and sat back on my haunches. Dave was bleeding to death. There was only one thing to do. I took off my shirt and tried to tear it. It wasn't easy. I felt around for the broken bottle and used it to start a tear in the shirt. It ripped.

"Do something," he cried.

"I am, I am. Give me your hand."

I started wrapping the piece of shirt around his hand and tied it tight. "There," I said.

We sat for a moment, Dave staring down at his bandaged hand, me just staring. Then I realized I had nothing on on top. I didn't wear a bra. After scrambling around in the sand, I finally found what was left of my shirt. Fortunately, what I'd ripped was at the bottom so most of me was covered when I put it on.

"We gotta go," he said.

I remembered the other kids and wondered what they'd think when they saw us dripping wet and me with half a shirt. But when we rounded the bend nobody was there.

"Early night," I said.

"Huh?"

"Everybody's gone already."

"It's almost twelve-thirty," he said.

I stopped as though I'd been kicked in the stomach. Twelve-thirty! A million things started whirring around in my brain. My mother—my father—Jack waiting at the wall—police—oh, God, what was I going to do? Say? I turned to face him, grabbing his arm.

"Thanks a lot," I yelled.

"Huh?"

"I was supposed to be at the wall at ten of ten."

"You didn't tell me."

Of course he was right. I had never said when I had to be home. But I was mad and still a little drunk. "You should have known."

"What am I supposed to be, a mind reader?" he said angrily.

"Well, I'm only a little girl," I said and almost before the words were out of my mouth we both began laughing.

"Some little girl," he said. "You sure didn't put that stuff away like a little girl."

"Okay, okay But this is serious. What are we going to do?"

"I don't know."

"Well, I know one thing. I'm never drinking again."

"Yeah, sure," he said.

"I'm not."

"Okay . . . who's asking you to?"

We walked into the parking lot. There was a phone booth and I guessed the only thing I could do was to call home and ask somebody to come and get me. But what would they say when they saw me? And what excuse would I give for being so late?

"Maybe we should run away," I said.

"I've got fifty cents. How much do you have?"

"Well, what should I tell them? What will you tell your parents?"

"I come and go as I like."

"What am I going to do, Dave?" I wanted to cry, but I didn't want him to know what a creep I was.

"Okay . . . okay, I got it. You call your parents and tell them where we are. We'll say we were sitting on the beach, minding our own business, when a gang of motorcycle guys came along and . . ."

"On the beach?"

"They came *walking* along the beach. They came along and beat us up and knocked us out. Okay?"

"And what about the booze . . . I mean, they'll smell it, won't they?"

"We'll say they forced us to drink it—or poured it on us, or something."

It didn't sound very plausible to me, but just as I was thinking we didn't have much of a choice, we heard a car. Two headlights were coming toward us and on top of the car was a whirling red light.

"Oh, Christ," Dave said.

"Say," I said, "what do you have in mind for our second date?"

"Just stick to the story," he said quickly, "but let me handle it."

Suddenly he was running toward the car and waving his arms frantically. The police car stopped and the policeman got out. I followed Dave over to the car.

"Oh, thank God you've come, officer. Thank God," Dave said. He sounded like he really meant it.

"What's the matter, son?"

"Oh, it was terrible . . . just terrible."

"What happened to your hand?" Then he looked at me. "And you, what happened to you? My God!"

I hadn't realized I looked that bad. But in the light I saw I was wet, ragged, my shirt was covered with blood and what I guessed was vomit. There were hundreds of little barnacle cuts on my hands and arms, my jeans were ripped and my leg was bleeding.

"I'd better take you two to the hospital."

"Oh, thank you, officer."

"No," I said at the same time. "I mean, I'm not hurt enough to go to the hospital."

"You may have a concussion," Dave said.

"I don't think so," I said tentatively.

"After all, Geri, that big guy gave you quite a knock on the head."

"Come on, kids," the cop said. "Get in and I'll take you to the hospital. You can tell me about it on the way."

"My parents," I said weakly.

"Is your name Peters?" he asked.

I told him it was.

"We got a call for you."

Oh, God. I could imagine what kind of hysteria was going on in my house. The cop called into the station that he'd found us.

Dave sat up front and I sat in the back. I had never felt so sick or frightened in my life. And the more Dave talked the sicker and more frightened I felt.

". . . so then this big one, with a tattoo on his arm that said 'Born To Be Bad,' broke a beer bottle against a rock and came at me with it. That's how my hand got cut. Then they dragged us down to the water and made us stay there for hours . . . just lying in the water bleeding."

"You say there were ten of them?" the cop asked.

"At least . . . ten or twelve, wouldn't you say, Geri?"

He turned around, grinned, and gave me a wink.

"Maybe more," I said. "Fifty or sixty."

He stopped grinning and turned back to the cop. "She's still woozy," he said. "There were ten or twelve."

"What about the booze? You two smell like a gin mill."

"Oh, that. Well, after they took us out of the water they made us drink some stuff . . . I don't know what kind because I'm not familiar with liquor, but. . . ."

I stopped listening and tried to make myself as small as possible in the corner of the back seat. My head ached and my stomach was growling and feeling very empty, although the thought of food made me sick. All I wanted was to be in my own bed. Dave had gotten to the part where the big guy konked me over the head. I wondered what the doctor would say when he failed to find a bump. For a moment I thought about stopping Dave and telling the truth but the consequences of that seemed so much worse than anything else that I kept my mouth shut. Then I thought of jumping out of the car but with my luck I'd break something and have to face it all anyway.

We pulled up to the emergency entrance of the hospital. Maybe I could pretend I'd passed out so that I wouldn't have to answer any questions until I got it together more—but a doctor would know right away that I was faking. The cop opened the door.

"Okay, little lady. We'll get you fixed up now."

Slowly, I got out of the car.

"Soon as the doc checks you over I'll want you to make a statement. Okay?"

I could have said "I have no statement to make" or "don't hang by your thumbs" or "just try and make me, buster." What would you have said? I said, "Yes, sir, officer."

7

"No, Geri, this is not what I meant by all-round popularity!"

We were driving home from the hospital; my father, my mother and me. I was sitting between them in the front seat. If there is anything I hate more than sitting between my parents, especially in a car, I can't think what it is. I wanted to sit in the back seat, but she insisted I sit in the front between them. When my father bought the car I'd urged him to get one with bucket seats just so this would never happen. But he said that soon they wouldn't be making cars with bench seats and he wanted to have one. Now, here I was, between my father, who was stiff and tense, and my mother, who was squirming and lighting one cigarete after another.

"I didn't think," my mother said, "that having all-round popularity meant going to the beach with a boy alone. When we used to go out we went in groups."

"Don't you call ten or twelve guys a group?" I asked.

"You didn't *go* with them, Geri . . . you went with one puny boy who couldn't defend you. That is the whole point."

"Don't blame the boy, Ginger."

"You always have to stick together, don't you?"

"Who does?" my father asked.

"Men," my mother said.

My father sighed and my mother lit another cigarette. I wanted to tell her that if she kept smoking I might throw up but at that moment I felt so sick I couldn't even speak.

"What I don't understand," my mother went on, "is if these boys hit you over the head then why didn't the doctor find any lump or anything?"

I said nothing. I knew by the way the muscle in my father's jaw was jumping that he had an idea why.

"This is what I don't understand," my mother said.

My father made a small grunting sound. I decided I'd better say something—and this was another turning point in my life. Before I tell you about it I have to explain that although I was never a real goody-goody —I mean, I've told little lies like everyone else—I never was a real big liar—until then. That night it just came out.

"Okay," I said, "I'll tell you the truth."

My father made a sound like "aha" and my mother turned and stared at me. I looked straight ahead.

"Dave made it up . . . I mean the part about the guys hitting me over the head. You see, he was ashamed because he fainted and he never really knew what happened."

"Very nice," my mother said sarcastically. "In my day a boy never would have. . . ."

"Let's hear what she has to say," my father said.

"Well, after he fainted I guess I fainted, too . . . I mean, I don't know what happened. But no one hit me over the head. You see, one of the boys, the one with 'Born To Be Bad' tattooed on his arm, said he was going to rape me and. . . ."

"Oh, my God," my mother gasped.

". . . and that's what made me faint."

"For all you know then, he did . . . he did rape you."

"No, he didn't."

"How do you know, Geri, if you fainted?"

"Mother," I said, "I know."

We pulled into our drive.

"How? How could you know if you were out cold?"

"Ginger . . . use your head. The girl would know."

"Anyway," I said, "that's the truth . . . that's what really happened." And there it was—so easy. It came as easily to me as it had to Dave. And it didn't even bother me. I knew that if the real truth came out I would probably never be able to see Dave again and I didn't want that to happen. So I told a lie. The first of many.

Inside, Grandma and Grandpa were sitting in the living room waiting for us. Grandma, of course, hugged too hard and Grandpa clutched at his heart when he saw me.

"This is the worst thing that ever happened to me," Grandpa said.

"Be quiet," Grandma said. "Be glad she's home in one piece."

Just then Jack came into the living room in his pajamas, which consisted of a pair of old pajama pants, cut off at the knees, and an old sweatshirt with the arms cut out. He looked terrible, as though he'd been up for days.

My mother gasped when she saw him. "What is it, darling?"

"I can't sleep," he said.

"Look at that," my grandmother said. "He's worried about his sister."

"Huh?" Jack said.

Fat chance.

"What's wrong?" Mother asked again.

"I have a sore throat and chills and I ache and look at this." He walked over to my mother and held out his arm for her to examine.

She looked—closer—closer—her eyes almost resting on his arm now. "What?" she asked. "I don't see anything."

My grandfather groaned. "I don't think I can take much more."

My father made himself a drink and I thought I might vomit just watching him pour it.

"Can't you see that rash?" Jack said.

"Let me look," Grandma said.

Jack went to her quickly. Grandma looked and looked and looked. "I don't see anything," she said guiltily.

"Red spots," he said.

I made a mental note of what night it was or had been. Tuesday. Marcus Welby night.

"Also," Jack said, "I have an intolerable headache."

Intolerable. That was the key word. He always used one word from the programs he watched that was completely unlike anything he would normally say.

"What is it you think you have?" My father asked. He was sitting in a chair smoking and drinking and not really looking at Jack.

"I think . . . it could be meningitis."

"Oh, my God," Grandma said.

"I knew it, I knew it," Grandpa said.

"Go to bed, Jack," my father said.

"George, how can you?" said Mother.

"With ease," he said.

"*I'd* like to go to bed," I said.

Grandma was feeling Jack's head. "He does seem a little warm."

"It's a warm night. Go to bed, Geri. You too, Jack."

"I'm probably dying and you don't even care."

I, for one, *was* dying. If I didn't get to bed soon I thought I might *really* faint.

"I might have convulsions," Jack said.

"Well, have them in your room," my father said. "I've had enough excitement for one night."

"We've raised a beast," my grandpa said.

"Yeah, a beast," my father said. He picked up *TV Guide* and flipped through it. "All right, listen to this." He read: " 'A young boy begins to have intolerable headaches, sore throat and fever. He refuses to get treatment because he wants to play in the big game. Dr. Welby attends the game where the boy collapses and meningitis is discovered.' Good night, Jack."

I took that as my cue to leave. Climbing the stairs was one of the hardest things I've ever done. The next hardest thing was getting undressed. But I managed and fell into my bed, literally. I heard Jack come upstairs and heard my parents and grandparents talking downstairs. I felt very creepy. My head ached, my throat was sore and every bone in my body ached. Is this what happened when you drank? Did everyone, after a night of drinking, feel like they'd been run over by a tank? If so, what was the point? Of course, maybe it was because the wine had been so sweet and sickening. Nevertheless, if the way I felt was the result, then that was that. NEVER AGAIN! If only it had been so simple.

8

Needless to say, I didn't go to school the next day. I slept until about two and when I woke up I felt perfectly fine. Of course, I didn't want my mother to know I felt fine because then I'd have to go downstairs and face a huge lecture. So I decided to stay in bed—or at least stay upstairs. As I tiptoed from the bathroom I heard voices. I knew it wasn't my grandparents because I'd found a note from them on my door saying good-bye. I had also found, slipped under the door, an article ripped out of the morning paper: the continuing story of the boy who had stabbed his girlfriend seventeen times.

Anyway, I heard these voices so I tiptoed down to the top landing of the stairs and sat down. Suddenly I felt four years old again. When my parents used to have parties Jack and I would sit on the landing and listen to everything that was going on. Occasionally, we'd get caught by a guest and they'd drag us downstairs and everyone would make a big fuss over us and feed us bologna and cheese and even Mother and Daddy seemed to enjoy it. Then we'd be taken back to bed, tucked in, and kissed good night. I could still remember the wonderful combination of smells of my mother in the middle of those party nights. Perfume and powder, whiskey and salami, cigarettes and silk. And just the plain smell of Mother, if you know what I mean. Then the feel of her skin next to mine, the brush of her hair against my forehead, her warm lips on my cheek, and her strong but gentle hug, reassuring me that life was wonderful and I was loved. I couldn't even remember the last time my mother hugged me like that—not that I wanted her to!

So now here I was, age sixteen, sitting on the landing, spying. Quickly I identified the voices: my mother and her friend, Lois Gilbert. Lois was a tall redhead and although she wasn't exactly a swinger, she was a lot more with it than my mother. I couldn't understand how they could be friends, except I noticed my mother never did her fifties number around Lois. Sometimes I wished that Lois was my mother. She had two sons and she was always saying she wished she had a daughter like me. I had a feeling that I could talk with her. But then her son Don, who was a year younger than I, always said he wished my mother was his mother. So who can figure it out?

"I know how you feel," my mother was saying. "It takes a long time to get over it."

"But it's been months, Ginge."

"It took me years . . . in fact, I don't think you ever *really* get over it. Time helps, the pain lessens, memories fade, but you never really forget."

"Oh, God," Lois said.

I couldn't believe my good luck! Was I about to hear really terrific gossip? Was I hearing it now? Lois must have had an affair with someone and my mother must have been referring to some affair she had had. If only they'd say the names. Then immediately my hopes of juicy revelations were shattered like fallen icicles.

Lois said, "There were so many things I never told her."

"I was fortunate. I had time with my mother before she died."

They were talking about their dead mothers. Lois's mother had died about six or seven months before. My grandmother had died when I was eight. I hardly remembered her. And I certainly didn't remember anything about her death. She lived in Pennsylvania and Mother went to the funeral alone. I remember though that around Christmas time that year, some carol was playing on the radio and Mother was sitting there with tears running down her face. I asked her why she was crying. She didn't answer, but Daddy said she was thinking of her mother. Then he went over and put his arm around her and gave her his handkerchief.

"I had that time with her in the hospital several months before she died, remember?" Ginger asked.

"Yes. You told me that you said you loved each other and you straightened out a lot of things from the past."

"Yes . . . we did."

There was silence for a moment.

Then Lois said, "Oh, Ginge, I didn't mean to make you sad . . . I'm sorry."

"It's okay. But you see what I mean? You never quite get over it. I still, to this day, every once in a while automatically think, 'Oh, I can't wait to tell Mamma,' or something like that . . . you know what I mean?"

"Yes . . . yes, that's what happened to me this morning. I guess that's why I got so depressed."

"Well, I know it's corny, Lois, but time does help."

Imagine my mother knowing something was corny! Imagine my mother comforting someone! Imagine my mother—I couldn't imagine my mother anyway but the way I knew her: "Queen of the Hop" and "Pain in the Ass"!

I knew she'd been different when Jack and I were kids. I mean, she'd always sort of lived in the past, but that seemed to accelerate when I got into high school. When I was little I actually loved her! Now the thought of loving her was—I don't know—strange, weird, creepy—odd.

"It's strange, isn't it, the cycles we go through?" my mother was saying. "When I was a little girl I loved my mother. Then, in my teenage years, I couldn't stand her. Everything she did either embarrassed me or drove me crazy."

What was she now, a mind reader?

"Mine, too," Lois said. "I used to hate to have my dates call for me because she made such a fuss."

All my mother said was, "Yes."

Now that was weird. There was a perfect opening for her to go on about her four million dates, and all she said was "Yes." That's what I mean. She never did her

Teenage Life with Lois—not that *I* ever heard anyway.

She went on: "And then when I got older, after I was married, I started to turn to her for advice, and later when the kids were born we became friends and I loved her again. I look forward to that time with Geri. I know she hates me now."

I felt like I'd been caught cheating on an exam or something. I could feel myself turning red and my stomach got all clutchy. I wanted to yell out that it wasn't true but I couldn't—one: because I shouldn't have been sitting there listening, and two: because it was true.

"My boys hate me, too," Lois said. "But they hate Bob more. That's my one consolation."

"Yes, I know what you mean. Jack favors me."

How could they just sit there like that calmly discussing how their children hated them? I would never understand parents—and I certainly never wanted to be one.

"Want another drink?" Mother asked.

"Sure."

Mother and Lois always drank sherry together when Lois dropped by during the day. Coffee before noon, sherry between noon and five, cocktails between five and seven and highballs or beer after dinner. They left the living room and went into the kitchen and I couldn't hear them anymore so I tiptoed back to bed.

I lay there for a while, both dogs and Sophie pressed against me, thinking about just who my mother was. I mean, it's funny how you can live with a person for sixteen years and not really know them. I decided to do one of my favorite things. When I was sick, or just hanging around, I often got out my mother's box of pictures, an old gray box tied with a string that she kept on a shelf in her closet.

The box contained pictures of my mother from the time she was born until she was about twelve and then it picked up again from the time she was married. The reason there were no pictures of her in her Fabulous Teenage Life was because she'd had her baby pictures (up to twelve) in one box and Fabulous Teens in another, and when her family moved from one house to another when she was eighteen and a half the Fab Teen Box got lost. It was one of the great sorrows of her life, and she was always moaning about it.

"Oh, Geri, if only you could have seen how I looked for the junior prom." Or: "The pictures of me and Glenn Schneider at the Sadie Hawkins Day dance were a riot. . . . Oh, I could just cry about losing all those great pictures."

But, of course, when she wanted to show me who anyone was she always had her trusty yearbook where things were written like:

> Dear Ginger,
> It's been great knowing you. You're a great kid.
> I'll never forget all the fun we had in typing.
> Love,
> Myra

With the yearbook she kept another book, smaller and soft-covered. It said 1954–1964 and was from her tenth high school reunion. A reunion she never attended. I guess that was even worse for her than losing all the pictures. She had all the plans made—suitcases packed, Grandma and Grandpa Peters coming to stay with us for the weekend—and then that Friday morning she came down with some terrible intestinal virus or something. I was only six at the time but I remember that she was sick all weekend and that between bouts of throwing up she never stopped crying. Daddy said we had to be especially nice to her because it was one of the great disappointments of her life and she'd have to wait fifteen more years before the next reunion. Anyway, the little book which they sent her from the reunion told about what everyone was doing in 1964. For my mother it said: "Virginia Burke (Peters). 'Ginger' married George Peters a year after graduation and has a son and a daughter. She is a housewife and he is an engineer." Except for the girls who didn't marry, it said something like that for almost every single female. Even if they'd gone on to graduate school it would say Willa or Audrey or Nancy or Peggy is a housewife. But that was 1964. I wonder what it would say now? I hoped it would say Willa is practicing law and Audrey is a mechanic and Nancy is selling insurance and Peggy's an actress and they all dumped their husbands who didn't understand them and tried to make them slaves! Please don't think I am a man-hater. I am not. I just face reality!

I opened the box and pulled out a handful of pictures. Naturally, they weren't in any order since they'd just been thrown in. My mother was always saying, "One of these days I'm going to organize those pictures even though the best ones are gone forever!"

The first one I looked at was my mother when she was about eleven. She was on the beach with her mother and father and she looked miserable. Although it was a black and white picture, the suit she was wearing looked like it was gold or silver and not a thing filled it out. One parent was on either side of her. Almost all of the pictures of Mother and her parents were like that. One on each side. I guess it was because she was an only child. I hadn't seen my Grandpa Burke for nearly five years. (He lived in California with his new wife, but the last time I saw him he didn't look too much different from the way he looked in the picture. I remember people were always saying how young he seemed and how handsome he was and how much he looked like Gregory Peck. I guess he did if you could picture Greg around five feet six!)

I went through a bunch of pictures of my mother when she was little—it was funny how she was never smiling in any of them—and then I came to one of her and my father when they first met. I know because it said on the back "George Peters and me my second month in Lancaster, Pa." Mother had moved from Herschey to Lancaster and met my father there. He was a senior at Franklin and Marshall College and she was a secretary in the administration office. He had come in to the office for something and took one look at Ginger and practically fell over in a faint—or so she tells it. Since she had only lived there a month and a half when they met, and had only had her job for two weeks, she didn't know anybody except some girl named Jennie who was the dean's secretary. So George was the first man who asked her out in Lancaster, Pa.! After having had all-round popularity for so many years in high school, I guess she really felt the pinch of loneliness in Lancaster and she probably would have gone out with a goat by that point. Not that Daddy wasn't cute. He was—if you like the type. He had straight blond hair, parted on the left, and a kind of straight nose, full lips and a long neck. In the picture he was wearing these horrible baggy tan pants with cuffs and funny pleats on the upper thigh, a white shirt with the sleeve rolled up, a white T-shirt showing at the neck, white socks and loafers. He was standing very close to, but not touching, my mother. She was wearing a short-sleeved sweater with a small scarf around the neck, a long skirt with a terrible-looking poodle painted or stitched on it, about an inch and a half of bare leg, and white socks and loafers. They both looked hideous. Neither was smiling.

I went through some more pictures of her childhood (Daddy's mother kept all of his baby and youth pictures) and her parents until I came to other ones of Daddy and Mother together. One said "George and Me on a picnic . . . July 1955." This time they were touching. He had his arm around her and she had her head on his shoulder and they were looking into each other's eyes and if you didn't know any better you'd think they were in love! You never saw such gooey, mushy looks. The next one was of them already married. Mother was holding me in her arms and Daddy had Jack on his lap. Both of them were smiling. There was one of Mother and me when I was about six months old. On the back it said "Geri at six months, my perfect little daughter." Then there were lots of family pictures when Jack and I were four and six or five and seven or ten and twelve or whatever. Neither parent was ever smiling. It was as though they had stopped smiling when I was about three.

There were lots of Jack doing everything and anything and plenty of me, too. But the ones I liked best were the ones of Daddy and Mother alone—especially before they got married and when they were first married. I couldn't believe they were the same people I lived with. Their looks hadn't changed that much—I mean, they were certainly recognizable—but what amazed me was how they looked at each other in those pictures. It was definitely love, unless I was crazy. I guess there was no doubt about it: She didn't think he had B.P. when she married him. And he certainly thought she was *it*. What the hell happened? Or was that just the way it went? Did everybody look all starry-eyed at first and then get that set look around the mouth and the droopy eyes and, let's face it, that bored expression? Maybe that's just what marriage did. Well, I wasn't going to fall into that trap. If that's what marriage did to a person then—

"What are you doing?" It was my mother.

"Looking at the old pictures. Look at this, Mother." It was a picture of her and Daddy sitting across a table from each other, mooning into each other's eyes.

"What about it?"

"Don't you notice anything?"

She looked at it carefully. "He's not wearing a tie. That used to drive me crazy. I used to beg him to wear—"

"No, no," I said. "Look at the way you're looking at each other."

"What about it?"

"You don't look at each other that way now. How come?"

"Put these away . . . it's time for dinner."

"How come you don't?"

"Geri," she said sadly, "to explain that to you I'd have to explain all of life and the pork chops might burn while I was doing it. Get dressed and come down to dinner." She closed the door behind her.

Well, that was either a dodge or she really didn't know why. At any rate, if she did know I was not going to be her confidante. The whole thing made me extremely sad and I vowed once more that I would never look at the pictures again. They always made me sad —I always took that vow—and I always forgot it. I knew I'd think about the pictures for days, wishing we could all be happy again the way we were when I was a baby. Even though I couldn't remember what it was like, the pictures told the tale.

I put on a pair of jeans, a shirt, and my moccasins and, with some apprehension, went down to dinner.

I was pleasantly surprised. Nobody said anything about the night before. No matter why they had decided to let the whole thing go, it was, I thought, a very intelligent approach! And by the time we reached dessert and I knew they weren't going to lecture me or even bring up the incident, I felt like we really were a happy family. Until I looked at my mother and father. Neither one of them was smiling.

The next day I went back to school. Dave seemed really glad to see me. I asked him if it was true that wine made you feel just awful and he said it was. He suggested I switch to vodka. I said I was planning never to drink again although, now that I was feeling better, I knew that somewhere I would. He just smiled.

B.J. and Carolyn had heard all about what had happened because I had talked to them on the phone the night before. Carolyn said it sounded like fun, except for the part with the police, but B.J. thought it was disgusting and said she hoped I wouldn't do it again. I said I wouldn't. Actually, I thought a few drinks might be good for B.J. They might loosen her up. Carolyn, I knew, would try anything. So whn Dave suggested we do something Saturday night, I suggested that we go over to Carolyn's house and have a party.

"You mean me and the three of you girls?"

"Why not?"

"Well, that's hardly a date."

"Her parents have lots of liquor and they'll never miss it."

"Oh," he said, "you mean a party, party."

I nodded.

"Well, sure," he said. "That sounds like fun."

I guess I knew instinctively that if liquor was involved Dave wouldn't care if it was twenty girls and him.

On Saturday afternoon I told my mother Carolyn was having a party and that I was going to stay overnight.

"What kind of a party?"

I guess I felt guilty about what we had planned because I said, too quickly: "A small quiet party with Cokes and stuff."

She looked at me strangely. "Is that boy going to be there?"

"What boy?"

"The one who wears a carrot in his ear."

So Jack *had* opened his big mouth.

"I don't know what you're talking about."

"Jack told me, Geri, so don't pretend. The one that was at the hospital the other night . . . what's his name?"

"You mean Dave? Well, you saw him. Did he have a carrot in his ear?"

"Is he going to be there?"

"No," I lied.

"Good. There's something about him I don't trust."

I couldn't understand why she said that because Dave had been very nice to my parents, very polite.

"He's a real smoothie," she said. "Too polite."

"Oh, Mother. If he hadn't been polite you'd tell me he was rude."

"There's a polite and then there's polite."

"Well, he's not going to be there so you don't have to worry about me being with a polite boy."

"What boys will be there?"

"None," I said. Big mistake.

"None? You mean it's a hen party?"

"I wish you wouldn't say that, Mother. It's so . . . so sexist."

"Don't start that."

One thing you have to understand about my mother is that she's completely brainwashed where women are concerned. She bought the whole role thing a long time ago and nothing I say or do has any effect on her. I gave her a subscription to *Ms.* magazine for her birthday and she said I'd just wasted my money because she wouldn't read anything written by a bunch of bra-burning ama-zons. Well, anyway, at least *I* got to read it.

"There's nothing wrong with having hen parties, Geri . . . we used to have them all the time. But you don't have them on Saturday nights. You have them on Fri-day nights."

"Why? What's the difference?"

"Saturday night is date night. Friday night you go out with the girls." Another of her fifties rules.

"It isn't like that anymore, Mother."

"We wouldn't have been caught dead with a bunch of girls on a Saturday night. If I didn't have a date on a Saturday night, and I can't remember that ever happen-ing, I would have stayed home by myself rather than being with a bunch of females."

"You really hate women, don't you?" I said.

"Don't be ridiculous."

"There's nothing wrong with *females* getting togeth-er."

"Of course not. On Friday night, not Saturday."

It was hopeless. "Well, we don't have dates so. . . ."

"If you'd stop hanging around with that necrophiliac and that crazy animal-lover you might have a date on a Saturday night. You've got to try and be *some*body. Why don't you try getting in with one of the good crowds?"

"Mother, please. Let's not go through this again."

"Your brother says you don't make any effort to get to know anyone. You've got to learn to smile in the halls."

The last time she'd said that to me was about two years earlier and the next day I'd tried it. Everyone thought I'd gone crazy. I walked around all day smiling at everybody and I heard later that some of the kids thought I was smoking pot. Some people just have faces that smile, even when they're not trying. They have natural smile lines and lit-up eyes. Like Dave. Like Jack. I have the opposite. If I don't actually make a smile, I look very serious and I can't see why I should go around smiling when I have nothing to smile about. Anyway, it didn't do me any good the time I tried it.

"The trouble with you, Geri, is that you have B.P. just like your father."

"Carolyn and B.J. don't think I have B.P.," I said.

"That is because, and I should think it would be obvious, Carolyn and B.J. have B.P. themselves. In fact, with the exception of your father, they have the worst cases of B.P. I have ever run across."

"I guess you're right. All three of us have the worst B.P. in America. In fact, that's why we're having a party. To celebrate. It's not every day that the worst cases of Bad Personality in America can be found in one room."

"You don't *have* to have B.P.," she said. "You could do something about it if you wanted to."

"Like what?" Why did I ask?

"Well, you could fix yourself up for openers. You could wear a little makeup and—"

"What does makeup have to do with B.P.?"

"Geri, if you start from the outside and work inward—"

"Nobody wears makeup anyway. You certainly don't want me to be different from everybody else, do you?" I knew I had her there.

"I suppose if that's the style . . . well, you could try being a little more feminine."

Inwardly, I groaned. "What does that mean?"

"Feminine? Surely you know what feminine means."

"No, I don't."

"You're playing games."

"No. Tell me what you mean by 'more feminine.' "

Have you ever noticed that when you ask someone to define what they mean by "feminine" they usually can't? The reason they can't is because what they really mean is helpless and nobody wants to say that. So they hem and haw and come up with the most ridiculous answers—or none at all.

"You know what feminine means. I'm not going to go into something you know."

"Do you mean wearing makeup and dresses?"

"That's part of it, but since you say that's not the style . . . look, Geri, you don't want to be feminine or popular because you prefer to torture me. So let's just drop it."

You see what I mean.

"So can I stay overnight at Carolyn's?"

"May I?"

"May I?"

"I suppose. What difference does it make anyway? If you want to waste the best years of your life with those two losers, why should I care? For a girl who lost being Most Popular in her graduating class by two votes a daughter like you is a heartbreak."

Before she started in on how the election was rigged and how Claire Cahill got Ben Davis and Bill Nowels to vote twice, I started toward my room.

"Thanks," I said. "I know we'll have a wonderful time. All that B.P. in one room makes for a really exciting night."

"When I think of how Claire Cahill got those two boys. . . ."

I closed the door of my room. Sometimes I thought if I had to hear one more of her stories, repeated one more time, I'd go crazy. She talked to Lois about other things. Why couldn't she talk to me about other things? Or better yet, why did she have to talk to me at all? No, that wasn't true. If I had a choice I'd rather have a mother who talked to me about *things* than a mother who wouldn't talk at all. But this mother was impossible. Was it always this way? I tried to remember. Maybe it was my fault. When I was little and she used to put me to bed I'd ask her to tell me a story. Nothing unusual about that. Then she'd start a make-believe story and I'd always stop her.

"No," I'd say, "tell me a story about *your* life."

Was that how it started? Did I bring it on myself? Anyway, that didn't matter now. The point was that I wasn't a little girl anymore and I'd heard all the damn stories over and over again. I didn't care about how they did things in the fifties. Couldn't she understand that? It was the seventies now and that's what was important. Her crummy old life was over. It was my turn now—my turn to do it *my* way and I hated her expecting me to live up to standards that were more than twenty years old. Even Thomas Jefferson thought the Constitution was going to be rewritten every ten years!

If only she'd join a consciousness raising group or something. I had suggested it once.

"Why don't you join a C.R. group, Mom?"

"A what?"

"A consciousness raising group."

"You mean those meetings where a bunch of women get together and talk about how awful men are?"

"That's not what goes on. They talk about everything . . . their childhoods . . . their teens." I thought that would appeal to her.

"I had a very happy childhood," she said.

"So talk about that."

"What for?"

"To share your feelings with other women. Women think they're all alone. . . . I mean, you have a terrible image of yourself as a woman. It's not your fault. . . . Most women do . . . that's what you'd find out."

"So you want me to go to some meeting to find out I'm a terrible person, hmmm?"

"That's not what I said. Why can't I ever talk to you like a human being? You just don't listen."

"I listen. I just don't like what I hear. I'll tell you something, Geri. You're going to end up an old maid if you don't watch it."

"Oh, God. Please don't use that expression."

"Expression or no expression that's what you're going to be. A woman is nothing without a man and you'd better learn that right now."

"What about Amelia Earhart?"

"She's dead."

"Okay . . . *you* have a man . . . what are *you?*"

"What do you mean, what am *I?*" I'd never seen her look so hurt.

"Just that. *You've* got a man . . . are you something?"

"Yes . . . yes, I am."

"What?"

"I'm a wife and a mother."

"Yuck."

"It may be yuck to you, Geri, but you'll find out someday that that's all there is." I thought she might cry.

"But it isn't," I said softly. "That the whole point, Mom. That's what CR teaches you. That's what Women's Lib is all about . . . it isn't all there is . . . there are other alternatives. I mean, I guess there's nothing wrong with being a wife and mother but that's not *all* there is. Being a wife and mother has to do with other people. What are *you* just for *you*? Huh?"

She looked at me for a long moment, then turned her back and started peeling carrots or something. I reached for her to turn her around but she began talking, her back still to me.

"I'll never forget the time Betty Fritz . . . she was head cheerleader . . . and Mac McLinchie . . . he was captain of the football team . . . decided that. . . ."

I couldn't believe it. Bing! Just like that she switched from a heavy rap to some dumb thing about two people I didn't know from her high school days. That's the way it always went. I'd given up trying after that one. She was just plain hopeless.

And I was hopeless for even thinking about her. The whole thing was a waste of time. Why think about Ginger? There were a lot more important things to think about . . . like tonight. All the arrangements were made. Carolyn's parents were going into New York and spending the night at a hotel. Ralph was staying overnight at a friend's and we would have the house all to ourselves. Dave said he might bring two of his friends who were coming to visit, so, we might be having dates after all. I hadn't told Carolyn and B.J. that part because they would have been too disappointed if it didn't happen. Actually, the truth is, they would have been too scared that it might and Carolyn probably would have called the whole thing off. As it was, Carolyn and I hadn't told B.J. that we were planning on a drinking party. We just said that we were going to watch this great Bette Davis movie on TV and that Dave might drop by. We knew that once B.J. was there and things got going she would probably join us. And if she didn't, she'd go into a bedroom and read one of her animal books.

I, for one, was looking forward to the evening like I had never looked forward to anything before. Carolyn's parents had this neat bar in their recreation room, and Carolyn said they had cases and cases of booze behind the bar. You see, Carolyn's father is a liquor wholesaler and so there's this endless supply. But the best thing is that her parents hardly drink, so they'd never notice that anything was missing. I couldn't understand why it had never occurred to us to try drinking before. I mean, the liquor had always been there, waiting for us. Now we were going to have all we wanted. Carolyn said she was going to try brandy because she read somewhere that all chic people drink brandy. Personally, I wasn't terribly interested in what chic people drank. I just wanted to see what I was going to drink. I mean, I'd decided that that night I would pick the ME drink. Everyone should have a favorite, something that can be identified with them, like a brand of cigarettes or a kind of perfume or something. Well, I was going to pick a drink that was me—and the only way I could see to do that was to try them all!

9

Dave had said one way not to get sick was to eat well before you started drinking. Line your stomach, he said. So that's what I did. That expression, "lining your stomach," has great possibilities for a cartoon, doesn't it? Anyway, I suppose you're wondering why, after everything that happened, I would *want* to drink again? I mean, I got all cut up and I puked and almost got in trouble with the fuzz and I could have drowned and I felt really lousy afterward, so why would I want to do it again? Well, the part I left out, I guess, was how I felt before all the bad stuff happened. How I felt was: wonderful, terrific, ecstatic, stupendous!

I'll try to be more specific. To start with, there was nothing I couldn't talk about. I was like the greatest conversationalist who ever lived. And funny? Lily Tomlin had nothing on me! And happy? I guess I'd never felt so happy. Like I didn't have a care or worry in the world. I felt I could say and do things I'd never have the nerve to say and do if I were straight. I couldn't remember what those things were, but I could remember the feeling. And I wanted to feel it again. Besides, this time I was sure I wouldn't get sick and we would be safe in Carolyn's house. Nothing bad could happen there.

Jack dropped me off around quarter to eight. The B. Davis picture started at eight. It was *Marked Woman,* a gangster flick with Humphrey Bogart as a DA who tries to convince Bette to testify against her boss. I'd seen it five times before, but it was a really neat picture and I didn't mind seeing it again. Not that we'd be seeing that much of it if we were going to have a party.

B.J. was already there and she and Carolyn were down in the recreation room. B.J. was drinking a Coke and chewing on one of those Slim Jim beef things that we call chemical sticks—have you ever read the ingredients on one of those things? Carolyn was behind the bar, her hand on a bottle of brandy.

"Well, thank God, you're here," B.J. said. "Maybe you can talk some sense into her."

"Into who?"

"Into Carolyn, of course. Do you see anyone else here?"

"B.J. is being a drag already," Carolyn said.

"Do you know what she wants to do, Geri? She wants to actually drink that stuff." She indicated the brandy.

"No! You can't mean it," I said with mock horror.

B.J., being her usual naïve and serious self, said, "You see, Carolyn, I knew Geri would be against it, particularly after you-know-what happened."

"I've been trying to tell her that brandy's too strong," I said.

"You see, I knew. . . ." B.J. looked at me, a slight glimmer of understanding passing over her face. "Just what do you mean by that?"

"I mean just what I said. Brandy's too strong."

"Oh, Geri, all the In-people drink brandy," Carolyn said.

"Since when do you know what the In-people drink?" B.J. asked.

"I read."

"Well, drinking brandy is not going to make you an In-person. It's just going to make you drunk and disgusting. I know it, you know it and God knows it."

I guess you should know that B.J. is not a religious person. Even though she's always saying that, it's not because she believes in God or thinks that God really knows it. It's just an expression.

"B.J.'s right, Carolyn."

B.J. nodded as if the whole thing were settled.

"I think you should start with something milder."

"What do you mean, 'start with'?" B.J. squealed.

"I mean, maybe she should work up to brandy."

"Hey, what's going on around here?"

"I told you," Carolyn said. "We're having a party."

"I thought we were going to look at a B. Davis movie?"

"We will, we will."

"Can't we do both?" I asked. "Are you so limited you can only do one thing at a time?"

She didn't like that. "I can do plenty of things at the same time."

"Then it should be simple for a contortionist like you to have a party while you watch *Marked Woman,*" Carolyn said.

"What do you mean by a party?" She squinted her already squinty eyes at me.

"We're just going to have a few drinks . . . have some fun."

"Like you did the last time, Geri?"

"It so happens," I said, "that I *did* have fun. The problem was we were out and so things got a little confused . . . but nothing can happen to us here in Carolyn's rec room. Use your head. We're just going to have fun."

"I don't know."

"B.J., it's time you got out of your cocoon."

"What cocoon?"

"The one you're in."

"Break out of your shell," Carolyn added.

"What shell?"

"B.J., trust us. Aren't we your best friends?"

She nodded.

"Would we do anything to hurt you?"

She shook her head.

"So then, trust us. All we want to do is have a good time."

"Why can't we have a good time just watching the movie?"

"Hopeless," Carolyn said.

"Okay. If that's the way you want to be, B.J., that's

your right. Stay a baby all your life." I turned away from her. "Bartender, what do you suggest?"

"Well, let's see what we got here." Carolyn leaned down behind the bar. "There's vodka, gin, bourbon, rum, tequila, rye whiskey, Scotch and then there's all these liqueurs . . . Dram . . . Drambu . . . I can't pronounce it. Anyway, if you want to see them come back and look."

"My mother drinks Rob Roys . . . but that's probably a fifties drink."

"My father drinks them," B.J. said.

We ignored her.

"I don't think I want anything sweet," I said, remembering the Annie Greensprings wine. "Is rum sweet?"

"Got me," Carolyn said.

"It's sweet in rum cake," B.J. said.

We ignored her.

"Should we have it straight or what?" Carolyn asked.

"It's almost time for the movie," B.J. said.

We ignored her.

"Maybe we should mix it. How about rum and Coke?" I said.

"That sounds good."

Carolyn got out ice and tall glasses and opened a bottle of rum.

"Should I put the set on?" B.J. asked.

We ignored her.

Carolyn filled the glasses halfway with rum. "Is that enough?"

"A bit more," I said.

Then she poured in about an inch of Coke and stirred it up. "Here you are," she said.

"I'll have a manhattan," B.J. said.

We looked at her.

"What's that?" Carolyn asked.

"It's what my mother drinks. Do you have any cherries? You get cherries in them."

Carolyn reached below the bar and brought out a bottle of red maraschino cherries. "These?"

"Those are the ones. You make it with whiskey and

sweet vermouth. I'll make it myself if you don't know how."

"How come *you* know how?" I asked.

"I make them for my mother sometimes. Here, I'll show you." She jumped off the bar stool and went behind the bar.

My drink was sitting in front of me and I was itching to start, but I didn't want to seem too eager. I knew it would look funny if I didn't wait for B.J, now that she had decided to join us. But I wished to hell she'd hurry up.

"Do you have a cocktail shaker or a big glass?"

I groaned. It was going to be a production.

"I'll use this big glass," she said. "After you put in the ice you put in this much whiskey." She poured. "Then sweet vermouth. You have it, don't you? No, that's dry vermouth. That's it. Then you put in this much sweet vermouth." She poured again. It was taking forever. "Now you stir until it gets nice and cold and then you pour it into . . . do you have a cocktail glass?"

Carolyn handed her a short round glass.

"That's not a cocktail glass, stupid. Let me look."

I could have killed her. What difference did it make what kind of glass it was in? There she was in those dumb blue overalls she always wore, searching around the cabinet for a stupid glass, and there I was, my glass in my hand, the ice melting.

"Come on, B.J., what's the difference what glass it's in?"

"It makes a lot of difference. If I'm going to drink a cocktail, then I'm going to drink it out of a cocktail glass. Of course, I shouldn't even be having a cocktail at this hour . . . particularly after I've eaten dinner. It's very gauche. But I like the cherries. Here it is. You see, a cocktail glass has a long stem."

"Fascinating," Carolyn said.

"Will you pour the damn thing, please?" I said.

"Hold your horses . . . what are you, some kind of alcoholic or something? You can't wait two minutes?"

"Yeah," I said, "I'm a real Bowery bum."

No one knew, of course, at that moment, the truth of

what B.J. had said. And I certainly didn't know that Bowery bums were the smallest percentage of alcoholics.

At last she poured the drink. There was a lot left over in the big glass.

"That's the dividend," she said. "And here's the best part." She dropped two cherries in the glass. "You actually should only have one but what the hell."

"Thanks very much for this bartending lesson," I said. "Can we drink now?"

"Let's make a toast," B.J. said.

Murder was in my heart.

"Let's toast to all the beautiful animals in the world."

"That is the dumbest toast I ever heard," Carolyn said.

"Oh, who cares?" I said.

We toasted and finally drank. My drink was very strong. I mean the Coke taste didn't do much to disguise the taste of the rum. Not that I didn't like the taste of the rum. I did. But it burned as it went down.

"*Ecch!*" B.J. said after taking a swallow.

"What's wrong?" Carolyn asked.

"It tastes awful. I've always just tasted the cherries and it wasn't so bad, but this is rotten."

"Let's see," I said. I took a sip of her drink. Talk about strong! But it was kind of good. Not too sweet, just sweet enough. "I like it."

"You want it?" B.J. asked.

"Sure," I said. "Take this drink." I handed her my rum and Coke.

"*Ecch,*" she said again. "This is just as bad."

"You're crazy," I said.

"Well, I'm not drinking it, crazy or not."

"Try something else," Carolyn said.

"I think I'll just stick to Coke."

"You really are a creep, B.J."

"I hate the taste," she whined.

"You're just afraid," Carolyn said.

"Right."

"I hate the taste. Why should I drink something I hate? Why is it, if I don't like something it automatically means I'm afraid of it? I hate the taste of cream soda and I don't drink that. Am I afraid of cream soda?"

"It's very different," I said. I didn't know then why it made me so furious that B.J. didn't want to drink with us, but the more I drank of the manhattan the more important it seemed that she drink also. Now I know the reason. When you're a drunk, it's important that everybody drink with you.

"Give her something else, Carolyn."

"I don't want something else, Geri. I'm very happy with my Coke."

"I never knew what a creep you were."

"Well, maybe I should just go home then."

Carolyn hated fights. "No, come on now. If she doesn't want anything then why force her?"

"Well, she just doesn't know what she's missing." I finished my drink and poured the "dividend" into my glass.

"I do know what I'm missing. A rotten-tasting thing. You're not supposed to drink a cocktail like that, Geri. You're supposed to sip it."

"It tastes too good to sip." And it did. "The point, B.J., is not so much the taste, although I think it tastes super, the point is what it does to you. Do you feel anything, Carolyn?"

Carolyn had a very peculiar smile on her face. Usually, when Carolyn smiled her mouth almost disappeared, but now her mouth was gone completely. "Yeah, I feel kinda nice."

"You see," I said to B.J.

"I feel fine just the way I am."

"Forget her," Carolyn said. "If she wants to miss out, let her miss out."

"I just can't see what you're afraid of. . . . I mean, you're staying overnight so your parents won't find out or anything."

"I'm not afraid. I just don't like it."

"I know," I said, getting a bright idea. "I bet B.J. would like something sweet." I went behind the bar and looked at all the bottles. "I'll bet you'd like this," I said. It was something called banana liqueur and if there was one thing B.J. loved it was bananas. Without waiting for any response, I poured some in a Coke glass. "Try this."

"Why do I have to?"

"Just try it. If you don't like this I'll drop the whole thing."

Reluctantly, B.J. took the glass and, screwing up her face and practically holding her breath, she took a tiny sip. Then another sip. Then a bigger sip. She started to smile.

"That's good," she said.

Carolyn and I cheered. "A toast to B.J.," I said clinking my glass against theirs.

B.J. was smacking her lips together and really digging it. I decided I'd better find out what was so good. I'm not a banana lover to begin with and it was much too sweet for me but I didn't want B.J. to know so I told her I thought it was very interesting. I think Annie Greensprings turned me against the sweet stuff forever.

"I think that now, I will turn the set on," B.J. said.

I don't know what it was, but that just broke up me and Carolyn. Maybe it was the way she kind of waddled out from behind the bar or maybe it was the way she was licking her lips or maybe just the way she said it. Anyway, it cracked us up.

"Just what is so funny?" she asked.

Well, that was even funnier. I guess we knew instinctively that drinking was going to make B.J. even more serious and proper and that's what struck us so funny.

"I do not see anything so side-splitting," she said.

Even funnier.

Carolyn and I were doubled over on our bar stools when we heard Dave's voice. He was standing on the steps.

"Sounds like fun . . . can I join?"

We stopped laughing or at least tried to.

"What's the joke?"

"They are maniacs," B.J. said, and that started us up again. Even Dave started laughing.

"Can I bring my two friends in?" Dave said when we were all laughed out.

Carolyn looked at me, panic on her face. I nodded yes.

"Okay," she said.

Dave put two fingers in his mouth and whistled. How I wish I could do that.

In a few seconds we heard the sound of feet coming through the living room overhead and then we saw them coming down the stairs. They were much bigger than Dave and they looked a bit older, too. They had long greasy hair, one blond, one dark. One guy had a lot of pimples on his face and the other one looked like his nose had been broken a few times. When they got downstairs they sort of looked us over and then the one with the funny nose said to Dave: "Dogs' dinners."

He meant us. Have you ever noticed that even the ugliest, crummiest-looking boys seem to think that all girls should be glamorous model types? It never occurs to them what *they* look like.

"Shut up," Dave said. Then he introduced us. The nose was called Chick and the pimples was called Bingo for reasons that were never explained. When Bingo raised his hand to wave a kind of hello, my heart almost stopped. There on his arm was a tattoo. You guessed it. "Born To Be Bad." Well, there was nothing else to do but make myself another drink and that's exactly what I did.

10

"You know, you drink like a guy," Bingo said to me.
"I suppose you think that's a compliment, don't you?"
"Ain't it?"
"It is a very sexist remark," I said.
"Huh?"
"Never mind."

Even in my very nice, high state I could see that Bingo was hopeless when it came to women and chauvinism. In fact, he was hopeless when it came to anything. At least this is what I thought at around ten o'clock. By midnight, according to B.J., who served as my Boswell that evening, I had either revised my opinion of him, forgotten or didn't care. Apparently, and I am embarrassed to tell you this, by midnight I was curled up in Bingo's arms on the love seat. I shudder to think of it now.

Carolyn, it seems, was off making out in a corner with Chick. Dave was sprawled on the floor, a bottle in one hand, a cigarette in the other. B.J. stayed at the bar, having switched back to Coke hours before, and observed us all—particularly me, as Bingo and I were closest to her. One thing about B.J. is that she has this remarkable memory. The next day she was able to regale us with almost every detail of that night. I, for one, would have been happier to remain the blank I was. But, oh no, B.J. insisted I hear every sordid detail. Such as:

BINGO: Why don't we go upstairs?

ME: What for?

BINGO: You know.

ME: I don't. Why don't you get me another drink?

BINGO: Sure. Then let's get it on upstairs.

ME: Get what on?

BINGO: You're kiddin'?

ME: Where's my drink?

BINGO: You sure can swill it down.

He got up to get me a drink and I suddenly had this mad urge to telephone someone. I lurched my way over to the phone on the bar and picked up the receiver.

"What are you doing, Geri?" B.J. asked. "Who are you calling at this ungodly hour? Don't you think it's time you went to bed?"

"Good idea," Bingo said, leering.

"You shut your filthy mouth," B.J. said.

"Who is this weirdo?" Bingo asked.

"You leave B.J. alone. She's my bestest . . . best . . . better . . . good"

"Here's your drink . . . you're really messed-up, you know that?"

Eloquently, B.J. came to my defense. "And you're the biggest mess I've ever seen."

"Messed-up means drunk, you moron," he said and walked back to the love seat where he plunked himself down with a fresh can of beer.

I started dialing.

"Who are you calling, Geri . . . it's twelve thirty-five in the A.M."

"Good," I said. It rang and rang and, eventually, was picked up. "Hello, there. Is this the famous Mr. Derrick who teaches shop at Walt Whitman High in Goose Bay, New York, in the United States of America, in the Western Hemisphere? Is that whom this is?"

B.J. was moaning and groaning, her head down on the bar, her hands covering her head.

"Do you know who this is, Mr. Potato White Derrick? This is. . . ."

B.J. pushed down on the black button cutting us off. "Leggo, B.J."

"No. You're going to get in a lot of trouble. Hang up."

"No."

"If you don't hang up, I'll pull the phone out of the wall."

"Oh, no, you won't." It was Carolyn, coming over with Chick for more drinks. "Who the hell do you think you are, B.J.? Do you think you're Humphrey Bogart or somebody to go around pulling phones out of people's walls?"

"Make her hang up," B.J. said. "She's calling California."

Before I could protest Carolyn screamed and tore the receiver from my hand, slamming it down and cutting me off from the Horrible White Potato.

"Who wants another drink?" Chick asked.

"I do," I said. "If I can't talk to my lover in California I'll drown my sorrows in. . . ."

"You already have a drink," B.J. said.

"What lover? What'll I tell my parents?" Carolyn squealed.

Chick poured himself a drink and said, "I don't see why you have to tell your parents about her lover . . . it's none of their bizzness."

"Right," I said. "My lover in California is my own bussness."

"I mean about the phone call? What'll I tell them when they get the bill?"

"I called collect," I said.

"Well, why didn't you say so? Why did you make me hang up, B.J.? If she wants to call her lover collect, who cares?"

"You're all disgusting," B.J. said. "I should just go home and let you wallow in your own disgustingness."

"Good idea," Chick said. "Why don't you?"

"Come on back here, Geri," Bingo yelled from the love seat. "I'm lonely."

"What the hell's goin' on around here? What's all the yelling?" Dave shouted from the floor. "Can't a person have any peace?"

"You said it, Dave," Bingo chimed in. "That's all I want . . . just a little piece!" He laughed lasciviously and a beat later we all got his meaning. The boys laughed along with him, but even in our drunken state

Carolyn and I didn't find it funny. And of course B.J.,
being sober, found it horrendously offensive.

"Well, that does it," B.J. said. "That just does it.
You boys can just get yourselves the hell out of here."

As much as Carolyn didn't like Bingo's remark she
liked B.J.'s takeover less. "Well, just who do you think
you are, Joan Crawford or somebody, throwing people
out of other people's houses?"

"Did you hear what he said?"

"This is my house, B.J., and I say who stays and who
goes and you can just go."

"I won't," she said. "Somebody has to look after
you. . . . I know it, you know it and God knows it."

"C'mon," Chick said, "ignore her . . . le's go back
over there." He grabbed Carolyn, who towered over
him, and dragged her back to the corner.

B.J. sat back down on a bar stool, manning her
lookout post, and I went back to Bingo.

B.J. says we immediately started making out. I don't
remember. The thought of making out with Bingo is
puke-provoking. But if B.J. says that's what I did, I
guess that's what I did. She would have no reason to
lie.

Besides, that is the least of it. B.J. says that after
making out for a while, which consisted of a lot of
noisy kissing, I jumped up, unbuttoned my blouse and
threw it across the room. As I told you before, I don't
wear a bra. B.J. screamed and tried to get me to put it
back on. She also tried to get Carolyn's help, but Carolyn was too engrossed in her own making out with
Chick. So B.J. turned to Dave, but he was out like a
light. Finally, she found herself in kind of a wrestling
match with Bingo. She was trying to get him not to look
at me—he was trying to get the shirt from her—and she
was trying to get me to put the shirt back on. Eventually, Carolyn heard the racket and screams and pulled
herself away from Chick. We'll never know exactly
what Carolyn thought was going on because she refuses
to discuss that night. What she did was to pick up a
wooden folding chair and bang Bingo over the head
with it. He, of course, went down and out. I, reluctantly,
put my shirt back on, Chick got Dave up and after

reviving Bingo, they helped him out to the car and left. We learned on Monday that they'd driven Bingo to the emergency room at the hospital where he had five stitches taken in his head. They didn't tell the truth about what happened.

After the boys left, Carolyn threw up all over the bar and then passed out on the floor. And what did I do? I made myself another drink. By this time I was drinking Southern Comfort and water. B.J. says I insisted that she sit up with me—she would have anyway, fearing I'd make some more phone calls or God knows what—while I raved and ranted for two more hours about everything from my mother to the lack of good artists in this country to the sex life of the ant, which I know nothing about. I also vacillated between hysterical laughter and downright sobbing. B.J. said I was revolting.

Finally, about three in the morning, I tapered off both booze and talk and started falling asleep. B.J. suggested I go upstairs to a bed but I insisted that if Carolyn was going to sleep on the floor it was my duty to do the same, a logic I can't explain today. Anyway, after bedding me down on the rug and covering both Carolyn and me, B.J. curled up on the couch and by three-thirty all was quiet on Beekman Avenue.

After four and a half hours of sleep I sat straight up and let out an uncontrollable scream of terror. I don't know what provoked it, a dream perhaps, but it woke both Carolyn and B.J. Carolyn crawled out from behind the bar on all fours, her blanket hanging over her huge hulk like some kind of green and yellow shroud. She said the inevitable. "What happened?"

That was all B.J. needed. She began to tell us. We tried to stop her, neither of us ready for all the horrible details, but she couldn't be stopped. We had played our starring roles the night before—now it was her turn. And, oh, how she loved it! Every decadent detail. We groaned and rolled about, tortured by her words and our heads and our stomachs. While B.J. went on and on I groped my way to the bar and opened a Coke. Pure nectar. I had never felt so awful in my life. I thought it had been bad last time, but this was a hundred times worse.

"I'm never drinking again," Carolyn said.

"Neither am I," I said and I meant it.

Even though I thought some of what B.J. was saying was really quite funny, I was also horrified by it. The part about calling the Potato turned my blood cold and I couldn't believe I'd made out with the hideous Bingo or that I'd taken off my blouse. I decided then and there it was the end of my drinking career. Well, nothing could have been further from the truth. It was only the beginning—and the things I had done that night were minor league compared to what was to come.

When I got home that day, about eleven-thirty, I told my mother I thought I was coming down with a cold and should spend the rest of the day in bed so I'd be well on Monday for school. She agreed—but only after commenting that I looked as though I'd slept in my clothes.

I dragged myself to my room, taking two Cokes, some Yankee Doodles and Spaghetti O's, which I ate straight from the can. My mother said that I certainly believed in feeding a cold. I put all my food next to me on the night table, got Max and Tansy onto the bed with me and waited for Sophie to join us. She did in about five minutes, looking at me with great disdain as if to say "A cold indeed . . . ha!" Then she turned her back on me, shook her right hind leg in my face and went to the end of the bed, settling down in a puff of indignant and disgusted orange fur.

The dogs were not as discriminatory and one cuddled up on either side of me—thank God. I needed their warmth and comfort. I had never felt so frightened and insecure in all my life. I had turned on the TV and I watched whatever came on that channel. I was too sick and too frightened to move to change it.

As the day wore on, my fears grew. I can't explain what I feared because I didn't know. It was a nameless dread like DOOOOOOOOOM! I wished I would fall asleep but I couldn't. I couldn't do anything but lie there with my dogs and cat and eat and drink and wish that it was tomorrow. That was the beginning of my wishing away time, a sad and senseless thing to do but something I would do a lot of in the months ahead.

My mother, very kindly, brought me dinner in bed. I would have preferred something Chinese or a pizza, but I ate my meat loaf silently. And as it grew dark the fear got darker, like a huge gnarled hand closing over me. Around nine-thirty my eyes began to close and the last thing I remember thinking was: If this is a hangover I never want to have one again.

11

I kept my vow not to drink for quite a while—quite a while being two and a half weeks. That's how long the horror of Bingo and my hangover lasted. How quickly we forget!

Well, actually, I didn't forget. I told Dave I really couldn't go through another hangover like that and he explained to me that there was absolutely no need for hangovers. First, he said, don't mix your grains. In other words, if I started out with bourbon I shouldn't switch to Scotch or vodka—stick with the same grain all night. Much, much later I found out that this had nothing to do with anything, but at the time it sounded good. Anything would have sounded good. You see, the truth is I *wanted* to drink. I liked the taste. I liked how it made me feel. And I didn't *really* mind what it made me do. So what if I made out with Bingo? So it was a little disgusting—I mean, I never would have done it if I hadn't been drinking—but, in the grander scheme of things, what was so bad about it? It gave me experience, character. And so what if I took my blouse off? That just made me a little more interesting, didn't it? Did it really hurt anything? No. And as far as calling old White Potato—well, nothing came of that either. Of course, B.J. had saved me from telling him who I was, but I probably would've said I was Jane Fonda or Gloria Steinem or somebody like that. I don't think I would have been dumb enough to just come out and say I was me. How boring!

Anyway, back to the hangover, which was the only

thing I didn't like about drinking at that point. Dave said that if, for some reason, you ended up with a bad hangover—he, apparently, didn't have one too often —you simply had a little hair of the dog that bit you! That meant you had a drink.

"In the morning?" I said, shocked.

"Well, whenever. I mean, if you're up at eight and you feel lousy . . . well, then, yes. What difference does it make what time it is?"

"I don't know. It just seems creepy. That's what drunks do, don't they?"

"They do it *every* morning . . . night and day."

"Oh."

"Anyway, it'll fix you right up."

"I can't imagine drinking Southern Comfort at eight in the morning," I said, feeling queasy just thinking about it.

"Why does it have to be Southern Comfort?"

"I dunno. That's just probably what I'd drink the night before."

"You don't have to drink anything that strong in the morning. A beer will do nicely."

"But you said, don't mix grains."

"At night, at night! Boy, sometimes you . . . look, if you don't want to drink, I don't give a damm. I just thought you dug it and we could go to this drag of a dance Saturday and put some life into it, know what I mean?"

"It sounds good to me."

So I had my first date for my first dance—and with practically the best-looking boy in school.

The best-looking and maybe the strangest. For example: When we were in school, like walking down the halls, he'd put his arm around me or hold my hand and stuff like that. But when we were alone, he didn't come near me. Of course, most of the time when we were alone he was drinking. Another odd thing was that Dave didn't seem to mind at all the night I was making out with Bingo. I suppose that was very liberated of him and I should've been glad I had a boyfriend who wasn't possessive and didn't believe in the double standard. But *was* he my boyfriend? The fact was, we'd never even kissed! Yet he kind of acted like my boyfriend. Everyone in school assumed it. You could tell by the way they looked at us. B.J. and Carolyn assumed it. Even my mother assumed it.

"Geri, when are you going to invite Dave for Sunday dinner?" she asked every morning at breakfast.

"I dunno. Why do I have to ask him to Sunday dinner?"

"As much as I think he's too smooth, he's obviously what you've chosen for a boyfriend so I'm just trying to be a good mother and have him to Sunday dinner. I always had my boyfriends to Sunday dinner."

"I'm not sure he's my boyfriend."

"Don't be ridiculous, Geri. Of course he's your boyfriend. Do you hear that, George? She doesn't even know she has a boyfriend when she has a boyfriend. What have I raised?"

My father said, "Ugh," or something like it.

I knew, of course, that Dave and I were friends and I guessed that that was more important than anything. So what if we never kissed? Maybe that's the way things were now? All I had to go by was my mother and she certainly didn't know anything about the seventies. I wished I could ask Jack what he thought, but I didn't trust him enough not to tell Barbara or somebody. Anyway, the point was that Dave liked me and wanted to take *me* to the dance—so why was I complaining?

I had something much more important to worry about. I didn't know how to dance! Not a step. And I had no sense of rhythm. And I had two left feet. At least that's what my mother always told me. So what should I do? Should I tell Dave? I was sure he was a good dancer. If I told him I didn't know how to dance, maybe he wouldn't want to go to the dance with me. I mean, who would? Who would want to go to a dance with a person who didn't know how? On the other hand, I could break the date. I wouldn't have to tell the truth. I could pretend I was sick. That, of course, involved waiting until the last minute and that wasn't exactly fair to him either. Maybe I could tell him right away that I had to go out of town that night. But I wanted to go. I had never been to a school dance before. Besides, I had done the dumbest thing ever. I'd told my mother I was going.

"A dance! Oh, my God! What will you wear? We'll go right down to Walsh's on Saturday morning and buy something. If we go at nine when it opens that'll give me time to shorten it if it needs it."

"Shorten what?" I asked.

"Why, your dress, of course."

"What dress?"

"The one we'll buy at Walsh's. You have to have something new. . . . You can't go in any old thing. It's not a formal, is it?"

"No."

"Well, then we'll just get some nice kind of cocktail dress and—"

"Mother, no dress."

"Hmmmm?"

"No dress."

"What do you mean, no dress, Geri?"

"I mean, it's not that kind of a dance."

"Well, what kind of a dance is it? You don't intend to go naked, do you?"

"I intend to go in jeans. That's the kind of dance it is."

"A jean dance?"

"Well, no. I mean, it's not called that or anything, but that's what everyone wears to these kinds of dances. It's informal."

"Informal? Informal to you means wearing clothes you'd wear in a coal mine? In a field? In a ditch? In prison?"

"It's what everyone will be wearing. I don't know why you act so surprised? You've seen the way Jack goes to dances."

"It's different for boys."

I groaned.

"A girl should look pretty, feminine . . . not like a common laborer."

And so it went. The point was, she knew I'd been asked—it made her whole week—and she'd have my head if I broke the date. So the only choice I had was to try and learn how to dance before Saturday night. That gave me three days. Carolyn and B.J. were no help because they didn't know how either. That left my family. Halfway through the lime Jello I dropped my little bombshell.

"Hey, listen, I don't know how to dance and if I don't learn I don't see how I can go to the dance on Saturday night. You know what I mean?"

"You don't know how to dance?" my mother asked, amazed.

"Right."

"How is that possible?"

Jack said, "Maybe it's because of her two left feet."

"Just how is that possible?" my mother went on, ignoring Jack. "*I* was the best dancer in my school. I won prizes. How could it be that you don't know how to dance?"

"No one ever taught me, I guess."

"Well, we'll rectify that right this minute." She jumped up from the table and practically ran into the living room. We all looked at each other, saying nothing. In a few moments music began blasting from the stereo. It was Tony Martin singing "Dance, Ballerina, Dance." Not only is that particular song revolting in its philosophy—a woman loses her man if she doesn't give up her career—it is also something known as a foxtrot, a slow cheek-to-cheek dance.

Mother stood in the archway between the living room and dining room.

"C'mon, what are you waiting for?"

"C'mon where?" I asked.

"Geri, really! I'm going to teach you to dance."

"To that?" I said, indicating the repugnant Tony Martin.

"Of course. You take off your shoes and stand on my feet and I move you around. That way you get the feel of it."

Jack started laughing. I felt like crying. My father finished his Jello silently.

"I don't see what's so funny. That is precisely the way my mother taught me. We danced round and round in the kitchen to Les Paul and Mary Ford singing 'How High the Moon.' I remember it vividly. And I turned out to be a superb dancer. Isn't that right, George?"

"You're a very good dancer, Ginger."

"Look, Mother, there's no point in me learning to dance to 'Dance, Ballerina, Dance.' I mean, where would I ever use it?"

"I realize, of course, that at your coal mining affair on Saturday night they won't be playing 'Dance, Ballerina, Dance,' but a fox-trot is a fox-trot."

"Exactly. A fox-trot is a fox-trot. Nobody does the fox-trot anymore!"

"I assumed when you said you couldn't dance you were referring to civilized dances. Anyone can jump around to those awful sounds, can't they?"

"Anyone but me," I said. "I don't know the steps."

"You mean those dreadful gyrations are actual steps . . . there are *steps* that go with those noises?"

"Mom," Jack said, "there are all kinds of dances. It's not exactly a matter of steps . . . you just have to be loose and go with the music."

"You mean to tell me that you never do a sane dance? Never get close? If so, I don't want to know."

"You want me to teach you, Geri?" Jack asked.

"How can you teach a rock to be loose?"

"Come on."

"Okay, but I know I can't."

As Tony Martin ended and Jack and I went into the living room, we could hear Mother raving on to Dad.

"They have no taste today, no style, nothing. They wouldn't understand the beauty of a waltz if they fell over it. Can you imagine how they'd react to Eddie Fisher singing 'Oh, My Papa?' "

"As a matter of fact, Ginger, I *can* imagine."

Jack put on the Beatles and started trying to loosen me up. Well, it was hopeless. *I* was hopeless. I felt like a fool. I kept tripping over my own feet and my arms felt like two iron weights at my sides. I couldn't get the beat and I couldn't move without feeling that every part of my body was sticking out at a different angle, looking enormous and clumsy.

My mother's comments didn't help: "Nice." "Graceful." "Pretty." "Very feminine." "Looks like two pigs at a trough." "What's this one called, the Saint Vitus' Dance?"

"I can't . . . I just can't," I said to Jack.

"You're not trying," he said.

"I am. That's what's so discouraging."

"Get loose," he said.

"This is as loose as I can get."

"Get up on the balls of your feet. You're tight all over, Geri . . . I can see it. Just go with the music."

"I can't . . . I feel like a fool."

"That's the first sensible thing you've said in years," Mother said.

"You're not helping, Mom," Jack said. "This is the way we dance today and you know it. Why don't you go look at an old movie or something and let me teach her alone?"

So Mother left the room, mumbling something about Vaughn Monroe, and Jack patiently continued to try. It was a bummer! I couldn't stop seeing myself through everybody else's eyes. I could see Beverly Maher and Joyce Fell watching me and howling with laughter, not to mention Stan Karanewski and Joan Goldstein. A million eyes were on me, a million mouths open in outright, prolonged laughter. Finally, Jack just gave up.

"You're hopeless," he said.

"I know."

"I think you should go to the movies with him instead."

"He wants to go to the dance."

"Well, why don't you break your leg or something?"

"Thanks."

"Tell him the truth."

"I guess," I said. "Thanks for trying."

"Yeah."

But I had no intention of telling him the truth. I didn't know then what I would do, but I knew I'd come up with something. As it turned out, I didn't have to. The next day while we were walking from history to study hall, Dave said to me, "I don't dance, ya know. . . . I mean, who the hell wants to dance? Dancing's a real drag. . . . I don't see the point, do you?"

I had never felt so relieved. "I don't see the point at all."

However, after relief came confusion. If he didn't dance, why did he want to go? The only way to find out was to ask. "Dave, I know this may seem like a peculiar question to you but . . . well, if you don't dance, how come you want to go?"

"I dunno." He shrugged. "I just thought it might be fun to watch the freaks."

"The freaks?" The word hit me like a wet towel on a gray day. Didn't he know he'd be going with one of the freaks? Didn't he know that yet?

"Yeah. Why do you look like that?"

"Look like what?"

"I dunno . . . all strung out or something."

I wanted to say, I look this way because *I* am a freak. But I didn't. I couldn't. Instead I said, "What freaks?"

"Any freaks. All freaks. The dancing freaks. . . . What's the matter with you?"

I was beginning to get the picture. "Oh, you mean the kids who dance . . . you mean kids who dance are freaks?"

"Yeah, sure."

I could have shouted with joy. Dave had his own terminology. I should have known. What he was saying was that we, the freaks (by Walt Whitman High standards—by now Dave must have been considered a freak since he was basically a loner and hung out with me), were going to watch the jocks, straights, etc. (by Walt Whitman High standards) be freaks! It was a bit confusing, but I loved it.

"Don't you think it'll be fun to watch them make jackasses out of themselves?"

"The most fun I can think of," I said.

"I figure we'll get fired up a little before we go and I'll have some stuff at the dance so we can get really bombed out. Sound like a good night?"

"Sounds like a great night," I said, and for the first time I really meant it.

12

The way my mother carried on the night of the dance you would have thought I was getting married. Though I was spared the new cocktail dress, Mother wasn't—or, I should say, she didn't spare herself. She just *happened* to drop by Walsh's that morning and they had just *happened* to have some cocktail dresses on sale and she had just *happened* to buy one.

For those of you who don't know what cocktail dresses are, let me explain. A cocktail dress is something fancy a person wears to a cocktail party and they are always ugly! They were very popular in the fifties and Walsh's is the only store for miles around that carries them. It is, of course, my mother's favorite store. Walsh's is the kind of store where if you went in and asked for a pantsuit the salesperson would look at you as though you were from another planet and then direct you down the street to Matthew's & Kaplan's, the men's store.

Anyway, after dinner my father and I were sitting in the living room—he, doing a crossword puzzle, I, doing a few sketches while waiting for Dave—when my mother appeared at the top of the steps in her new pink taffeta and lace cocktail dress. We knew she was there because she cleared her throat several times until we both looked up. When she had our attention she descended grandly. We stared. When she reached the bottom of the stairs she did a little twirl, pretending she had forgotten something and was going back up the stairs. Then she laughed in a peculiar way, said, "Oh,

dear," as though she just remembered that she *hadn't*
forgotten anything and swept into the room in a very
bad imitation of Bette Davis.

"What are you supposed to be?" my father asked.
He was never very tactful.

"I beg your pardon?" she said.

"Are you going somewhere?"

"Isn't that just like a man?" she said to me. "Just
because a girl gets dressed up to look nice for her man
he—"

"Woman," I said.

"What's that?"

"Woman. You're a woman, not a girl. I'm a girl."

"Please, Geri, don't start that."

"I'm not going out," my father said. "I'm very tired."

"Why, who said anything about goin' out. Gracious,
ah've never seen such a fuss over nothin'."

I had a sneaking suspicion that I heard a slight
Southern accent in my mother's voice.

She went on: "My land, is there somethin' wrong
with a girl wantin' to look pretty?"

"Why are you talking that way?" my father and I
said in unison.

"What way, for heaven's sake?"

"That way," we said.

"Ah don't know *what* you're talkin' about. It is a
real pity when a person is attacked and criticized by
her own family and must depend always on the kindness of strangers."

My father and I looked at each other and nodded.
The night before the movie *Streetcar Named Desire*
had been on TV and one of Blanche Dubois' lines is, "I
have always depended on the kindness of strangers."
Blanche is a Southern woman. My father went back to
his crossword puzzle and I to my sketching.

In a moment I heard Mother's own voice.

"Are you going to pin your corsage on your sweatshirt, Geri?" she asked sarcastically. Then: "You look
like hell."

"Thank you. You've filled me with confidence."

"Look at her, George."

"I've seen her."

"Can you imagine me going to a dance looking like that?"

"I didn't know you when you were the belle of the ball," he said, not looking up.

"Well, she looks just awful . . . like some kind of phys. ed. instructor or something. It's disgusting."

"This is a brand new sweatshirt I've never worn before."

"I offered to buy her a new dress, but, no, she'd rather look like a garbage collector," said the mother of the bride.

"Leave the girl alone, Virginia."

"And that hair . . . it just hangs there."

"It's supposed to hang there," I said.

"And what are you doing sitting here in the living room?"

"Huh?"

"What are you doing here?"

"I live here."

"Don't you know anything, Geri? Go upstairs this minute."

"Why?"

"You can't be sitting here when Dave arrives," she said, trying to pull me up from the sofa.

"Why not?"

"What will he think?"

"He'll think he came to the right house," I said, pulling out of her grasp.

"He'll think you're crazy," she said. "Now go upstairs immediately. Listen to your mother for once . . . if anyone knows how to trap a man it's me."

"Nice talk," my father said.

"I don't *want* to trap a man," I said. "I think that kind of thinking is disgusting."

She started pulling at me again and my pencils and sketch pad fell to the floor. "Mother . . . please."

"Leave the girl alone, Virginia," my father said, filling in a word in his puzzle.

"You know nothing about this, George . . . you're as bad as she is. Geri, please, listen to your mother. It's important for you to keep the boy waiting."

"Why?"

"Do you want him to think you can't wait? You must never appear eager."

"I like being punctual."

"That's a lovely trait but not when it comes to men." She gave me a final yank and as she did the sound of her ripping dress filled the room. "Oh, my God!"

The seam on her left side had completely opened and the doorbell was ringing.

"Oh, my God," she screamed again. "I can't let him see me like this." She ran for the stairs as I started toward the door.

When I opened the door I screamed.

My father said in the background, "Leave the girl alone, Virginia."

Dave stood in the doorway wearing a horrible green and purple rubber mask, the face of a beast.

"Uh, I come ta take da maiden ta da dance," he said in a low moronic voice.

"Uh, ya come to da right house," I said, laughing. Actually, I wasn't laughing so much at him as I was at the thought that my mother would have opened the door if she'd succeeded in getting me upstairs. "Uh, come on in," I said.

He pulled off the mask and stood grinning at me. As the mask came off, the smell of liquor hit my nostrils.

"Whew," I whispered, waving the smell away.

"Sorry about that," he giggled. "I'm a few ahead of you."

I put my finger to my lips indicating that he should be quiet and brought him into the living room. "Daddy, you remember Dave, don't you?"

"Hello, sir," Dave said, extending his hand.

My father took his hand and grunted something unintelligible.

"Well, we'll be going now," I said.

"Don't be too late," my father said.

"No, sir, don't worry."

As we got into Dave's small truck which said BOB'S FISH MARKET on the side, I heard a strange knocking sound. I looked up at my mother's bedroom window and saw her rapping on the glass and motioning us back. She kept trying to open the window but it was obviously stuck.

"What's that sound?" Dave asked, getting in.

"It's the sound of the past," I said.

"Huh?"

"Never mind." I closed the door. "Let's go." I looked up again and saw that she was still waving her arms frantically. Dave pulled away. For a moment or two I felt very sad. After all her preparations and excitement about me going off to a dance and being the mother of the bride and all that, she had completely missed it. Sometimes my mother was pathetic. Dave interrupted my thoughts.

"We're gonna have to buy some booze," he said. "Do you have any money?"

I told him I had five dollars.

"Good. I have enough for some vodka, but you probably want your own, right?"

I said I did and asked how we could buy it. He smiled and said to trust him. When he pulled up in front of Gordon's liquor store a man was just going in and Dave jumped out of the truck and stopped him. I rolled down my window so I could hear.

"Excuse me, sir. I wonder if you would do me a favor? My girl and I are going to a party and I left my proof home, which is an hour away, and well. . . ." His voice got low, very buddy-buddy, but I could still hear. "I don't want her to think I'm a complete goof. You know how it is. Anyway, sir, I was wondering if you would purchase the liquor for me?"

The man, who was about forty, looked Dave over, then glanced toward me. "You left your proof home?" he asked Dave.

"That's right, sir."

"How old are you?"

"I just turned eighteen last month."

"And the girl?"

"She'll be eighteen in three weeks."

"She looks pretty young."

"Well, sir, if you'd like to see her driver's license she'll be glad to. . . ."

My heart stopped.

"No, no, that won't be necessary," the man said. "Okay, what do you want?"

I rolled up the window. It seemed like a very close call to me. When Dave got back in the truck with the booze he was grinning madly. "Never fails," he said.

"You mean people always buy it for you?"

"Sure. Of course, you have to know which ones you can ask. Almost anybody between eighteen and twenty-five will do it, but the rest have to be big boozers themselves. Women over twenty-five, whether they're boozers or not, will never do it."

"How do you know who's a boozer?"

"The face, the eyes, the color of the skin. When they get to be over thirty they start to show it. . . . They get puffy-looking for one thing."

"That man looked perfectly normal to me."

"You didn't see him up close. Besides, you should have seen the way his hands shook when I gave him the money. He was a drunk, all right. There was a real sad, desperate look in his eyes."

"Are we going to get like that someday?"

"Are you kidding? Not me. I got it all planned out. When I'm eighteen I quit everything and start leading the healthy life. I'll take my last drink the last day I'm seventeen so that gives me just about another year. I intend to do all the unhealthy stuff like drinking and smoking while I'm young. That's why I'm packing it in as fast as I can now."

He pulled the truck into Bohack's parking lot way back under the trees.

"Enough talk," he said. "Let's drink."

Dave had brought some plastic glasses and a thermos of water. He gave me my bottle of Southern Comfort and opened his own bottle of vodka. We poured the booze, toasted to the dance ahead of us and started drinking. When we were ready to go to the dance he opened two cans of Coke, poured them out onto the parking lot and told me to fill my can with booze.

"That way you can take it into the dance and nobody will know what you're drinking. Cool, huh?"

I did what he said and walked into the dance carrying

my can of booze/Coke and though I felt a lot more relaxed than I had when we'd started out, I still had plenty of anxiety about the evening that stretched ahead of us.

13

The gym was decorated in typical school-dance fashion. I'd seen enough movies to know that. There were crepe paper streamers and posters and two big signs strung over the basketball nets saying "Colour My World," the theme of the dance. The band, called Lords of the Rings after the Tolkien book, was blasting away. A lot of kids were dancing but just as many were not. Plenty of kids were standing around watching, drinking Cokes and talking. There were lots of girls there without dates—boys, too. B.J., Carolyn and I had talked about coming to dances together but had decided not to because we couldn't dance and thought it would be very embarrassing if somebody asked us to and we had to say no. The real truth, though we never admitted it to each other, was we were afraid *nobody* would ask us.

Dave and I walked over to a corner, passing the chaperons: Potato Face Derrick, dreadful Mr. Kelly with his wife, Mr. Stanton, the principal—the type who wears his pants under his armpits—and Ms. Laine, my humanities teacher. She was new this year. Nobody knew too much about her but she was pretty young and seemed okay so far. Dave smiled and made a big thing out of saying hello to them all. I just smiled.

"That's insurance," he said, when we got to our place in the corner. "You gotta act open and aboveboard so they don't suspect anything."

"I have to admit," I said, "I feel nervous carrying this." I held out the Coke can.

"Well, don't. Nobody knows what's in it but you and me . . . and about a dozen other kids," he said.

"Huh?"

"Don't look so scared." He laughed. "I'm talking about them." He gestured across the room.

A bunch of kids, most of them known as juicers, were standing around talking to each other. All of them had Coke cans in their hands.

"You mean . . . ?"

"Right."

"How do you know?"

"I can tell. Just watch them for a few minutes."

I did. They just looked like they were drinking Coke to me. "What am I supposed to see?" I asked.

"You know, for an artist you're pretty unobservant."

I felt very stupid and took a big swig of my Southern Comfort.

"Can't you see?" he went on. "The way they hold the can . . . the way they sip at it? How about the way they're acting? Christ, you must see that?"

"Maybe I ought to have my eyes checked," I said.

"Yeah, maybe."

"How come you can tell all that?" I asked. "How come you know so much about it?"

"I've seen it all my life," he said in a kind of dull, flat tone.

"What do you mean?"

"Nothing. Never mind."

I realized when he said that that there was no sense pursuing it. I didn't know Dave all that well yet, but there were some things I had learned very quickly. When he said *never mind,* he meant it.

"Why don't we go over and join them?" he asked.

"Join who?" I felt panicky. I wasn't sure who he meant but it didn't matter. The idea of joining anyone panicked me.

"Those kids," he said, gesturing toward the juicers again.

"Do you know them?" I, of course, knew them all by name but I never spoke to them or anything.

"Well, sort of. I mean, I'm in gym class with a couple of the guys and—"

"Let's not," I said quickly.

"Why?"

"I . . . they don't like me."

"How do you know?"

"I have a feeling." First of all, I couldn't imagine just going over and barging in on them. I mean, they all knew I was a freak. What would they think? And besides, I really never wanted to be part of them. I mean, they were juicers and juicers were just plain ordinary drunks. Why would Dave want to associate with them anyway?

"Well, let's find out."

"No," I said vehemently, pulling at his sleeve.

He looked at me a moment. "You scared, Geri?"

I nodded.

"Oh."

We stood there looking at each other for a few seconds.

"Well, why don't you drink up?" He said. "Drink up and then maybe we'll go over, okay? But if you really don't want to, we won't." He smiled sweetly at me.

He was terrific. Not many boys would have been so understanding.

"Thanks," I said. I was just about to clink Coke cans with him when Beverly Maher and Joan Goldstein came walking by us.

"Want a drink, girls?" Dave asked, holding out his can to them. "There's more to this than meets the eye," he said.

I almost fainted. Why was he telling them? They could report us and probably would.

"Buzz off," Beverly said.

"You're such a phony," Joan added. They kept on walking.

Dave was smiling very smugly when I looked back at him. "More insurance," he said. "Now nobody'll think there's a thing in here but Coke."

"But what if they'd stopped and taken a sip?"

"I knew they wouldn't," he said. "They hate me . . . you know . . . ever since that day with you. They think I'm crazy or something and that's just the way I want it."

"Why?"

"So they won't bug me. I know they're supposed to be the big deals of this school, but to me they're squares with a capital S. I can't stand their type . . . never could. They think they're such hot shit with their money and country clubs and all that stuff. They make me sick. Snobs."

"But they weren't snobby with you," I said.

"That's 'cause they didn't know me . . . they would have been snobby soon enough."

"What do you mean?"

"Nothing. Never mind."

There it was again. I let it go. But I vowed I'd find out more about Dave. He couldn't remain a mystery man forever.

"Hey," he said, "we're getting heavy here . . . c'mon, let's drink."

We both drank. It was strong without any water or anything, but I didn't mind. Mind! I liked it. I was starting to feel very good now. The Lords of the Rings were really socking it to us and almost everybody was on the dance floor. I really wished I could dance then. I could feel the music going through me and it was sort of like I needed it to come out somehow. All of a sudden I found myself keeping time to the music with my foot. Surprisingly enough, I discovered I was with the beat. I started moving in place.

"You wanna give it a whirl?" Dave said.

"I thought you didn't dance?" I said.

"I don't." He grinned. "Except sometimes."

I started to tell him I didn't know how, but then I realized I *did*. I was sure I could do anything anyone else was doing. "What'll I do with this?"

"Drink it."

"I can't just chugalug it."

"I'll help."

He grabbed the can from me, took a big swig and gave it back to me. He'd almost finished it and for a moment I was angry that he'd drunk my booze. But, basically, I was feeling too good to let anything really bother me. I took the last swallow, Dave grabbed me and we kind of ran onto the dance floor.

"Let's show them how it's really done," he said. Almost immediately it seemed like the most natural thing in the world, as though I'd been dancing all my life. My feet began doing things I never thought they could do. I was loose, looser than my brother had ever been. My arms were light and my hips moved like they were on a swivel. In short, I was *great!* At least I felt great and that was all that mattered. Besides, I looked around me and nobody was watching us or laughing or anything, so I guess we didn't look any worse than anyone else. But the really funny thing was that even if they had been looking at us—I mean, to laugh at us or something—I don't think I would have cared. That was the best feeling of all. I didn't care what anyone else thought. *I* felt GREAT! For the first time in my life, except for when I was drawing, I felt in tune with myself. My body wasn't some kind of beast, separate from my mind. I was all one and the one I was was Beautiful, Graceful, Witty, Brilliant, Sexy, Talented, and just plain Terrific. There I was, dancing away in the Walt Whitman High gymnasium—Geri Peters—The Great Me!

Dave and I kept dancing for hours, stopping every once in a while to go outside and have some more booze. When the dance was over, we were practically the last ones to leave. We walked, arms around each other, tired and happy, back to the truck. I groped around on the floor for my bottle. When I found it I saw it was almost empty.

"I wish we had more," I said, unscrewing the cap.

"Me, too. Too late now to buy any, unless you wanna break in someplace."

I lowered the bottle after draining the last drop—I'd long ago misplaced the glass—and looked at Dave. He had what you might call a glint in his eye.

"Are you kidding?" I asked.

He shrugged. "Ya said ya wished we had more . . . just a suggestion."

I knew he meant it. If I said yes, let's break into a liquor store, we'd do it. For a second the idea really appealed to me and then Dave started up the truck and began babbling about some kid in the school he used to go to who walked down the halls on his hands. The idea of the liquor store caper was gone before it even got a hearing.

Dave hunched over the wheel and started driving slowly out of the lot. That was a funny thing about Dave. When he was drunk he never drove fast like a lot of other kids. He just crept along, his eyes glued to the road. I guess I was lucky he drove that way. I looked down in my lap and saw the empty Southern Comfort bottle. I don't know why, but suddenly I found myself throwing it out the window. I heard it crash behind us and I loved the sound. It didn't occur to me at the time that it was a terrible thing to do. It just seemed natural. Then Dave took the last swallow from his bottle and did the same thing. We both started laughing when we heard his hit the road. I wished I had more bottles to throw out.

"You wanna go to Crawford's Woods?" Dave asked.

The question startled me. Crawford's Woods was a place everyone went to make out. If I said no, I was rejecting him, saying I didn't want to make out. If I said yes, I was letting myself in for God knew what? I mean, it would have been a lot easier if he'd just driven to the Woods without asking. Once there, I would have been confronted with the same decision but that would be easier than making it in advance.

"You hear me?" Dave asked.

"Yes."

"Yes, what? Yes, you heard me or yes, you wanna go?"

He sounded angry.

"I don't know," I said, my nice high fading fast.

"You don't know what? If you heard me or if you wanna go?"

"Will you stop that? I heard you."

"Well?"

"I said, I don't know."

"Well, if you don't know then we won't go." He swung the truck around and started toward my house.

I had no idea Dave was so—so what? So sensitive? So touchy? I really didn't know what his behavior meant. I just knew he sounded awful and he looked

awful, too. His face was filled with hate and anger.
When we pulled up in front of my house I felt lousy.

"Look, Dave. . . ."

"Get the hell out," he said.

"What's wrong with you?"

"Out!"

I had never felt so hurt in all my life. I climbed out
and before I could even shut the door, Dave started
driving away. I watched him go, feeling creepy and
crazy. What was so awful about saying that I didn't
know whether I wanted to make out or not? Didn't he
have enough sense to know that I was scared? I guess
I'd been giving Dave more credit than he deserved.

As I started up the walk I could see the blue light
from the television in the den. That meant my mother
was up. I felt really lousy now. If only I had another
drink. Why not? She wouldn't hear me come in if I
was very quiet. As the plan grew in my head, I began to
feel better.

I opened the front door and carefully tiptoed through
the living room into the kitchen where I opened the refrigerator and took out a Coke. As slowly as possible,
I opened the flip-top can. Even so it made a small
phhht which sounded to me like a bomb going off.
I poured three-quarters of the Coke down the drain
and tiptoed into the dining room where the liquor was
kept. It was very dark when I opened the liquor cabinet
door and I couldn't see the labels on the bottles. I
decided it didn't matter, took the bottle closest to the
front, uncapped it and began pouring it into the Coke
can. This wasn't as easy as it sounds. It was dark and I
wasn't all that steady. I spilled some on the floor and
some dribbled down over my hand. When I licked it off
I discovered it was vodka.

After putting the bottle away and wiping the floor
with the inside of my sweatshirt, I took a big gulp from
the can and almost instantly I started to feel better.
Then I walked into the den. My mother was looking
at an old movie. Normally, she would have kept on
looking—nothing could tear her away from one of her
old flicks—but tonight was different.

"Well?" she said, looking up at me eagerly.

I sat across the room from her so she wouldn't smell the liquor. I was kind of surprised to be there. I mean, usually I just checked in and beat it upstairs as fast as possible so I didn't have to answer any questions. But tonight I felt like talking, even if it was to old Ginger!

"Well what?" I didn't want to seem too ready to talk. I had to play it cool.

"How was it? A mother likes to know how her daughter's first dance went."

"It was fine," I said, taking a swig from my Coke can. Understate, I told myself. That's what she expects.

"Geri, I wish you would learn to express yourself better. What do you think 'it was fine' tells a person? It tells a person nothing."

Instinctively, I knew I shouldn't talk too much because I might slur or something, but my need to talk overrode my fears of discovery. So I started.

"Well, Dave and I were the hit of the dance. It was just like a movie, Mom. When we got out on the dance floor everybody else stopped and formed a big circle around us and clapped and cheered and everything. We were great. Then all the boys wanted to dance with me . . . so I danced all night . . . a different boy every dance and all the other girls were jealous and then the boys voted me Queen of the Dance."

She looked at me strangely on that last piece of information. Maybe I had gone too far. But after all, it *was* what she wanted to hear, wasn't it?

"Queen of the Dance?" she said.

I didn't blink an eyelash or miss a beat. "Queen of the Dance," I said. "I was just as surprised as you." I had to elaborate. I couldn't stop. "The thing was that they weren't even planning to vote for a queen or anything, that's why I don't have a clown . . . crown or anything. But when they saw how good I was and how everybody wanted to dance with me and all . . . the boys just got together and voted. It wasn't official in the sense that it was pranned . . . planned . . . but it still goes in the official Queen Book."

"What's that?" she asked, getting into it again.

"They have this book they mark all the Queens down in. It goes back to Nineteen twenty-two or something." They had no such book.

"And your name will be in it?" Her eyes said, tilt!

"Right . . . Queen of the Colour-My-World Dance: Geri Peters."

"Oh, that's wonderful, Geri . . . tell me more. What did the other girls have on? No, never mind, you can skip that. Tell me . . ." And she stopped, looking at me in that peculiar way again. "Geri," she said slowly, "you can't dance."

"But I can," I said. "I did."

"What was it, some sort of magic?"

I smiled. In a way she was right. It was magic, the magic of Southern Comfort. But, of course, I couldn't tell Ginger that. "Dave taught me."

"Tonight?"

"Well, no . . . he gave me some lessons in the last few days. When a person really cares about you, he can teach you anything . . . even if you do have two left feet!"

She believed me. "Yes, yes, I can see that. Well, what else happened? Who did you dance with? What did you talk about?"

And I was off. I told her everything I thought she'd like to hear and she loved every minute of it. I knew she was completely taken in because when *Gilda* came on at one-thirty, a movie with Rita Hayworth and Glenn Ford and one of her very favorites, she didn't even notice. By the time I finished with all the details I was really believing it myself. I'd finished my can of Coke and had a sudden urge to draw so I told her I was sleepy. She was reluctant to let me go.

"How many of them asked you for dates?" she asked.

"How many what?"

"Of the boys?"

"Oh, almost all of them," I said, inching toward the door.

"So which one are you going out with first?"

"I'm not going with anyone . . . Dave and I are going steady." That was a really dumb thing to say because, for all I knew, I might not see Dave ever again.

"Oh. Well, don't you think you should play the field?"

"I like Dave . . . I gotta go bed . . . to bed. Tired."

"Okay. We'll talk about it tomorrow."

"You goin' up?"

"In a while. . . ." She glanced at the set and saw that *Gilda* hadn't been on long. "Geri," she said, as I was almost out the door, "you made me very happy tonight . . . I'm very proud of you."

"Yeah." I left the room and for a moment I felt a twinge of guilt. Then it passed. Why should *I* feel guilty? She should feel guilty for having such rotten values that she'd be proud of me because I was made Queen of a stupid dance and all the boys danced with me. Is that something to be proud of? NO. Now I was mad. I went back in the kitchen, got another Coke and repeated the procedure I'd followed earlier. I carried it up to my room.

The rest of the night is really a blur. I know I drew some terrible pictures because they were there to horrify me in the morning. I think I made some phone calls, too. Fortunately or unfortunately, depending on how you look at it, I have a phone in my room. My father had it put in when I was twelve and had mononucleosis and had to stay in bed for six weeks. Anyway, that morning I had a vague memory of talking to somebody on the phone. The thought gave me the fears down to my toes. I suspected the worst. Maybe it was Potato Derrick? Or maybe this one? Or that one? I lived with that horror all day and night until I got to school on Monday and nobody said anything. The point is, I really couldn't remember much about the last part of the night.

I lay in my bed Sunday morning, Sophie staring at me with disgust—God knows what she'd witnessed— and tried to piece it together. All I could come up with were fragments and even they were elusive. The Coke can was empty on my bedside table and besides the awful drawings, that was really the only tangible evidence I had.

As I lay there, feeling just terrible, the phone rang. I picked it up.

"Hello," I said.

"Oooooooooooh," a male voice groaned. At least I thought it was a male voice. It was hard to tell.

"Who is this?"

"Oooooowooohaaaah," it said.

A certain tone in the *aaaah* gave me a clue. "Dave?" I asked, tentatively.

"Yeeeees."

"What's wrong?"

"Hung-o-ver."

"Me, too," I said and we both groaned at the same time.

Dave said there was no point in us suffering by ourselves—he'd pick me up in half an hour.

I thought it was odd that he'd even called after the way the evening ended, but then it occurred to me that maybe he didn't remember it.

My mother was in the kitchen when I came downstairs. I was walking very slowly, very carefully because every movement felt as though a spike was piercing my brain. The one thing I had to have was a cold Coke. A real one. As I reached into the refrigerator, my mother said, "Well, if it isn't Ginger Rogers?"

Suddenly, everything I'd told her the night before came rushing in on me. For those who don't know, Ginger Rogers was one of Fred Astaire's famous dancing partners in the movies and also who my mother was named after, I think. I could tell by the tone in her voice that the jig was up. She'd probably talked to Jack.

"Queen of the Dance, huh?" She was tapping her foot.

I opened my Coke and tried keeping my back to her. She came around in front of me.

"I'm talking to you, Geri."

"I hear you."

"Queen of the Liars, is more like it."

"Well, that's better than Queen of Nothing, isn't it?"

"I hate a liar," she said and there was a tone in her voice that I'd never heard before. She really meant it. "I should have known that a girl who goes to a dance in a truck that says BOB'S FISH MARKET on the side couldn't be the Queen of anything."

"We didn't take the truck into the dance," I said.

"Don't get fresh with me . . . I want to know why you lied to me?"

"I just exaggerated a little."

"Exaggerated? The hell you did. You lied. Jack told me everything."

"What? What did he tell you?"

"That nothing happened. You danced with Dave and that was all. And he said the one time he noticed you, you looked like you were doing acrobatics instead of dancing."

"So what?"

"So what was all this you gave me about being a great dancer and everybody asking you to dance and . . . ?"

"I don't want to talk about it." I started out of the kitchen.

She grabbed me by the arm. "Where are you going?"

"Dave is picking me up."

"For what?"

"We're going for a ride."

"You're going nowhere."

"Oh, yes, I am," I said. I had never spoken to her like that before. But I knew I had to get out of there. Besides, I wanted to be with Dave. I needed to be with somebody who understood how I felt.

"I want to know why you lied to me, Geri. There's nothing worse in this world than a liar."

"Okay," I said, "I'll tell you. I went to the dance and I had a really neat time. No matter what Jack said, I liked dancing and I was good . . . I know I was. But I knew that wouldn't be enough for you, so I told you what I thought you wanted to hear and it made you happy . . . you even said so. Nothing I do is ever enough so I told you what you wanted to hear," I screamed.

"I never wanted you to lie," she said, in a peculiar small voice. "I never wanted you to start that."

For a moment I thought she was going to cry and then I heard the sound of Dave's horn and I didn't care whether she was going to cry or not. I pulled away from her and ran out the door. When I got to his truck I realized she hadn't called after me or anything. I thought that was slightly peculiar, but I quickly pushed it aside.

"You look lousy," Dave said when I got in.

"Thanks, so do you." And he did. We both laughed and were off down the road, headed toward my first shared hangover day. It began with the devouring of an enormous pizza from Yolanda's, the only thing I could have eaten, and moved on to revelations that both amazed and shocked me.

14

I don't think there is anything in the world that is more satisfying for a hangover than a huge, gooey pizza. No anchovies or onions or peppers or sausage or mushrooms—just extra cheese and sauce. And plenty of cold beer.

Yolanda's was on a side road in South Hollow. It was a large run-down house, badly in need of paint. With the exception of a tiny red neon sign that said *Beer* in the corner of a window, there was no indication that it was either a bar or a restaurant. In other words, if you didn't know it was there, you wouldn't know it was there. Inside, it was just as rundown as outside. The paint on the walls was peeling and the linoleum buckled and was cracked all over. There were two rooms. The first room you entered housed the bar, which ran the length of the room. Three tables were placed near the windows. The second room, which was much smaller, had a few tables and a beat-up pool table. What the place had to recommend it were steins of draft beer for twenty-five cents, terrific pizza and a surprisingly good jukebox. Also, it had Yolanda!

Of course I don't suppose everybody would have found Yolanda an asset. In fact, I'm sure her presence kept people away. But I thought she was heavenly—heavenly in her horror, if you know what I mean. She was about four feet nine or something. I knew she had to be under five feet because she was a lot shorter than I. I felt like a big galoot standing next to her and looking down. I guess she was in her late fifties. Her hair was that short wiry gray kind and she had very deep brown eyes which looked like the button eyes from a teddy bear I once had. Her mouth was very small but one reason you knew it was there was because she wore a deep purple lipstick. Another was because it was open a lot of the time—talking. But the voice was the best part. If you closed your eyes you would have sworn it was John Wayne. I had never heard a voice like that on any woman and it was particularly funny coming out of such a tiny one. However, I think it was Yolanda's manner, rather than her appearance, that put people off.

"Well, here comes two bums if I ever saw two bums," she said in her bass voice as we walked in.

The three men at the bar looked at us and laughed.

"And what do two baby-bums want in a high-class joint like this? Hallo, Davy. Who's the bird? I know the puss but not the moniker."

"This is Geri," he said. "Yolanda."

"Hi," I said.

"Hi? High is what the cheese gets if I leave it out of the fridge. Ain't ya got no manners? Hallo . . . how-do-ya-do, Miss Yolanda . . . that's what yer supposed ta say, ain't that right, Davy?"

"C'mon, leave her alone," he said, grinning.

"Like you do, I suppose, huh?" She slapped the bar with her tiny hand in front of one of the men, making his head snap up out of his glass. "I'll bet he leaves her alone, huh . . . Richie . . . he leaves her alone all right, ya get my drift?" Then she laughed a great, deep laugh which sounded as though it was coming directly from her knees.

"How about a pizza?" Dave asked, the tips of his ears starting to turn red.

The funny thing was Yolanda didn't really embarrass me because I thought she was so unusual. I'd watched her before when I'd been in there with Carolyn and B.J. but she'd never spoken to me.

"How about it?" Yolands said.

"We want one . . . just cheese . . . extra cheese and extra sauce. And two beers."

"Two beers for two bums," she yelled as though

there were someone waiting to fill the order. Then she got two steins and filled them herself.

Dave took the steins and we went to a table.

"One cheese pie, heavy on the cheese, heavy on the sauce," Yolanda growled to the invisible pie-maker. Then she disappeared into the kitchen to make the pie herself. The place was a one-woman operation.

Neither of us said a word. The beer was the only important thing at that moment. We took long cool swallows. Nothing had ever tasted so good. Suddenly, Dave's expression completely changed. For a second I thought maybe he'd been poisoned. He was facing the door and I turned, following his eyes.

A woman had entered and was walking toward the bar. Now that sounds like nothing, but it wasn't quite nothing. This woman was a weirdo. I'd seen her around town a few times in the last couple of months and I'd been meaning to ask someone who she was. She was medium height and had platinum blond hair which she wore in kind of a pageboy (my mother would have loved it). Her makeup looked as though she were about to go onstage. For one thing, the eyelashes, even at a distance, seemed at least two inches long. But even weirder than the makeup and hair was her outfit. Today she was wearing a red silk blouse with ruffles at the wrists and neck, a gray and green skirt, black tights and very high-heeled silver shoes. I had seen her in other outfits equally bizarre and whenever I'd seen her she was riding an adult three-wheel bicycle—really.

In a very loud, raspy voice she said, "Have no worries, have no fear, your friend Amorette is here! Hiya fellas. Hey, Yo-lan-da, we're dyin' of thirst out here ... get your ass movin'."

"Oh, Christ," Dave muttered.

I looked back at him and saw that he was hunched way down in his chair, looking worse than I'd ever seen him.

"What's wrong?"

He didn't answer. There was a lot of laughter at the bar so I turned back to see what was going on. Just then Yolanda came out of the kitchen, wiping her hands on her flowered apron.

"Well, look what the cat drug in," she boomed. "Where you been the last few days, huh?"

"Been down t' my sister's place . . . couldn't take it . . . it was dry as a bone, know what I mean?"

"I get the drift. One boilermaker comin' up," Yolanda yelled.

The woman started bantering with the men at the bar and I turned back to Dave. His hand covered the side of his face nearest the bar.

"Do you know her?" I asked.

He nodded.

Suddenly, the whole thing became clear to me. It was pretty obvious what kind of a woman this Amorette character was. I mean, I don't usually make superficial judgments like that, but in her case—well, if she wasn't, she was certainly made up to make people think she was. Anyway, I thought she was and I figured that one night Dave had gotten real fired up and he'd probably done something with her and now he was ashamed of it, particularly in front of me.

"You don't have to be embarrassed," I said in my most sympathetic voice. "I understand."

He said, "Huh?"

"It's all right," I went on, "I'm not as naïve as you think I am. I know that these things. . . ."

I never got to finish because just at that moment the subject of our discussion let out a howl as she spotted Dave.

"Oooooohboy . . . look who's here. Hiya, Davyboy."

"Christ," Dave muttered again, realizing the hiding game was over.

She came over to the table, leaned down and kissed him on the top of the head. "How're ya doin', kid? Oooooohboy, this yer little girlfriend, huh?" She switched her drink from her right hand to her left and held out her hand for me to shake. "Hiya. I'm Amorette. It means 'little love or sweetheart' but everyone calls me Bunny so you can, too. What's yer name, honey?"

"Geri," I said, pumping her hand.

"Geri. Comes from Geraldine . . . means 'mighty with the spear.' Hiya, Geri."

"Hi. It doesn't come from Geraldine," I said. "It's just Geri." I spelled it for her.

A dark look came over her face as she let go of my hand. "No such name as G-e-r-i. It's a diminutive of Geraldine. I know all about names, kid."

"It's on my birth certificate," I said stubbornly. Then I felt a kick under the table from Dave.

"Honey, if there's one thing I know it's about names. It comes from Geraldine," she said in a way that made me feel I would forever after tell anyone who wanted to know that my name was a diminutive of Geraldine!

"Yes," I said, "you're probably right."

"Probably? I am right and that's all there is to it. You tell her, Davy."

"You're right," he said sullenly.

"Now take the name David . . . know what that means? It means 'beloved one.'" She laughed, reached out and ran a fattish hand through his hair.

"Cut it out," he said, pulling away.

"He don't like to be touched," she said. "At least not by me." Then she winked at me in a conspiratorial way. "Bet he lets you touch him though, huh?" She laughed, clapped her hands together and stood up. "Yolan-da, bring us another round here, will ya? We're dry as three turds in the desert."

I have to admit I was shocked even though it was a kind of funny expression. I'd never heard anyone talk that way. But although she shocked me, she also fascinated me. I couldn't take my eyes off her. She wiggled her way over to the jukebox.

"What we need in here is some music . . . music to soothe this savage beast," she said, laughing.

While she was making her selection Yolanda brought us our pizza.

"Extra sauce, extra cheese," she said. "Ya want the same thing ta drink, or ya want boilermakers, too?"

"Just beer. Maybe you ought to bring her just beer, too," Dave said, indicating Bunny.

"Yeah, well, as long as she behaves I gotta bring her what she wants. If she don't get it here she'll get it somewheres else, ya get my drift?"

"Yeah."

Yolanda walked away just as the music from the jukebox began to play.

"That's more like it," Bunny shouted over the music, beginning to dance around by herself to the beat of an old Beatles song.

As I watched I couldn't help wondering about what Dave had said to Yolanda. He had to know Bunny more than casually to suggest that Yolanda not give her the drink she wanted. I had read *The Affair of Gabrielle Russier* the past summer. Could it be that Dave and Bunny were lovers? Of course, Bunny was no Gabrielle Russier and, for that matter, Dave wasn't much like Christian Rossis. Besides, Gabrielle had only been thirty and this Bunny person was at least fifty. Even with all the makeup you could see how old she was. Could Dave really be having a thing with a woman who was more than thirty years older than he? The whole thing was weird and I didn't understand.

Yolanda put our drinks down on the table and Bunny was there in a flash.

She poured the shot of whiskey into the beer and raised her glass. "May the wind be at your back, may ya always take the right turn in the road and may God take a likin' to ya." She took a long swallow and sat down.

"Would you like a piece of pizza?" I asked.

"No thanks, honey . . . I'm a purist." She laughed.

I looked at her, not getting the joke.

"I don't want to interfere with the booze," she said slowly, as if I were a retard.

"Oh." Feeling like a retard, I turned away from her and bit into my piece of pizza.

"When did you eat last?" Dave asked her.

"Knock it off, kid," she said.

Well, there was no question in my mind now. If he was interested in her eating habits they must have been very close. Her next statement clinched it.

"You mind your biz and I'll mind mine, okay, lover?"

Lover. I mean, there it was—right there in plain English. I couldn't have felt more depressed. How could he?

Bunny turned to me, putting a hand laden with cheap

rings on mine. "This kid and his father drive me cuckoo ... they're always after me."

"His father?" I asked. It was getting worse. Did they have a threesome going?

"Yeah. Howard. Ya know what Howard means? 'Chief warden or guardian.' Chief warden ... can ya believe it? How the hell could I have married somebody whose name means chief warden? I must of been outta my box." She shook her head and took another slug of her boilermaker.

I sat there, a slice of pizza held in midair. Married? His father? It was slowly beginning to dawn. Bunny was Dave's stepmother. She had married his father. I felt relief. So much relief that, smiling, I said it out loud.

"Oh, you're Dave's stepmother!"

"Dave's stepmother? Hell, no. Where'd ya get that?"

I started to get that sinking feeling again. "But you said you married his father?"

Once again she looked at me like I was a real boob. "That's right. Howard's the father and Bunny's the mother. Father, Mother and Baby makes three," she said, pointing at Dave. "Where'd ya find this one?" she asked him.

"You're ... his ... mother," I said slowly. "His *real* mother."

"Give this girl a white owl cigar," Bunny shouted to the room. "Better yet, let's have another round. Yo-lan-da."

"You buying?" Dave asked.

"Yeah, any objections?"

"Where'd ya get the money?"

"None of yer goddamn beeswax. Yo-lan-da!"

His mother! I couldn't believe it. Nobody had a mother like Bunny. I mean, women like Bunny just couldn't be anyone's mother.

"What the hell are you looking at, Geri?" It was Dave, his voice snappish.

"Huh?"

"Why are you looking at me like that?"

"I'm sorry," I said. "I didn't know I was looking at you any particular way."

"Yo-lan-da," Bunny screamed and pounded the table. "We want booze."

Two hours later Dave and I were half dragging, half carrying Bunny down the path from Yolanda's to his truck. We weren't in the greatest shape ourselves, but Bunny was really out of it. Her head hung loosely on her neck and she babbled incoherently.

Dave propped her up against the side of the truck and I held on to her while he opened the door.

"I'll get in and pull and you push," he said.

We placed Bunny at the open door, her hands on the seat. I stood behind her to keep her from falling backwards and Dave ran around to the other side and got in. He took her hands in his and began to pull.

"Whatthehellthisis," Bunny mumbled. "Heytherehurts."

"You're hurting her," I said to Dave.

"Tough. Push."

He pulled, Bunny mumbled, I pushed and finally we got her in. She sat slumped over, her head resting on the dashboard. I got in next to her.

"I'd take you home first," Dave said, "but I need you to hold her up so she won't bang her head, okay?"

"Sure."

We pulled Bunny back in the seat and I held onto her so she wouldn't fall forward onto the dashboard. The more I looked at her, her head lolling drunkenly, her mouth handing open, her makeup smeared, the more my own mother looked good to me. Of course, Ginger was no prize either, but if I had to choose, Ginger would win hands down.

The truck slowed down and stopped in front of a small yellow house in Eastport.

"Open your door," Dave said. "Now *you* pull and I'll push."

"Maybe we'd better switch," I said. "I'm afraid I might drop her."

"Yeah, I guess you're right."

As he was coming around to change places with me, a man in a plaid shirt and jeans came out of the house. I assumed he was Howard, Dave's father, because Dave looked a lot like him. Although his dark hair was receding, I could see he was a lot younger than his wife.

"Hi, Dad," Dave said.

He nodded at Dave and then looked at Bunny. "Where'd you find her?"

"Yolanda's."

His father nodded again and looked very sad.

"Dad, this is my friend Geri."

"How do you do, Mr. Townsend."

"Hello. Excuse me," he said, indicating he wanted to get to Bunny. I jumped out of the truck.

He reached in, got one arm under her legs and one around her back and dragged her out. Once out of the truck he kind of hitched her up and looked down into her face.

"Ya make me sick," he said.

"Itsthewarden," she said. "Godgivemestrengthandabeer."

"Shut up," he said softly as he carried her up the path to the house.

"I'll be right out," Dave said. "Wait in the truck, okay?"

I climbed back in and shut the door. I felt horrible. I still had my hangover. The drinks at Yolanda's had helped, but they were beginning to wear off. And the whole scene with Dave's mother had depressed me terribly. Poor Dave. What a horrible home life he must have had. And I thought mine was bad. Then Dave was back, opening the door on the driver's side. He had a sixpack with him.

"I thought we might need this," he said.

"I could use one," I said. *Use* one. *Use* one? I didn't even know where that came from—some movie probably—but it felt right. I *could* use one.

I took two from the plastic holder, flipped the tops, handed one to Dave and drank from my own as we drove to Crawford's Woods.

We each opened our second beer. I was beginning to feel better. Some of the heaviness was lifting.

"Well," Dave said, trying to laugh, "she's pretty far out, huh?"

"Yeah," I said. "But then, so is my old lady."

"Oh, come on, Geri . . . you can't compare them."

"You don't know my mother, Dave . . . you only saw her that once. She's really very. . . ." But I couldn't go on. He was right. As buggy as my mother was, there was no comparison. "I'm sorry," I said softly, putting my hand on his.

"Don't be sorry for me," he said, a slight edge to his voice.

"I didn't mean it that way." But I did.

We slugged at our beers.

"Listen," he said, "I want to thank you. I mean, you were really cool."

I shrugged.

"I never thought I'd run into her or I wouldn't have taken you there. She was supposed to be at her sister's in Millington. I guess she hitchhiked back or something. I didn't plan for you to know about her. Of course, sooner or later you probably would have. Wherever we live people eventually get to know her or about her. But I didn't want you to know so soon."

"It doesn't make any difference, Dave." And it really didn't. "I mean, even though my mother's not like yours I sure would hate for you to judge me by her, you know?"

"Yeah. But people always do."

"Well, not me."

"She's not a bad person really . . . she just . . . she just can't handle the booze. Let's face it, she's a drunk."

"Yes," I said. That knowledge, spelled out like that —just plain and simple—made me feel very uneasy and I didn't know why. One thing I did know was that if my mother drank like that I'd be very nervous about my own drinking. I asked Dave about that.

"I told you, I'm gonna quit when I'm eighteen. I'll never drink like her. I wouldn't let anything run my life like that."

"How come your father married someone so much older?" I asked.

Dave smiled sadly. "He didn't. My mother's three years younger than him. She's thirty-nine."

A year older than Ginger. I couldn't believe it. What had happened?

Dave read my mind, or my eyes. "It's the booze. The booze's made her look like that. She used to be pretty . . . I've seen pictures."

"Well, I can see that," I said. But I really couldn't. Underneath all the makeup was terrible skin, heavy lines and small broken veins. Even her features didn't seem like they'd ever been pretty. I learned much later that alcohol abuse can even change your features.

"Can't . . . can't you do anything for her?"

"Like what?"

"I don't know. Doctors or something."

"She's seen plenty of doctors. They never helped. Plumbers make plenty of bread but my old man has spent so much on her it isn't funny. She's been to hospitals and drying-out joints and you name it, we've tried it."

"What about Alcoholics Anonymous? Did she ever try that?"

"Yeah, some blue-haired old ladies came to the house once after she got drunk and called some AA place. They took her to one of those meetings and when they brought her home she jumped into the car and we didn't see her for three days. As a matter of fact, that's when she lost her license. Now she goes around on. . . ."

"I've seen her."

"Yeah. Well. Anyway, that was her AA bit. But I can see why she wouldn't dig that. All those Holy Rollers and everything."

"Yeah, I guess." I didn't know anything about Alcoholics Anonymous except the ads I sometimes saw on television and little bits of things I'd heard here and there. "How come . . . I mean, your father . . . doesn't he get . . . well, how come he stays with her?"

"I guess he loves her. 'Course they have plenty of fights about it. Like later tonight they'll probably have a big one and then she'll cry and promise to be good and she will be too, for a while . . . a few days, a week . . .

they'll be real happy together. Then, bing, she's back on the bottle again and it starts all over. Sometimes he drinks with her. I guess it's easier that way. But I hate it when he does 'cause they always end up in really terrible fights. Fistfights."

Inwardly, I shuddered. I couldn't imagine my parents hitting each other. It must be awful for Dave. I wanted to say something to him but I didn't want to say or do anything that would make him feel that I pitied him. I didn't know how to handle it so I opened my third beer.

"It's a heavy scene," he said, taking his third beer.

"Yeah."

We didn't say anything for quite a while. We just sat quietly drinking our beer. Then Dave took my beer from me and put it on the dashboard along with his own. Next he put an arm around me and turned me toward him with his other hand.

"Geri, I want you to know . . . I mean, I think you're . . . listen, I really dig you. Shit, that's not what I want to say. What I mean is . . . I think I love you."

"I think I love you, too," I said.

And then we kissed for the first time. No bells started ringing and I didn't see any stars or anything but it felt really good. I had imagined what it would be like to kiss Dave but no imagining can take the place of the real thing. Writers are always trying to describe kisses and it always sounds silly, as far as I'm concerned. I'm not even going to try. The only thing I'll say is it felt like more! And there was more. We kissed for what seemed like a long time and then we realized it had gotten dark out and I figured I'd better get home. I was in enough trouble as it was.

We didn't say much on the way home but Dave drove with one hand and held my hand with his other one. When we got to my house we just sat, smiling and staring at each other. I couldn't seem to look at him enough. I knew my mother was probably peering out at us and that thought began to make me uncomfortable.

"I'd better go in."

He nodded. "See you tomorrow."

We didn't really kiss good-bye in case anyone was watching. But we kissed good-bye with our eyes.

I watched him drive away and then prepared myself for the attack I would get from my mother. But when I got inside no one said anything to me. My mother acted as though nothing had happened. I had dinner and watched some television and then went to my room to do some homework. It was hard to concentrate and I gave it up. I knew I had study hall first period and I could do it then.

When I got into bed I couldn't think of anything but Dave. I *really, really* had a boyfriend! And he thought he loved me! What would Ginger think of that? I toyed with the idea of telling her and I imagined how the conversation would go.

ME: I have something to tell you, Mother.

GINGER: What is it?

ME: Dave thinks he loves me.

GINGER: Thinks? Thinks? In my day a boy *knew* if he loved you. Thinking a thing like that doesn't count, Geri. Can't you get anything right?

What would you have decided about telling her? I decided my lips would remain sealed!

15

There were no really major events in the next few months—until right before Christmas. But before I get to that I think I should fill you in on the development of my cast of characters.

Ginger—For almost a week after the Queen of the Dance incident, there was absolutely no mention of all-round popularity. Then it, and things like it, began to creep back into her conversation. One day about two weeks after the Q.O.T.D. affair, apropos of nothing, she looked at me and said: "You know, Geri, you *are* the president of a lot of leftover people."

"Better than being *vice*-president," I said.

After that little exchange her fifties campaign seemed to take a turn for the worse. Of course, what was going on in movies and on television didn't help. It seemed like every time you turned around somebody was glorifying the fifties. That was pure adrenalin to my mother. But the worst thing that happened was that some television station offered five LP's of the late forties and fifties—practically every song that was ever made. Naturally, she sent for them even though she already had 78's of a lot of them. Now she could put the five albums on all at once and we would have an uninterrupted hour and a half of Eddie Fisher and Vaughn Monroe and Patti Page and—well, you get the idea. Then, with the flick of the wrist, we had the flip side of the uninterrupted hour and a half of pure hell. The worst part of all this was that she had become extremely selfish and possessive about the stereo. For instance:

"Mom, do you mind if I take off Doris Day for a while?"

"Yes."

"You've been playing your records for two hours now."

"So what?"

"Well, I just thought it might be nice to hear something else . . . something from the present."

"It wouldn't be nice at all . . . it would be dreadful."

It finally got to the point that if for some odd reason she wasn't using the phonograph Jack or I would quickly put on one of our records, even if we didn't feel like hearing it, just so she wouldn't put on Dick Haymes or Vic Damone. After a while even that didn't work because she would just take off whatever we were playing and replace it with Tony Bennett or Bing Crosby or somebody. It was very annoying and very rude and very unlike her. She had always been big on manners.

"Hey, Mom, I was listening to that."

"Too bad. I want to hear something sane."

"Couldn't you at least wait until the record's over?"

"No."

It was as cut and dried as that. But even worse than her music trip was her date trip—her "datalogue," as we called it. No matter what anyone tried to talk about Ginger interrupted and twisted the conversation her way. Her way was to talk about the wonderful boys she had dated before she met my father. For example:

GEORGE: Anything new at school, Jack?

JACK: Nothing much. I'm going to write a paper on Henry Kissinger for my. . . .

GINGER: Henry Barker took me to see *Moulin Rouge*. Afterwards, we went out for something to eat and some old man sketched me for fifty cents. I wonder what happened to that sketch? I wonder what happened to Henry? He was a wonderful boy. He lived in New York and was going to become. . . .

And on and on. None of us discussed what was happening but I think somewhere we all knew it wasn't so funny anymore. Instinctively, we realized something was wrong but nobody wanted to say anything because nobody knew what to do about it.

George—He seemed to be saying less and less, if that was possible. And he seemed to be out more—I mean, like coming home really late from work and even going into his office on Saturdays. And when he was around the house, with the exception of meal times, his nose was never out of a mystery or a crossword puzzle. It occurred to me that maybe my father was seeing another woman. I asked Jack about it.

"Jack, can I come in a minute?"

"Sure. What's up?"

"I was wondering something about Daddy. Do you think maybe he's seeing somebody?"

"What do ya mean, seeing somebody?"

"Another woman?"

"You gotta be kidding," Jack said.

"I do?"

"Dad, seeing another woman . . . come on, Geri!"

"I don't see what's so unbelievable about that."

"Dad's forty-one."

"So?"

"Well, what would he do with another woman at his age?"

"Now *you* must be kidding?"

"Well, think about it," Jack said. "I mean isn't the idea of Dad doing it with someone disgusting?"

"Even Mom?"

"Well, it's not a pretty picture," he said. And he was serious.

I don't know what that is with some people. I mean this thing about age and lovemaking. I have to admit the idea of my parents making love did not sit too well with me either—not because of their ages. It was more because I didn't think they loved each other. I've noticed that with most kids the idea of anyone over the age of thirty making it is repulsive. At the movies, when a couple that age or over starts to make it, all the kids in the audience groan and pretend they're throwing up. I don't feel that way about it. If two people love each other what difference does it make how old they are? Anyway, Jack was no help on that score. He just laughed off the idea that Daddy was having an affair so I tried to forget about it.

Jack—Nothing much happened with him except that he started a school newspaper called *Pizzazz* and was convinced that he had phlebitis, Hodgkin's, tuberculosis, Bright's disease and measles. Once when I came in from a date with Dave, and he was nursing his imaginary TB, he looked at me strangely and asked if I'd been smoking pot. I told him I hadn't and then he said something was wrong with my motor control because I was moving funny. After going through a list of diseases he thought I might have, the truth occurred to him.

"Have you been drinking?."

"What do you mean, drinking?"

"Drinking. Booze."

"I had a beer or two." Or twenty or thirty, I thought.

"I hope you're not going to get in the habit of that," he said.

"My habits are my own," I said. "God, that's terrific! Isn't that terrific?"

"What?" he asked, giving a series of little coughs.

"What? What? Sometimes you're really stupid, you know that. A person says a really great, profound thing and you, the big genius, don't even recognize it. I'm going upstairs and write that down."

"Write what down?"

"Forget it . . . you wouldn't understand."

The next morning I found this big piece of paper on my night table that said "MY HABITS ARE MY OWN!" and the whole conversation came back to me except that I couldn't see what was terrific about "MY HABITS ARE MY OWN!" In fact, it really didn't mean anything and I threw the piece of paper with the bright red and green letters into my wastebasket.

Carolyn & B.J.—After the night at Carolyn's house, B.J., of course, never took another drink. She said that she thought what drinking did to people was disgusting and she didn't want any part of it. So I never told her about my escapades or the fun I was having with Dave. Well, sometimes I told her things, but I left out the drinking part. Carolyn, on the other hand, sometimes joined Dave and me, but she never had more than one or two drinks, which we didn't mind because that left more for us. Often she didn't drink anything. She said she could take it or leave it. I couldn't understand that. I mean, how could a person take or leave something that made them feel so good? I didn't see as much of Carolyn and B.J. as I used to because I spent most of my time with Dave. But during October and November the four of us always had lunch at Carolyn's house and Dave and I always had a few drinks from her father's stock before we ate. Mostly, we drank Scotch in milk. B.J. always looked very disapproving as though she was smelling something really bad. Dave kept a thermos of Scotch and milk in his locker, but I was too scared to do that. At least at the point I'm talking about I was too scared. Later things like that didn't bother me at all. After the first week in December I didn't see Carolyn and B.J. socially anymore. But I'll get to that later.

Dave—As I said, he kept his thermos in his locker and I noticed that he was drinking a lot more than when I first met him. Also, he was doing lousy in school—just barely passing. He said he didn't care because he couldn't afford to go to college anyway and all he wanted was to get his diploma so he could get some kind of job that would pay well, like maybe driving one of those big rigs coast to coast. Mr. Townsend wanted Dave to go into business with him but Dave said he had to get away from home as soon as possible. He couldn't go on nursemaiding his mother or watching the fights. For the moment, to make some money, he got a job with Will Bless, who was a junk and antique dealer. Dave used his truck to help Mr. Bless haul furniture. He also learned how to strip and stain old pieces. It was a pretty good job and he always had plenty of money for booze and that's all that seemed to matter to him.

A lot of the kids found out that the crazy lady they saw riding around town on a three-wheeler, dressed in short shorts or vinyl jumpsuits, was Dave's mother. And most of them made mean remarks to him about her. Although I know they hurt him he never swallowed the bait and fought over it. He said he'd learned a long time ago that fighting over his mother solved nothing —it didn't change anyone's opinion and it certainly didn't change Amorette. The only thing it ever got him was a black eye and a chipped tooth. I thought his attitude was very mature and it made me love him even more.

Me—Nothing terribly exciting or important happened from the end of September until the beginning of December. My mother was involved in her own head and my father wasn't home much so nobody seemed to notice that I was going out a lot on school nights. I guess my mother was just glad I had a boyfriend, even if it was Dave whom she didn't particularly like. I managed to get my homework done and to keep a B average but I really didn't have much interest in school work anymore. Also, I never seemed to find any time for my cartooning. I didn't hang around with B.J. and Carolyn after school anymore because I used that time to do homework so I could go out with Dave at night. I had licked the hangover problem by always having a little Scotch and milk in the morning. I kept a thermos of it way back in my closet and that's how I started at least four days out of seven. Also, I had joined Dave in the wonderful world of mouth sprays! The truth of the matter was that I wasn't really doing much of anything but going to school and drinking. But it seemed great to me. Dave and I always had a good time when we drank. We'd get into really heavy raps and end up solving all the problems of the world. It didn't matter if the next day I couldn't remember most of what we'd talked about or if it wasn't quite as earth shattering as it seemed the night before.

The only really unusual thing that happened during that period was that Ms. Laine asked me to stay after humanities one day. I'd had a couple of extra drinks before lunch and it had been really hard to concentrate during class.

"Geri," Ms. Laine said, "I've been meaning to talk to you for a few weeks now, but something always came up. Anyway, I've been wondering . . . is something bothering you?"

I stepped back from her. I hadn't had a chance to squirt myself with the wintergreen. "No, nothing," I said.

She looked directly at me and I tried looking straight back at her. "You used to sit in the first row," she said.

"I see better from the back," I said, "I'm near-sighted."

"Have you seen an eye doctor?"

"Yes," I lied. "He said I should sit in the back row in all my classes . . . you know, like an eye exercise."

I knew she didn't believe me but let her prove it.

"I'm going to be late for my next class," I said.

"I'll give you a note. Look, Geri, if something is wrong I'd like to help you."

"What makes you think something is wrong?"

"You've changed since the first month of school. Maybe you aren't even aware of it."

"Is something wrong with my work?" I was sure I was doing the same work I'd always done.

"Not really, I guess. I mean you hand in your assignments on time but . . . well, I just wanted you to know that I'm here if you need someone to talk to."

"Thanks."

That shook me up a little bit because in all my years in school no teacher had ever come on like that with me. I was never considered a problem kid or anything. But by the end of the next period I'd put it out of my mind.

During the first week in December Dave told me that he'd gotten to know the kids we had seen at the dance. The juicers. He said they were real swingers and he'd like us to start going places with them. He said he knew I was nervous about meeting new people but once I got past the initial meeting it would be fun. I told him that it wasn't just shyness that made me apprehensive. He asked me what else it was.

"They're juicers, Dave," I said.

He started laughing.

"What's so funny?"

"What the hell do you think you are?" he asked.

I can't tell you what I felt like when he said that. It was a mixture of shock and shame and horror. But, of course, he was right. I just had never thought about myself that way before. Still, I didn't want to hang around with them.

"Just try it once," he urged. "They're really great kids. You'll like them once you get to know them."

When I saw he was really set on hanging out with them, I gave in. I hated to think I was being snobby, and, after all, what difference did it make who you drank with? It was bound to be more fun than drinking with Carolyn and at least nobody would give me a look that said: "You're disgusting! I know it, you know it and God knows it."

So that first weekend in December we went to a party at Linda Scott's. I was really nervous about it—I had a few extra Scotches in my room before Dave picked me up—but when I got there I found that all my nervousness was for nothing. Dave was right. They were really neat kids. Nobody put me down or treated me like a freak or anything. I felt like one of them right away. It was a great party and the beginning for me of belonging to a crowd.

Two of the girls I liked a lot were Linda Scott and Ceil Nardone. I started hanging around with them all the time. And one day they asked me to go over to Linda's house for lunch. I didn't know what to say to Carolyn and B.J. so I didn't say anything. I just didn't meet them that day at the usual spot. In homeroom the next day Carolyn asked me what happened.

"Do I have to tell you what I do with every minute of my time?" I snapped.

She looked at me as though I'd punched her in the mouth. "I just wondered, that's all. We waited and waited and then. . . ."

"Well, don't wait anymore," I said. "I have other things to do besides hang around with you two all the time . . . I mean, where is it getting us?"

"Getting us?" B.J. asked. "What does that mean, Geri?"

"Oh, B.J.," I said, "you really *are* a drag." And I opened a book and pretended to read.

There was silence for a while and then Carolyn said softly, "You mean you're not going to have lunch with us today either?"

I slammed my book shut. "Not today or any other day. I'm just not interested in morticians and vets anymore and I'm not interested in being a freak anymore either."

Fortunately, the bell rang and I walked off without them. I felt awful all morning and when I saw Carolyn in my English class I could tell she'd been crying. But I wasn't going to give in. For the first time in my life I had real friends, a real crowd to hang out with, and I wasn't going to let Carolyn or B.J. spoil it. Still, I couldn't get rid of that nagging feeling in my stomach. At least not until lunch time when I went to Linda's and we made a batch of daiquiris in the blender. After a few of those I knew I'd made the right decision and all thoughts of Carolyn and B.J. vanished.

And that brings me up to December 21 and the horrible beagle incident.

16

December 21 was a snowy Saturday. My mother played Bing Crosby singing "White Christmas" practically all day. Daddy went into his office and Jack went to work as usual. I had a very slight hangover. Dave and I and the gang had spent the night before in The Village Smithy, a bar that catered mostly to young people and the occasional fisherman. There wasn't much chance anyone would see me there who shouldn't. Dave had gotten me some false proof through Bingo for only ten dollars. Anyway, we had a neat time singing Christmas carols, of all things, and playing pinball for beers. I didn't get too drunk, just high enough to really have fun. I know I spent a lot of the night with Linda talking about—well, I couldn't remember exactly what we talked about, but I knew it was important because I remembered her looking very serious and I think she even cried a ilttle. I'd have to devise some subtle way of finding out what it was she was so upset about.

I was still lying in bed when my mother knocked on my door. I told her to come in.

"Oh, still in bed, hmmmm?"

I nodded. How I hated people who point out the obvious.

"Going to lie in bed all day?"

"Nope."

"What *are* you going to do with this beautiful, cold, snowy December day?"

I looked at her. Who talks like that? I asked myself.

My mother was getting more unreal all the time. "I'm going over to my friend Linda's house and help her get ready for the party tonight."

"Another party," she said softly and shook her head. "It seems like that's all you do these days . . . party, party, party."

"I thought that's what you wanted . . . I thought you'd be thrilled that I got in with a new crowd and had lots of swingy friends."

She found a tiny place at the end of the bed and carefully sat down. "Oh, I am thrilled, Geri, I think it's wonderful that you have all these nice new friends only . . ."

"Only what?"

"Well, why haven't you brought any of them around here? I was beginning to wonder if they really existed until Jack told me that they did. So why don't you bring them over . . . have a party here."

I knew, of course, that what she meant by having a party was Coke and cookies. Wouldn't that be just super? If she and my father would just go away for a weekend I certainly would have a party. Fat chance of that.

"Oh, Mom, you wouldn't want all that mess in the house. You know how sloppy kids are . . . Cokes spilled and cigarette ashes and all."

"I don't care about things like that, Geri . . . I'd love to meet your friends. Jack said they're very . . . very interesting."

I could tell by the look on her face that Jack had said nothing of the kind. "Okay, what did Jack say about them?"

"Nothing of importance. Why don't you have a party here next week?"

"The parties are arranged all through the holidays. Just what did Jack say?"

"Don't you feel that you should reciprocate? It isn't polite to keep accepting invitations without returning them. I don't know what your friends will think," she said, twirling a piece of her hair around her fingers. This was a new habit she'd started in the last few weeks and she did it constantly while she talked. Sometimes she even did it when she wasn't talking. Several times I'd found her sitting and staring and twirling.

"Mother, please tell me what Jack said about my friends."

"Well, you won't like it . . . please don't tell him I told you."

"I promise."

"He said they were juicers. Naturally, I didn't know what that meant so he explained. He said they drank a bit."

"Really? He said they drank *a bit?*"

"Well, actually he said they drank a lot, but I'm sure he was exaggerating."

I had a terrible impulse to say they drank like fish and so did I and what was she going to do about it. But of course I didn't. I said, "Well, Jack doesn't know everything, you know."

"I'm sure he doesn't. There's nothing wrong with having a little wine or beer now and then. Your brother is such a health nut with his athletics and all . . . when I was your age I often had a glass of wine or a beer when I went out on dates. Of course, I never overdid it . . . everything in moderation, I always said. I haven't forgotten what it's like to be sixteen, you know."

"Yes, I know."

"I'd much rather have you have a little beer now and then than smoke pot."

"I never smoke pot," I said. And I didn't. I tried it once and I didn't like it at all. I liked what booze did for me much better.

"So I want you to know, Geri, that you have my permission to have a little something to drink now and again. I know you're grown up enough and sensible enough to handle it properly."

I almost laughed in her face. What would she have done if she'd known about the Scotch in my closet? I wanted to say, "Well, let's drink to that, Mom!" What would she have said? I said, "Thanks, that makes me feel really good knowing that you trust me that way."

"Anyway, the point is, if you'd like to have your friends over I'd be glad to serve them a little wine or beer."

That'd go over big, I thought. "Maybe after the holidays," I said. "Thanks a lot."

She stood up then, twirling her hair, and started toward the door. When she reached it she turned back and looked at me. "You don't see Carolyn and B.J. anymore, do you?"

I really didn't like to think about that. I shook my head.

"I guess they're a lot less mature than you, hmmm? Still, it seems odd not having them around anymore."

"I thought you didn't like them. I thought you thought of them as leftover people."

"Leftover people," she said strangely. "Yes, they're certainly that." And she left the room.

I lay there for a minute thinking about her. She was acting stranger and stranger. And it all seemed to date from the time I lied to her about being Queen of the Dance. Now when she talked to me, which wasn't too often, she said funny little things that I didn't understand. It was as though she thought I was lying all the time. Of course, I was doing a lot of lying in a way. I mean, lying by omission. But the point was why would she think I was lying *all* the time just because she'd caught me in a lie once? Maybe my mother had lied to her mother! Or maybe she was lying now! I've noticed that sometimes when people are doing or thinking something that isn't too hot, and they're guilty about it, they accuse someone else of that very thing. I think it's called projection. Maybe my mother was projecting. But about what? I mean, what in hell could she be lying about? She didn't go anywhere or see anyone. Let's face it—Ginger's life was so boring she had nothing to lie about. That couldn't be it. But maybe that *was* it! Maybe because her life *was* so boring she was flipping out. Who knew? Sophie jumped up on the bed and nuzzled into my neck. I began to pet her.

"Sophie," I said, "do you think my mother is flipping out?"

For an answer she began to knead and purr. How nice to be a cat, I thought, never having to worry about anything. I hoped that in my next life I would be a house cat so all my needs would be provided for.

"Sophie, you don't know how lucky you are." She licked my neck as if to say she did.

In the afternoon I went over to Linda's. Her parents had gone to Connecticut for the weekend to visit her married sister so the house was all ours. The night before each of us put five dollars in the hat and Saturday morning Pete Stanzini went to the liquor store and bought our supplies. I guess maybe you're wondering where we got the money for all the liquor we drank. I'm not sure about anyone else, except the kids who worked, but I got mine several ways. First of all, I got ten dollars a week allowance. That was supposed to cover milk and dessert at school and anything else I wanted. I used to buy a record a week but I hadn't done that for months. I don't smoke so I didn't need money for that. I'd stopped wasting money on desserts even though Jack made some cracks about me eating too many of them. I'd gained over ten pounds in two months and it worried me a little. I was going to start dieting the first of the year. It was all those pizzas Dave and I were always eating on Sundays! And maybe I'd have to drop the milk from my Scotch.

Anyway, back to my finances. My father had a habit of carrying quite a bit of money and at night he always put it on his dresser. I discovered that, in the morning, while he was taking his shower and my mother was making breakfast, it was very easy to slip into their room and just take a little. I started with quarters, but by December I'd worked up to a dollar or two a day. He never missed it because he never knew exactly what he had. Once I even took a five-dollar bill, but I didn't want to do that too often. I never thought of it as stealing. I told myself I was just borrowing the money and, after all, he was my father so it really belonged to me too, didn't it? I know now that was a rationalization because, no matter how you look at it, I *was* stealing. But I couldn't face that then any more than I could face anything else.

"I guess we won't open the potato chips yet," Linda said. "Let's just put the bags in the bowls and we can open them later."

I noticed when Linda took the bowls down from the

shelf that her hands were shaking. I also noticed that her eyes were red like she'd been crying and that her white, white skin was pink and blotchy. Usually, Linda looked terrific. She was one of the best-looking girls in school, a natural blonde with almost violet blue eyes. But today she looked awful. I wanted to ask what was wrong but I had a feeling I was supposed to know. I didn't want her to realize that I didn't remember anything about our conversation the night before so I tried to word my question to her in such a way that she'd think I'd remembered.

"How are you feeling today?" I asked.

"How *should* I feel? How would *you* feel?"

No clues in that. I tried again. "No better, huh?"

"Geri, how can I feel better? I still didn't get it."

Get it! Get what? A letter? A phone call? Her period? Yes, that was it. Something was coming back to me, I decided to risk it. "How long has it been?" I asked.

"I told you last night . . . six weeks. Oh, God, I just don't know what I'll do if I'm pregnant."

That was it! Now I remembered. Linda thought she was pregnant by Pete Stanzini. That's why she had been crying. "You'll just have to have an abortion," I said.

A look of anger flashed across her face. "What's wrong with you, Geri? I told you last night that I don't believe in abortions."

I tried desperately to remember the conversation. I couldn't. I found it really hard to understand why she would be against abortions and I had to know her arguments. I started laughing.

"What's so funny?" she asked.

"Me," I said. I had to make this look right.

"Huh?"

"You're not going to believe this but, well, I don't remember a thing about last night . . . I must have been really messed up."

"I guess so. You didn't seem that stoned. That happened to me once . . . I mean not remembering. It's awful, isn't it?"

"Yeah, terrible. I hope it never happens again," I said. It happened to her *once!* I couldn't believe it. Secretly, I'd hoped she would say it happened to her all the time, too. This *once* business was a shock to me. Having what's known as a blackout was commonplace to me. I thought everybody who drank the way we drank had them. What I didn't understand then was that although Linda drank a lot we didn't drink the same way. Linda was not an alcoholic. . . . I was.

"So, anyway," I went on, trying to sound as casual as possible, "why don't you believe in abortions?"

"I'm not going to go through the whole damn argument. . . . I don't care if you don't remember. I do. Suffice it to say, I think it's murder."

"But, Linda. . . ."

She held up her hand. "Please, Geri. I know what you're going to say. I heard it last night. You didn't convince me then and you won't convince me now. Help me put these bottles out on the table."

Actually, I didn't need to hear it from her. I knew what she'd say. I'd read the arguments in countless newspaper and magazine articles. It was hard for me to understand how anyone could feel the way Linda did. It seemed so clear to me, especially in this overpopulated world, that it was a much greater wrong to give birth to an unwanted child. I wished I could convince Linda of that, but apparently I had already tried and failed. "So what are you going to do?"

"I don't know . . . I just don't know. I guess Pete and I will have to get married."

A fate worse than death, as far as I was concerned. Imagine getting married and having a baby at seventeen! "You mean you'll both have to quit school?"

"Well, what else?"

For a second I thought about having to marry Dave at this point in my life. The thought was horrifying and I wished Linda would suggest a drink. Of course, I had my own bottle there and I had the right to have a drink whenever I wanted. But something made me know that if I suggested a drink then, at three in the afternoon, for no reason, she might think it was strange. It was different when we drank before lunch somehow. Then I got an idea.

"Linda," I said, "I want you to know something.

Whatever happens, I mean if you should be pregnant, I want you to know that whatever you decide to do I'll stand by you."

"Gee, Geri, that's really great of you."

"Let's have a drink on it," I said. And before she could answer I opened my bottle of Scotch—Scotch was practically the only thing I drank now, the cheapest I could get—and poured us both a drink. "Here's to friendship," I said, raising my glass.

The glass was halfway to my mouth when she spoke.

"Geri, I hope you won't be insulted, but, well, I hate Scotch. Do you mind if I pour one of my own?"

"Of course not," I said trying not to smile. I knew Linda hated Scotch. I knew she wouldn't drink it. While she poured her vodka I poured her glass of Scotch into mine. After all, I couldn't waste it, could I? How good I was getting at these devious little games —a real pro!

Linda and I had our drinks and then I went home to shower, change and have dinner. Actually, I didn't shower. I took a bath because one of the things I loved doing was sitting in the tub, drinking a Scotch and milk and listening to my favorite rock station. By the time I sat down to dinner with Ginger, George and dear old Jack I was feeling pretty good. Meals were a lot easier to get through since I'd started having my own private cocktail hour. I understood completely why my parents always had a couple of drinks before dinner. The only problem I had was that booze made me want to talk and I knew it was a lot safer if I didn't. I mean, it would be harder for them to detect anything in me if I kept quiet. On the other hand, they were a bit high themselves so I'm not sure they would have noticed. But I wasn't taking any chances. Anyway, there was the straight-jock to contend with. The booze helped me to just sort of sail through meals. If Ginger got on one of her fifties kicks, or if she and George were sniping at each other, I really didn't give a damn. I felt too good to care. I didn't even care when they talked to Jack like he was some kind of a prince or something. Not caring was a neat feeling.

Dave picked me up at seven-thirty and we stopped off at The Village Smithy for two drinks before we went to the party. I almost wished we could stay there because now I really preferred drinking in bars to drinking in houses. I liked the atmosphere and the smell and everything about it. And what I liked best of all was actually sitting at the bar. It made me feel terrific—important. But our booze was waiting for us at Linda's and everyone was expecting us so off we went.

The party was fun. We sat around and talked for a while and then we danced and later on we sort of broke up into couples in different parts of the house and made out. Dave and I, preferring for the moment to continue drinking, stayed in the living room at one end of the couch. A girl named Marcelle and her boyfriend Bob were at the other end of the couch. She had a look in her eyes that made me know she was a lot more interested in drinking than Linda was. Actually, she reminded me of me even though I didn't know her very well.

Dave and I made out a little bit and then we drank some more and just got into rapping. Bob and Marcelle joined in and then, suddenly, Marcelle suggested we go down to The Village Smithy. I could have kissed her. The four of us took our bottles and split—in two cars. Bob was a maniac driver when he was drunk so Dave let him pass us and go ahead. I really was grateful that Dave had this built-in thing about driving slowly.

When we got to the V.S. Marcelle and Bob were already at a table. The place was packed even though it had snowed that day. Of course, the roads were clear because Goose Bay took great pride in clearing roads after snowstorms; keeping lawns trimmed and leaves raked and all that kind of stuff. Also, I was beginning to learn that Goose Bay was a drinking town and that neither rain nor sleet nor anything else kept the citizens from their booze. I guess one of the reasons was that there wasn't much else to do. That was certainly true for us kids.

We usually drank beer when we were in the V.S. because that's all we could really afford. Anyway, that night we were already pretty messed up. Draft beer was twenty cents a glass and Bob suggested we play a game with matches for beers. I was a little low on funds that night because the bottle of Scotch had kind of wiped me out. But, fortunately, I kept winning. Dave and Bob kept losing. It made them furious and that just broke up Marcelle and me. Even in a game of chance they couldn't bear losing to girls. Will it ever change?

After about eight games and eight beers, Marcelle and I excused ourselves and went to the bathroom. While we were combing our hair, Marcelle said, "Whadya think would happen, Geri, if we took all our clothes off and walked back out into the bar, huh?"

I started laughing.

"Ya wanna do it?"

"You're kidding!"

"No. I think it would be cool."

"It would be cool all right," I said.

Marcelle didn't get my joke.

"C'mon, Geri, let's do it, huh?"

"We'll just get kicked out."

"You're chicken, huh? C'mon, naked is beautiful."

The idea of going out into the bar nude actually did strike me kind of funny and the more Marcelle kept talking about it the funnier it seemed. Before I knew it thoughts of getting kicked out or arrested were replaced by thoughts of what a turn-on it would be. I became convinced it was a matter of freedom and, then, that it was my duty. There was only one small beat between the thought of duty and removing my clothes. I've often wondered if we weren't the original streakers—except that we didn't streak. We very slowly and calmly opened the bathroom door and nonchalantly headed toward our table.

It's hard to remember exactly what happened. I know that the place got quiet—at least conversation stopped. The jukebox kept playing but that was the only sound. Then, I think, there was a lot of noise and a lot of people rushing around. Suddenly, a coat was around me and Dave's face was there and Bob's and I felt pulled and pushed and almost crushed. And then I saw her. I don't know how because she was back in a corner but I saw her all right. I broke away from whoever was holding me and stumbled through the people until I was leaning over her table. Dave told me the next day what happened then.

I put both hands on her table, the coat swinging open. "Well, well, if it isn't Ms. Laine. What're you doin' here?"

"Hello, Geri," she said.

I looked at the man with her. I didn't know him. "Is this your lover?"

"This is John Wilson," she said. "Geri Peters."

Then she reached out and tried to button the coat. I pulled away.

"Don't be so uptight, you bitch."

Dave tried to drag me away from the table. I slapped him in the face and kicked at him, but he overpowered me and started dragging me through the bar toward the door. Once outside, I got free and started running through the snow. I don't even remember the cold although my feet were bare and the coat was still open. The next thing I knew Dave and I were rolling around in the snow and then I was on my back and he was straddling me and holding my hands over my head.

"Cool it, Geri, just cool it. You crazy or what?"

"Leggo, you rotten. . . ."

"C'mon, cut it out."

He wrestled some more and then I felt kind of tired and gave up. We walked back toward the truck, my feet feeling a little prickly by now. I held the coat around me. When we got to the truck Ms. Laine was standing there, holding something in her arms. It turned out to be my clothes.

"What do *you* want?"

"Shut up, Geri," Dave said.

"Here are her clothes," she said to Dave.

"Here are her clothes," I imitated. "Goody Two-shoes, that's what you are."

"Thanks," Dave said, taking them from her. "I'm sorry."

"Why don't you two run off together . . . you're both too good to live."

"I think you'd better take her home," Ms. Laine said. "Do you need any help?"

"I can manage," he said.

"This conversation sucks," I said. I tried pulling away but Dave had a good grip on me.

"Come on, Geri." He gave me a pull and a push and I was in the truck.

I rolled down the window while Dave ran around to his side of the truck.

"You know what, Laine . . . your humanities class sucks, that's what."

"Drive carefully," she said to Dave as he started the motor.

"And you're a goddamn bitch," I went on.

"Thanks, Miss Laine," he said. We started driving away.

I stuck my head out farther and yelled back at her: "Up yours with a rusty meat hook."

Dave pulled me back in and told me to shut my mouth. I tried grabbing the wheel then and he slammed me hard with the back of his hand. I started to cry. I guess I kept on crying because I didn't notice where we were going. When the truck stopped I looked up. We were at the beach parking lot. It was completely empty except for us.

"Put your clothes on," he said.

"No."

"Look, you're gonna catch cold. Put them on and we'll have a drink."

That did it. I'd forgotten we had our bottles in the truck. Slowly and clumsily I put on my clothes. When I was dressed he handed me my bottle of Scotch. I was cold and the Scotch made me warm. We didn't say anything for a while and then I remembered Marcelle.

"What happened to Marcelle?"

"Bob got her in his car. She went peacefully . . . not like some people. What the hell got into you?"

I shrugged.

"Jesus, you were like a maniac out there."

"So what?"

"What made you do that, you and Marcelle? How come you did that?"

I started laughing, remembering. "We thought it was funny."

"A real hoot," he said sarcastically. "Well, toots, they'll never let you back in there, ya know."

"Who the hell cares? It's a dump anyway."

"I thought ya loved it."

"Dump," I said and took another swig from my bottle.

We were silent again for a bit and then Dave started the motor.

"I guess I'd better take ya home . . . it's late."

He put on his lights and there, sitting in the snow, was a dog.

"Hey, look at that." I opened my door.

"Where ya goin' now?"

"Don't ya see him?" I got out of the car and walked slowly toward the dog. He was sitting there shivering and looking like all the problems of the world were on his brown and white shoulders. He was a beagle— or she. I didn't know. Dave was standing next to me.

"Careful," he said. "Go easy."

"His tail's wagging." I went closer, putting my hand out, palm upward. He sniffed and started licking my hand. He was very wet and bedraggled and wasn't wearing a collar.

"I'm gonna take him," I said.

"Take him where?"

"Home."

"What about Max and Tansy and Sophie?"

"So? Max and Tansy love other dogs. And Sophie's used to the two of them so I don't think . . . I'm taking him." I picked him up and staggered back to the truck. Once we were settled inside I saw that he was a male.

"Beagles chase other dogs, ya know," Dave said.

"I'll handle it . . . have no fear."

All the lights were off in my house except on the porch and one in the living room.

"Ya sure ya wanna take him in? I'll take him home with me if ya think it might be too much here."

"No, he'll be fine."

"You better watch out for Sophie . . . Beagle's chase—"

"You said that. Don't be such a worrier . . . Sophie can take care of herself."

I said good night to Dave and carried the dog up the walk. I tried to open the door as quietly as possible but with the beagle in my arms that wasn't easy. Tansy heard me and came bustling down the stairs, Max behind her. I sat down in a chair, holding the dog while Max and Tansy sniffed around him. He wagged his tail and gave a bark. I shushed him and was just about to go get him some food when he suddenly leaped from my arms. At first I didn't know what was happening. Then I realized that Sophie had come into the room and he was chasing her. He was barking and she was yowling and they were both knocking things over. Lights went on upstairs as the chase continued. I started screaming as the animals went around and around the room. Finally, I ran for the front door and opened it, hoping the beagle would dash out. He did, chasing Sophie who went past me in a streak of orange. Max and Tansy started out too, but I quickly closed the door. I felt sure Sophie would be all right once she got to a tree. There were lots of them on our lawn.

"What's going on?" my father asked, coming down the stairs in his pajamas.

"What is it?" Mother asked, right behind him.

Daddy snapped on a light. "Are you all right, Geri?"

"Fine, fine," I said.

"What was all that noise?"

I didn't know what to tell them so I said nothing.

"Geri, answer," my mother said.

"Nothing, forget it, let's go to bed." I started toward the stairs and tripped over the hassock falling on my face. My mother gave a little scream and my father helped me up. When I was on my feet again he looked at me closely.

"You've been drinking," he said.

"So?"

"Don't talk to me like that. Have you been drinking?"

"A little. Mother said it was all right to have a little."

"A little wine or beer never hurt anyone," Mother said.

"This girl's drunk, Ginger. Look at her."

"Don't be ridiculous, George. Go to bed, Geri."

"Wait a minute," he said, his voice rising. "Just wait a damn minute. This child is drunk. Are you blind? Look at her."

He had a firm grip on me and I couldn't get away. I tried to pull myself together but my head was spinning and I kept hearing the beagle barking in the distance.

"All the children drink a little these days, George . . . don't be so old-fashioned."

"I don't care what they do . . . and she didn't drink just a little . . . she's drunk."

"I'm not drunk," I said, trying hard to sound sober. But I guess it didn't come out the way I wanted.

"Listen to her," he yelled.

"Well, just be glad it's not pot," she said. "Anyway, there's nothing you can do about it now. Let her go to bed."

He looked at my mother, amazed, and then he looked around at the messed-up room. "I want to know what happened here."

"A dog chased Sophie around," I said and suddenly the whole thing struck me very funny and I started laughing.

"What dog?" he asked.

"A beagle," I said through my giggles.

"Let her go to bed, George."

He let go of me then and somehow I got to my room, fell on the bed and passed out.

The next thing I knew it was daylight and Jack was standing over me. His face was set in a hard expression and his eyes were red. We looked at each other for a few moments and then he threw something at me which landed on my chest. I looked down. It was Sophie's red leather collar. I looked back up at him, my stomach turning over. I knew what it meant, but I didn't want to know.

"She's dead," Jack said. "A car hit her. Mr. Lewis found her at the side of the road. You killed her. I hate your guts."

He walked out, slamming the door. I lay there staring down at the collar. The bell was bent. Sophie. Sophie.

17

When I finally came downstairs that morning my parents and Jack were sitting in the living room as though they were waiting for me. The fact was they *were* waiting for me. On top of everything else I had an absolutely colossal hangover. If I'd have drawn me that morning I would have drawn a tiny little bent figure with a huge tongue hanging out to the floor and a crown of spikes around the head. Whatever happened I had to get to the kitchen for a Coke. A beer is what I really wanted—I would have killed for one—but I knew there was no chance. I had finished my closet Scotch with my bath the night before so there I was with absolutely no fortification and no hope of any. Coke was the only possibility. If I stopped to say anything I would never get to my Coke so I kept walking right past them into the kitchen. I knew all their eyes were on me and when I got to the refrigerator I could hear them mumbling to each other. I opened my Coke and drank half of it in one long swallow. It quenched my thirst for a moment, but it did nothing for my head or my shaking hands. I knew I couldn't stay in the kitchen forever, but the last thing I wanted was to go out and face the triumvirate. Still, I had no choice. Another swallow of Coke and I slowly made my way back to the living room.

They were still sitting there, still staring at me with their hideous beady eyes. I felt as though my body would shake apart. My kingdom for a beer!

My father broke the eerie silence. "Sit down, Geri, we want to talk with you."

I sat at the end of the sofa, the farthest point from all three.

"You shouldn't be drinking Coke the first thing in the day," my mother said.

"Never mind that now, Ginger. We want to talk with you," he said again.

I waited. No one said anything. Ginger sat twirling her hair, staring out the window, and my father kept looking down at his feet and clearing his throat. Jack was the only one who kept his eyes on me. They were two brown rays of hate. I kept sipping my Coke, looking down at my feet and away from Jack's stare.

"Well, go on," Jack finally said in a tone I'd never heard from him before. "Either you say something or I will."

My father raised his hand to quiet him and cleared his throat again. "Geri," he began, "you were drunk last night, weren't you?"

I knew that this time it was pointless to lie. I nodded, trying to look repentant. Of course, I *was* repentant in terms of Sophie.

"That was the first time you've ever been drunk, wasn't it?" he asked.

Somewhere in my life I had learned that when people phrased things that way they told you what answer they wanted. I mean, if he had said, "Was that the first time you were drunk?" it would have been different. He was really making a statement rather than asking a question. I said yes, it was the first time. Jack groaned. He was going to be my real problem.

"Does he have to be here?" I asked.

"He's a member of this family, such as it is, and he's had a loss, too." Daddy said. "Now, I want to know why you got drunk, with whom, where and how?"

"I don't see what difference that makes, George. Isn't the important thing making sure she doesn't do it again?"

"Ginger, please."

She twirled her hair more furiously.

"Well?"

I didn't know what to say. How could I answer those questions? *Why* did I get drunk? I mean, that didn't even make sense. What did he mean, *why?* You drink—you get drunk. That was all. That's just the way it was. Wasn't it? I couldn't tell him with whom because I knew he would forbid me to see those people again. The same with where. And *how?* That I didn't understand at all. How did he think? By drinking, of course. I just didn't know what to say and without planning it —at least I don't think I planned it—I started to cry.

"Oh, Christ," Jack mumbled.

"I can't help it," I sputtered. And I didn't think I could. I felt frightened and lonely and I wanted Sophie. How could I have brought a dog into the house like that? My stomach turned over and I thought I might throw up. Maybe I should eat something. But just the thought of food made me feel even worse. I wanted to curl up into a little ball—and this was the strangest thing of all—I wanted to curl up into a little ball on my mother's lap! Inside my head I kept calling "Momma, Momma," something I had never called her, ever. It didn't make sense. There she sat, twirling her hair and staring into space, and in my head I was calling to her, knowing she'd never hear me. This made me cry even harder and that made my father clear his throat more and made Jack shift in his chair, uttering funny little noises. It didn't seem to affect my mother at all. She just kept staring and twirling. I thought if she twirled another minute I'd scream. I had to stop looking at her so I covered my face with my hands.

"All right, all right," my father said. "There's no need to cry."

Why do people always say that or things like it? It's not true. If you're crying there is a need to cry, isn't there?

"The point is," he went on, as though I'd stopped crying, "we know that every young person gets drunk now and then, although I have to say I'm not used to the idea of girls doing it . . . nice girls. Anyway, I suppose things are different now. So you've had your experience and I trust you've learned a lesson. It's too bad that Sophie had to die to teach you a lesson."

"Did I have to be taught a lesson, too?" Jack said angrily.

"Life isn't always fair, Jack," he said. "I'm sure your sister is sorry."

"Sorry doesn't bring Sophie back."

"Well, what do you want," I screamed, "my life for hers?"

He looked at me disgustedly. "Don't be so dramatic."

"Well, what *do* you want?" I asked through my tears.

"I want you to tell them the truth . . . the least you can do is that."

I felt more frightened. "What truth?"

"Oh, Geri, you know what truth. They think this is the first time you ever drank and got drunk for one thing."

I wiped my eyes and looked straight at him. "Well, it is," I said with conviction.

His mouth fell open slightly and I think he realized there was no use trying to pressure me into the truth. He stood up and walked toward the front door.

"She's conning you, Dad," he said turning back to my father, "and you want to be conned. She's a disgusting slobby liar." Then he left the house.

There was a moment of silence before my father said, "Are you lying?"

I began to scream. "You always take Jack's side . . . you always believe everything he says . . . you hate me . . . you've always hated me."

I ran up the stairs into my room and threw myself across my bed, sobbing. I hadn't cried that way for years. I felt very little and all I could think about was Sophie. She'd been so beautiful, so sweet. She'd never done anything to anyone. As far as I knew she'd never even killed a mouse or a bird. Poor little thing. Why? Why did it have to happen? Deep down I knew Jack was right. I *had* killed her. And I also knew that I never would have brought that dog into the house if I'd been sober. But I couldn't stand to dwell on that for long. Oh, Sophie, forgive me.

I couldn't believe I'd never see her again, feel her

soft fur, hear her purr, or feel her rough little tongue on my neck. How could she be gone? Finished—over—ended? Never again in all the days of my life would I ever see Sophie. It was almost impossible to contemplate. Twenty-four hours ago she was alive, I thought. Then twenty hours ago—fifteen hours ago—twelve hours ago. If only I could go back in time. If only Dave hadn't driven to the beach. If only the dog hadn't been there. If only, if only, if only, if only. Maybe it was a mistake—maybe it hadn't been Sophie. But then, of course, there was her collar. Maybe they were just saying that she was dead to punish me—but I knew that wasn't true. There on my pillow was her collar, the bell bent where she had been hit or where she'd landed. A bent bell on a worn red leather collar was all that was left of that dear, sweet animal. Is that what it was all about? What would *I* leave behind *me*? Some clothes and shoes, some drawings—what? Would anyone grieve for me? The horrible fear and finality of Death cornered my mind and held it captive. I heard myself wailing, griving for the loss of Geri. Where was the Great Me now?

My bedroom door opened and I recognized my father's footsteps. I felt him sit down on the bed. He cleared his throat.

"Geri, don't cry," he said softly, touching my back.

"Why not?" I asked.

He had no answer for me. He went on. "We know you're sorry about last night. About getting drunk . . . about Sophie. And it's not true that we take Jack's side. You and Jack are very different . . . we know this. And we know you won't do it again . . . get drunk. And we've decided that if you want you're old enough now to have a drink with us before dinner. We want you to learn to drink properly. There's nothing wrong with alcohol if you don't abuse it. So from now on, anytime you'd like to have a drink with us, you just say so. We told Jack that when he was sixteen, but he never wanted to. I don't know why we didn't tell you the same thing when you turned sixteen . . . I guess it's our old-fashioned ideas about girls. Okay, Geri?"

What I hated most of all was this "we" thing. Why

couldn't he just speak for himself? Were he and my mother the same person? I suppose that's what marriage did to you. If I ever got married I would never be a *we*.

"Geri?"

I tried to think about what he'd said. He was telling me I could drink at home. A few weeks ago I would have been thrilled to hear that. Even yesterday. But now it didn't matter. Once I got past this hangover I was never going to drink again. I knew I'd have to have a beer or two later with Dave, just to get me through, but that was it. My drinking had killed Sophie, and if that was the result I didn't want any part of it.

My father was waiting for some kind of answer. I turned over to look at him. He looked tired. "Okay, Daddy. Thank you."

He patted my hand. "Grandma and Grandpa will be here any minute so maybe you can get cleaned up for dinner, okay?"

I nodded.

After he left I began to sort things out. I had completely forgotten my grandparents were coming for dinner. In fact, I had forgotten it was Sunday and that we'd be having our dinner at three—which meant the cocktail hour would begin at one, fifteen minutes from now. Things started clicking into place. If my father meant what he said, I could have my much needed drink right here in my own house, right in the open. Naturally, he meant that I could have *a* drink. But that was fine. I just needed one to get myself together. How funny, I thought, that I would have my last drink in my very own house with my very own parents! Yeah—real funny!

My father took everyone's drink order and then he turned to me. "Would you like something, Geri?"

I tried to play it very cool. Inside I was shaking like mad. "Well, if you think it's okay," I said. "Maybe I would have some beer."

"Beer? Beer?" my grandfather said. "What do you mean beer? You're going to let this tiny child have beer, George?"

"Please, Papa," he said.

"Do you know how old that makes me feel? My little granddaughter drinking beer?"

"You *are* old," my grandmother said. "Besides, we let George drink when he was Geri's age. Better they should drink at home."

"I remember the first time George drank at home. Do you remember, George?" Grandpa asked.

"No," my father said quickly.

"I remember," Grandma said.

"I remember, too. You sure you don't remember?"

"No, I don't remember and I don't think anybody cares."

"I care," I said.

My father glared at me.

"Well," Grandpa started, "it was some kind of occasion. What occasion was it, Alice?"

"I don't remember that," she said, looking away from him and fussing with her handbag.

"Oh, come on . . . you must remember. You're always bragging about what a wonderful memory you have. What was the occasion?"

"I don't know, Ted. What difference does it make? Are you going to tell the story of the occasion or the story of George's drinking?"

"Why don't we just skip the whole thing," Daddy said. "Geri, want to help me make the drinks?"

"Now she's a bartender," Grandpa said. "I'd like to remember what the occasion was. It's all a part of the story."

"Just tell about George's drinking, Ted." Grandma had a funny look on her face.

"I just want to know what the occasion was. I can remember that there were a lot of people milling around. Was it a wedding?"

"Yes, yes, a wedding," Grandma said. "Go on."

"Whose? Whose wedding was it, Alice?"

"I don't know," she said. "This is really boring, Ted. I've lost interest in the whole thing now. Haven't you?" she asked my father and me.

"I never had any interest in it," he said.

"Let's talk about something else," she said.

"Or was it a birthday?" Grandpa said.

"Oh, for God's sake," Grandma said, "it was a funeral. Your father's, to be exact."

With that Grandpa began to cry.

"I knew it," Grandma said. "You couldn't just tell the story without the details . . . oh, no, you had to delve. Sometimes I think you do that to make yourself sad."

"Well, how did I know it was my father's funeral?"

"You didn't. But you probably hoped."

"You're crazy, you know that. You're really crazy," he said.

"So what happened when Daddy drank?" I asked.

"He got drunk," Grandpa said.

"Is that the story?" I asked.

"I don't feel like telling it now," Grandpa said.

Grandma said, "He made his first drink a martini. He had two and before you could say Jack Robinson he was drunk and then he threw up all over Mrs. Edwards who was asking him how he was doing at school. He opened his mouth to answer and just threw right up on her . . . all over the front of her black dress. It was disgusting. Then he ran upstairs. I found him later lying on the bathroom floor. That's the story."

"Oh."

"We paid the cleaning bill on Mrs. Edwards' dress," Grandpa said.

"Naturally," said Grandma.

"That's a really fun story," my father said. "Why don't you and Papa try and think of some more terrific stories like that while Geri and I make your drinks?"

As we left the room I asked Daddy if he had really forgotten throwing up on Mrs. Edwards. He admitted it was something he'd never forget and that if I was smart I'd stay away from martinis until I was a lot older. I didn't tell him I thought martinis were a very establishment drink and that I had no intention of drinking them ever. I just grunted and he took that as agreement.

We went to the liquor cabinet in the dining room and I helped him carry the bottles into the kitchen where he always made the drinks. Mother was cutting up vegetables for the salad.

"What would you like, Ginger?"

"I'll have the usual."

The usual was a Rob Roy—Scotch and dry vermouth. I would have liked that myself, but I knew it looked better for me to have beer.

"You can get your beer from the fridge."

I did what he said and put it down on the table, not wanting to appear too eager. What I really wanted to do was open it and pour it down my throat. Daddy showed me how to measure a shot. That was something we never did—we just poured. My grandmother drank manhattans and he explained the proportions to me. That made me think of B.J. and I felt kind of sad. Then he made Mother's Rob Roy and a Scotch and water for himself. Grandpa's martini was next.

"You stir it gently," he said, "so you don't bruise the gin." Then he kind of laughed. When he was finished he put all the drinks on a tray. I picked up my beer and opened it. I can't tell you how much I wanted to drink it, but I knew I'd better wait until we were all seated in the living room. I started toward the door.

"Where are you going?" he asked.

I looked at him, puzzled.

"A glass, Geri, a glass."

"I can drink it out of the can."

"Ladies," my mother said, "do not drink out of cans."

"I drink Coke out of cans."

"That's different," he said.

And she said, "You certainly do and I've never liked it. A lady should sip from a glass . . . particularly an alcoholic beverage."

"But it's all right for a man to drink beer from a can, huh?" I said.

"That's a whole other thing," she said.

"I don't see what the difference is. I think it's very sexist to make that kind of—"

"Don't start," my mother said.

I decided to let it go. The longer I talked the longer it would be before I got to drink my beer. I got a glass from the cabinet.

"Not one of those," Ginger said disgustedly. "If

you're going to learn to drink properly then you must learn to drink from the proper glass. Here." She handed me what's known as a pilsner glass. It's a tall V-shaped thing with a short stem.

"You tip the glass and pour slowly so you don't get too much head," my father said.

Finally, the beer was poured and we were on our way into the living room.

Thank God. At last I could drink. I knew I had to be careful not to gulp but I really needed more than just a *ladylike* sip! Nevertheless, that's all I could have because my father was watching me closely.

Then my grandmother said, "Where's that rotten cat?"

Nobody said anything. Grandma had always called her "that rotten cat." She liked to pretend that she didn't like her, but it was just a game. The truth was she was crazy about Sophie and Sophie had been crazy about her. She always sat in Grandma's lap when she came to visit.

"What's the matter, cat got your tongues?" Grandma said and roared with laughter.

I took a big swallow of beer, not caring what anyone thought.

"The cat's dead," my mother said bluntly.

"No!" Grandma said.

"You see," Grandpa said, "death is all around us."

"Shut up, Ted," Grandma said. "What happened?"

Daddy told her, leaving out the part about the dog.

Grandpa kept shaking his head. "You never know . . . it could come at any time. Here a cat goes out for a walk and *phhht*, it's over. You should never have let that cat go outdoors. We've got to be careful. Let that be a lesson to you, Geri."

"You mean I should never go outdoors?" I asked.

"Just don't think you're immortal. It could happen to you, *phhht* . . . like that."

"Could we change the subject, please?" Mother said.

"I feel awful," Grandma said. "She was a nice cat."

She had tears in her eyes and it made me feel like crying all over again. I couldn't shake the empty feeling Sophie's death gave me and now Grandma was making it worse. I drank some more beer. It really wasn't doing much. I felt a little less shaky but that was all. I should have had something stronger. Now I'd blown my chance. I definitely should have had something stronger, particularly since it was my last drink. My last drink! Well, maybe one more. After all, what I'd said to myself was that I'd quit after I got some relief from my hangover and that hadn't happened yet. But how? I knew Daddy would never offer me another. And then it came to me. If I could make the drinks alone I would have access to the booze. I could take some for myself—just enough to get rid of this awful, empty, lousy feeling. Otherwise, I'd never get through dinner. I'd fall apart and then everyone would be upset. Actually, I'd be doing them all a favor if I could just have a little bit more and pull myself together.

I looked around the room to see how close they were to their next drinks. Pretty soon. I poured the remainder of my beer into my glass and took another sip. I looked at my watch. One-thirty. Twelve hours ago Sophie was alive. My stomach felt like somebody was kicking it, over and over.

"Ready for another?" I heard Daddy say. "Papa! Mom?"

All were ready. And so was I.

I jumped to my feet and tried not to sound too eager. "Daddy," I said, "I have a neat idea."

"What's that?"

"Well, nobody ever serves you . . . I mean, you always have to make all the drinks . . . so why don't I do it?"

"Isn't that cute?" Grandma said.

"I saw how you did it . . . I'm sure I know how."

"So adorable," Grandma went on.

My father thought for a few seconds. Then he said yes. Relief flooded through me. I picked up all their glasses and put them on the tray. My grandfather grabbed my wrist when I got to him.

"When you were a little girl, five, six," he said, "you used to bring me my martini on a tray . . . a white towel draped over your arm. You said you were the waitress."

I had forgotten all about that. Every Saturday we

visited them and that's exactly what I did. I also used to have a *cocktail* with them. Ginger ale with a cherry floating in it—always in a cocktail glass. It made me feel very important and grown up.

"First a waitress and now the barmaid . . . where did the time go?"

I started toward the kitchen. Suddenly, I realized my father was in the kitchen with me. I looked at him.

"I'll supervise," he said.

He might as well have killed me. All hopes of getting anything more to drink were smashed. Fortunately, the beer had steadied my shaking hands so I didn't spill anything as I made the drinks. I had fantasies of knocking him out and pouring the booze down my throat. But, of course, I didn't do anything except make the drinks perfectly.

"You have a good memory," he said.

Everyone oohed and ahhed about how well I'd made their drinks and I sat in silence, seething with envy at every swallow they took. I only had a tiny bit of beer left and I finished it, my whole body calling for more. Finally, my chance came. When it was time for their third drink my father sent me into the kitchen alone.

Quickly, I took gulps from the Scotch bottle before I started. Then I drank from each of the other bottles so no one would be able to detect what I'd done. I had to be careful because I never knew when someone might come in the kitchen. Thank God, Jack was having dinner at Barbara's. I moved as fast as possible and by the time I went back to the living room I was feeling terrific. But within twenty minutes or so I knew I wanted more. I said I was going to have a Coke and casually headed for the kitchen. I couldn't take the time to do my old Coke and booze trick, but I managed to get a few swallows of Scotch before going back into the other room. That helped for a while. Now I was feeling pretty good, but I wanted to feel better. I couldn't wait for dinner to be over with so I could get out of the house and meet Dave.

I got through dinner all right and when Dave came by at four he told me what had happened at the V.S. and I told him about Sophie. We went to Yolanda's and drank beer and got into a heavy rap about death. By the time I got home I was pretty high. I got past my parents by going to my room immediately to do my homework. Of course, homework was the last thing I could do. Dave had given me his flask of vodka and I sat in my room sipping from it and thinking about how I'd killed Sophie and how everything happened to me. I even called B.J. to tell her about it. I thought of all people she'd give me some sympathy. But she said I sounded funny, made some dumb excuse about having to nurse a sick rabbit and got off. How could people be so callous? Didn't she understand what a burden I had to carry? I made some other calls—Marcelle —Linda—but I don't remember much about them. My life, I decided, was nothing but sadness and tragedy and before I went to sleep I knew that the only thing that would keep me sane and give me a little happiness once in a while was a drink now and then. After all, the terrible tragedy of Sophie could have happened to anyone and I couldn't be expected to punish myself forever, could I?

18

One more significant thing happened before Christmas vacation. At the time I didn't view it as significant —just as an interesting piece of information.

My last class on Monday the twenty-third, the last school day, was humanities. I desperately wanted to skip that class and planned to but Ms. Laine caught up with me in the hall beforehand and said we'd walk to class together. There was no way out. I couldn't look at her. Not only had she seen me roaring drunk, she had seen me naked. She babbled on about the coming holidays and then just before we entered her room she said she'd like to talk to me after class.

During class we listened to a lot of Christmas music and discussed its origins and stuff like that. I said nothing. All I could think about was the impending talk. Obviously, she was going to talk about what had happened Saturday night. I wondered how many of the other teachers she had told. I thought Mr. Kelly had looked at me funny that morning in homeroom but then he was always looking at me funny. What could I possibly say to her? I couldn't deny that it had happened. It occurred to me to pretend I was sick and get sent to the nurse. But then I realized I'd have this little talk hanging over my head all through vacation. Laine was not the kind to let something like this drop. She'd be sure to nab me the first day back. Barring faked illness, there was no way out of the confrontation.

The class dragged on through "The First Noel," "Good King Wenceslas" and "Silent Night." And then the last bell rang and everyone cheered as they always did on the last bell before vacation. I did not join in the shouting. I stayed in my seat after telling Linda to ask Dave to wait for me. When the last kid left the room, Laine looked up from her desk and smiled at me.

"Are you going to stay way back there?"

I had taken to sitting in the last chair in the last row in all of my classes. Slowly, I got up and walked to a seat in front. I might as well get it over with.

"How are you feeling?" she asked.

"Fine." I was not. My stomach was turning over with anxiety at what might be coming.

"Geri," she said softly, "I'm sure you know that I asked you to stay to talk to you about what happened Saturday night."

I nodded, looking down at the scratched desk. "Marion loves Perry" I read. Who were Marion and Perry, I wondered, and where were they now and did she still love him?

"I understand your problem, Geri."

I looked at her. "What problem?"

"Your drinking problem."

"Look, I know I was drunk Saturday night . . . I mean, there's no point in denying it, but if you think I make a habit of that kind of thing you're wrong." Problem, for God's sake!

"Am I?"

"You think I go around taking off my clothes in public any old time of day or night?"

"I was referring to your drunkenness." She held up her hand as I opened my mouth. "Before you say anything I want to tell you something." She shifted uncomfortably in her chair. "I'm taking a chance telling you this, Geri, but I think basically you're someone I can trust. Am I right?"

"Sure." I thought I was. Actually, I didn't give a damn whether I was or wasn't. Now I was curious.

"I'm going to tell you this because I think there may come a time when it will be helpful for you to know it. I'm taking a chance because if you told the wrong people it might hurt me. Most people don't understand."

I wished she'd get to the point.

"I'm an alcoholic. A nondrinking alcoholic."

I was shocked and confused. "How can you be an alcoholic if you don't drink?"

"Because once an alcoholic, always an alcoholic. It's a disease that can't be cured. Only arrested. And the way it is arrested is by not drinking. I haven't had a drink in four years, but if I were to pick up a drink now I'd get drunk again."

I didn't like this conversation. I felt uncomfortable and wanted to get the hell out of there. "Why are you telling me this? You don't think I'm an alcoholic, do you?"

"I don't know. Only you can really decide that. I suspect you may have a problem with alcohol . . . not just because of Saturday night. I've watched you change since the start of the school year and I know there have been times in my class when you've been high. Don't bother denying it, Geri. I'm very tuned in when it comes to drinking."

"Look," I said defensively, "everybody does it."

She smiled. "First of all, everybody doesn't do it. Yes, I'm aware that there are plenty of kids drinking and I'm also aware that you're not the only one with a possible problem . . . but you're the only one in my classes . . . the only one that maybe I can help."

"I think you're making something out of nothing," I said. It was so typical, I thought. Laine was a drunk so she thought everybody else who took a drink was a drunk. A real holier-than-thou type. She probably belonged to Alcoholics Anonymous, too. "Do you belong to AA?" I asked.

"Yes, I do."

Just as I thought.

She laughed. "Why the face?" she asked.

I hadn't been aware that I'd made a face but I guess I had. "Creepy," I said before I knew it.

"AA is creepy or I'm creepy?" she asked.

Both, I wanted to say, but instead I shrugged.

She said, "Or maybe you think both are creepy. I can understand that. I thought that once myself. The point is, Geri, I'm not looking for recruits . . . I don't have to. There are plenty of members, believe me.

I'm telling you this because I want you to know if you ever do think you have a problem with booze, or you just want someone to talk with, I'm here. I'm going to give you my home phone number but please don't abuse that privilege."

Privilege, I thought. Who the hell does she think she is?

"I'm also going to give you this pamphlet." She wrote her name and number on the outside and handed it to me. The title was *Young People and AA*. "You don't have to read it if you don't want to. There won't be any quiz on it. Just put it in a drawer somewhere and maybe sometime you might want to look at it. Who knows? If nothing else, it's interesting."

Interesting! I bet! What I wanted to do was to tear the pamphlet up in tiny pieces and throw it in her face. But I knew the smartest thing to do right now was just to yes her. I would tear it up later. She stood up and I did the same.

"I hope you have a very nice holiday, Geri, and I also hope what I've told you will be our secret. I'm not ashamed of being an alcoholic, but most people just don't understand."

I nodded and started toward the door. Then something hit me. "Ms. Laine, if you don't drink anymore what were you doing in a bar?"

"I was having a Coke and enjoying myself. My life didn't stop when I stopped drinking, Geri. As a matter of fact, it began. Merry Christmas and Happy New Year."

I mumbled the same back to her and left. I shoved the pamphlet between the pages of a book so no one would see it. I'd get rid of it later. As I hurried through the halls toward the parking lot I couldn't wait to tell Dave that Laine was a drunk. But, strangely enough, when I met him at the truck I didn't say that. He asked me what she wanted and I said she gave me a lecture about drinking, but that was all I said. I didn't know why I didn't tell him about her but something made me skip it.

The whole gang was going to the movies that night and before I went out I took the pamphlet out of my book. But instead of ripping it to shreds, I opened the first page and read the first paragraph on the inside cover. It said:

ALCOHOLICS ANONYMOUS *is a fellowship of men and women who share their experience, strength and hope with each other that they may solve their common problem and help others to recover from alcoholism.*

I quickly closed it. What crap, I thought. But still I did not destroy it. I put it in the bottom drawer of my desk under a bunch of papers. And then I promptly forgot about it.

Christmas vacation turned out to be one big blur. With the exception of Christmas Eve, which I had to spend with my family, I was hardly sober at all. I guess I had a ball, but I really don't remember it. I guess, too, that nothing awful happened because somebody would have told me. My parents never noticed what was going on because they were either in bed by the time I came home or my mother was watching some old movie on television and didn't pay any attention to me. I thought they'd be watching me like hawks after the Sophie incident. But I guess they had their own problems or else they just didn't want to know what was going on with me.

Dave and I got really drunk New Year's Eve and I was still hungover from it two days later. When school started again The Big Boozer, as I had come to think of Ms. Laine, asked me to stay after class. I was really bugged. Was she going to hound me now?

"I waited for you to call me all day Thursday, Geri, but you never did."

What the hell was she talking about?

"I would have called you but your number is unlisted. Are you all right?"

"I'm fine," I said.

She looked at me a moment and then she smiled slowly, sweetly. "You don't remember, do you?"

"Remember what?"

"You called me Wednesday night . . . well, Thursday morning really . . . it was after four."

So that's why I'd found that stupid pamphlet in my bed on New Year's Day!

"You sure it was me?" I asked, knowing it must have been.

"I'm sure. I knew you were drunk, but I didn't think you were *that* drunk. I mean, well, I guess you were talking to me in a blackout."

I didn't like her knowing I'd had a blackout. I wanted desperately to know what I'd said to her but I didn't want to appear that interested. The whole thing was making me mad. I wanted Laine off my back even if I had brought it on myself. I started to shake with anger.

"Look," I said, "maybe I called you, maybe I didn't ... I really don't give a damn. All I care about is that you leave me alone."

"What would you like me to do if you call me again?"

"I won't."

"If you should?"

"Hang up ... have your number changed ... go to hell!" I started to leave the room.

"Geri, don't you want to know what you said to me?"

"No. And if you don't stop bugging me I'm going to tell everybody you're a goddamn drunk." I slammed out. I was shaking with rage and the first thing I did was to go to my locker and open my thermos of Scotch and milk. Yes, I had begun to stash booze in my locker. That was the way I'd started the new year.

19

The heavy dark months of January and February, usually unbelievably tedious and boring in Goose Bay, seemed to fly by. I sat through my classes in a haze and mostly concentrated on seeing Dave, nursing hangovers and planning where and when I'd have my next drink.

I'd like to say a word about hangovers. Although for me they were always pretty bad—shakes, headaches, queasy stomach and the HORRIBLE FEARS—there were times when I was able to have fun with them. I know that sounds like a contradiction, but it really isn't. If I had to be alone it was never fun. But when I shared a hangover day with Dave it could almost be a groove. I'd still feel like hell and have the same symptoms but eating pizza or heros, drinking beer and sometimes watching an old movie in Dave's room made it pass faster and easier.

Of course, these hangovers were the early and middle stage hangovers. Near the end of my drinking no amount of sharing helped. Then it was almost impossible to get food down and if, by some miracle, I did, it never stayed down. The HORRIBLE FEARS, of course, couldn't be lessened or changed by anyone or anything. If you've never had the H.F.'s it's pretty hard to explain. I mentioned earlier a feeling of DOOOOOOOM and that's part of it. But H.F.'s are much more than that. The fears can be specific, like a fear of death. Or, if you happen to be out, a fear that something will fall on you from a window or some stranger will come up and stab you. For instance, one hangover Saturday Dave and I drove fifty miles to the Sandhaven Mall to get Friendly's cheeseburgers and Swiss chocolate almond sundaes (the only things we could possibly eat). As we walked along inside the mall, making our way to Friendly's, a child of about six months, riding in a papoose thing on its mother's back, happened to look at me. I was convinced this child was going to beat me up! I was terrified of this six-month-old killer! In fact, I was so afraid that I grabbed Dave's arm and started running (an extremely difficult thing to do with a hangover) to get out of range of the six-month-old hit man! That is a specific fear. However, if you think that's bad, let me tell you something about unspecific fears.

Unspecific fears are impossible to be specific about. They are all-pervasive and they float. They pass over, under and through you. They are very black with oozing green spots. They kick holes in your brain with heavy-cleated shoes and grip your viscera with rotting fingers. They are the worst and there is nothing you can do about them. Drinking lessens them slightly but only time and sleep can make them disappear completely. Unless, of course, you quit drinking! But even the unspecific fears are not hideous enough to make you do that until you're ready.

So that is the hangover. It may seem strange to most people because almost everyone has experienced what is commonly known as the hangover and it is nothing like what I've described. Right? Well, the common hangover known to the nonalcoholic drinker is another banana all together. In fact, that type of hangover is often funny. At least we see it portrayed that way on television, in movies and sometimes in books. The man or woman awakes, groans, grabs the head, gets out of bed unsteadily, looks in a mirror, groans again, takes some aspirin, drinks coffee, holds the head again and in an hour or so it's gone. That's what a hangover is for the nonalcoholic. But for the alcoholic or the problem drinker it's serious business and almost always no laughing matter—although now I can see that something like the six-month-old maniac is pretty funny. At the time, however, it was seriously terrifying. I guess

I've said more than a *word* about the hangover, haven't I? Oh, well.

So January and February went by without major incident and I floated into March.

In March, Dave's mother freaked out.

Very often on hangover days, after we'd gone to Yolanda's for pizza or Friendly's for burgers and sundaes, we'd come back to Dave's house and look at television. This was usually on Sunday afternoon and either his mother was out drinking or conked out in bed, and his father was over at a friend's house, working on a boat they were building, or out looking for his mother. But even if they were home they didn't seem to mind if we lay on Dave's bed and looked at an old movie. My mother would have had ten thousand fits!

Anyway, on this particular Sunday in March, we were lying there looking at *The Blob,* a sci-fi flick with Steve McQueen, when Dave's father, looking very tired and distraught, flung open the door.

"Heard anything?" he asked.

"No," Dave said.

"Nothing?"

"Nothing."

His father started to close the door, then threw it open so hard it smashed against the wall. Even though we both saw it coming we jumped.

"Well, maybe you'd know something if you got your ass out of bed and helped me," his father yelled.

"C'mon, Dad, what do you expect me to do?"

"You could help me look instead of lying around here all day with your chippy."

Dave jumped up. "Hey, Dad."

Mr. Townsend's face was flushed with anger, his lips pressed together. "Okay, okay. I'm sorry." He looked at me. "Sorry," he muttered.

"That's okay," I said. I didn't know what a chippy was, but I figured it wasn't something terrific.

Dave and his father stared at each other for a few seconds. Then Dave spoke.

"You want me to go looking?"

"Nah. I've looked everywhere. She must be holed up in somebody's house."

I was beginning to get the picture. Obviously, Bunny was missing and not to be found in any of the bars. I wondered how long she'd been gone.

"Should we call the police?" Dave asked.

"What are you, nuts?"

"I don't know . . . she's never been gone this long before."

"She'll turn up," Mr. T. said, sounding as though he wasn't sure he wanted her to. He started to leave again.

"What are you going to do now?"

"Wait."

He sounded so forlorn and lonely that I blurted, "Would you like to look at the movie with us, Mr. Townsend?"

He looked at me like I was crazy. "Uh, no thanks, kid," he said.

When he was gone and closed the door, I put my arm around Dave. "How long has she been missing?" I asked.

"Since Tuesday. She left Yolanda's around one in the morning. She probably got a ride with somebody."

"But, Dave, I mean, she could be. . . ." I couldn't say it.

"Yeah, I know. But she isn't. I mean, even though she's never been gone quite this long before I'm pretty sure she's safe."

"But how do you know?"

"You want a beer?"

"Sure."

He went to get it. I did want a beer very much . . . almost as much as I wanted to know how he could be so sure his mother hadn't been killed. What did it mean that she got a ride with somebody? And why didn't Mr. T. want to call the police? Dave was back with the beers.

"Dave," I said, "why are you so sure she's okay?"

"I'm not *sure*. I just think she is. Look, sometimes . . . oh, hell. She's probably shacked up with some guy somewhere." He turned his back to me.

That had not occurred to me. And now that he'd said it I was shocked. I was glad he'd turned away because I was sure he would have seen it in my eyes. I moved closer to him and rested my head on his back. I didn't want to crowd him, but I wanted him to know I was there. Neither of us said anything for a while. Then, from outside, we heard a screech of tires that seemed to stop in front of the house. Dave jumped up and ran to the window. I followed.

An old souped-up Buick, its back lowered, a foxtail flying from the aerial, a red stripe painted around its green middle, had pulled up. The door on the passenger side opened and Bunny, pushed by a disembodied man's hand, came flying out and landed hard on the sidewalk. The door was pulled shut and the car squealed off.

Immediately, Dave ran from the room. I stayed at the window. First his father appeared, running down the path toward his wife. She was conscious and beginning to try to sit up. Then Dave ran down the path. They both knelt over her and, finally, Mr. T. picked her up and all three came toward the house. When they were out of my line of vision I left the window and went to the top of the stairs. I wasn't sure what I should do so I waited. I heard them come in. Bunny was mumbling and Mr. T. was saying things that sounded as though he were trying to soothe her. Dave said nothing. I finished off my beer, ran back to Dave's room, put the can on the table, snapped off the TV set, and went back to my place at the top of the stairs.

"My God, Bunny," Mr. T. said.

"Godbunnygodbunnygodbunnygodbunnygodbunny," she mumbled.

"Look at her," he said.

"I see," Dave said softly.

"I've never seen anything like it," Mr. T. said.

I decided *I* wanted to see so I came down three steps and looked over the banister. Bunny was lying on the couch and they were standing over her, blocking her face. I could see that her clothes were torn and filthy, but that was all.

"Drink," she said.

"I think you've had enough," Mr. T. said.

"Drink," she yelled and sat straight up. That's when she saw me. And screamed.

Dave and his father turned to look at me. Bunny pushed them out of the way, with great effort rose to her feet, took a few steps toward me and held out her arms.

"Betty," she said. "Oh, Betty, help me." She was crying and limping closer and closer to the stairs, her arms outstretched.

Mr. T. grabbed for her. "That's not your sister," he snarled.

"Leggoame." She pulled out of his grasp. "Betty, Betty, help me." She was at the bottom of the stairs now.

I didn't know what to do. I looked to Dave for help, but he said nothing. Mr. T. had sunk down into a chair, his head in his hands. I could see that Bunny was determined to climb the stairs to reach me so I met her halfway. She flung herself at my feet, her arms wrapped around my ankles.

"Betty, Betty," she sobbed.

I sat down on the step and looked through the spokes in the banister. Mr. T. raised his head and said to Dave, "Call."

Slowly, Dave left the room. Bunny had raised herself and her head was in my lap. She looked up at me with two huge black and purple eyes.

"Oh, Betty," she cried, "I've been a bad girl . . . sucha bad girl."

I wasn't sure what I was supposed to do but, instinctively, I reached out and stroked her hair which was greasy and filthy. Now I saw her mouth. It was caked with blood where she'd obviously been beaten. And the smell of her was enough to make me gag. I leaned back and away from her.

"Betty," she went on, the tears continuing, "get me a drink and I'll be good, I promise. Oh, I've been so bad. Are ya mad at me, huh? Why don't ya answer?"

I didn't know what to say. I looked through the spokes again. Mr. T. was walking toward us.

Bunny screamed as Mr. T. grabbed her. She held onto me, her arms tightly encircling my waist, as he dragged us both bumping down the last four steps.

"For Christ's sake, Bunny, let go of the girl," he yelled.

"Get that man away, Betty. Help me."

"Leggo, Bunny."

She held on tighter. Dave appeared and tried breaking his mother's grip. Mr. T. was shouting at her to let go, she was screaming for Betty to help her, Dave was softly begging her to let go of me, and I had begun to cry. I don't know why I was crying exactly, except that it was a terribly ugly and pathetic scene and I guess I was frightened. After several minutes of this, Dave's father punched the wall.

"This is it. This is it. This is the last time . . . I can't take it anymore." He pulled at her again.

"Betty, get the man away from me."

"Dad, let go of her. She's not hurting anything." Then Dave looked at me and saw the tears running down my cheeks. "Oh, God," he said and started pulling at her, too.

"It's okay," I said, "let her go. It's okay."

I guess they were startled that I'd spoken because they stopped pulling at her and stared at me. For some reason that made me cry all the more.

"Don't cry, Betty. Bunny'll be good from now on. Let's have a little drink, okay?"

"What should I do?" I asked Dave.

"I . . . I don't know," he said.

"Jus' a little drink," Bunny said.

"This is really it," Mr. T. said. "I've had it."

There was a knock at the door and we all looked toward it except Bunny, who grabbed me even tighter when she heard the sound.

David opened the door. There were two men in white hospital suits. One had a folded-up stretcher under his arm and the other one carried something else that was also white. Immediately, a phrase came into my mind: "Look out or the men in the little white jackets will come." I knew that's who these guys were and realized that Dave had called them.

They came over to where we were lumped together at the bottom of the stairs.

"Which one?" asked the one with red hair.

Oh, thanks a lot, I thought. I guessed I looked pretty awful, sitting there and crying. Then the other one poked him and said: "You're kidding, man? The blonde, dummy."

"Oh, yeah, sure."

"What's her name?"

"Bunny," Dave said.

The dark-haired one, who seemed a little brighter than the redhead, leaned down and touched Bunny on the shoulder. She jumped and burrowed her head into my breasts, murmuring and crying.

"Hello, Bunny," Darkhead said. "Wanna go for a nice ride?"

She didn't answer but nuzzled in even deeper.

Redhead leaned down on the other side. They looked at each other. Darkhead nodded and they began to pull at her. Bunny fought them, pushing against me and pulling away from them. Redhead reached behind me and broke her grip as Darkhead lifted Bunny away and up.

"Nooooooo," she screamed. "Betty . . . help me."

She started to swing at Darkhead and he grabbed her wrists as Redhead opened up the white thing he carried. It was a straitjacket. Even though I'd only seen one in the movies I knew that's what it was. I didn't want to watch, but I couldn't help myself.

They struggled and fought with her as she scratched their faces and tried to bite them. It seemed to take hours but it was really only a few minutes. As they carried her out, wrapped in the white straitjacket, she was still screaming for me—for Betty. I thought I would hear that scream forever. Sometimes, even now, I do.

Bunny stayed in the hospital for two weeks and when she came out she was *good* (that meant not drinking) for six days. Then it started all over, although it was quite awhile before she disappeared again for several days. Of course, Mr. T. was still around and, according to Dave, would always be around. I didn't know how any of them stood it. Now I know.

By April, my mother was going through her own changes. She seemed to have slipped completely into a world of her own. For years, of course, she had been in her world of the fifties but this was different. She seldom left the house for anything besides marketing and she stopped seeing her friends. If the phone rang and I was home she always made me answer. If it was one of her friends, I was forced to say she was out. I asked her about it.

"Why don't you ever want to talk to anyone anymore?"

"I have nothing to say to those people."

"What do you mean *those* people? I thought *those* people were your friends."

"Friends? Friends have things in common. I have nothing in common with them."

Well, I could see that that was probably true. After all, most people were living in the seventies. Had I been a sober person, I think I would have tried to do something about my mother—at least spoken to my father about her. I noticed her withdrawal but, beyond an occasional question, I really couldn't get involved in it. I was only interested in when, where, and how I would get my next drink—although I wasn't aware then that that was my only interest. I knew what was happening to her wasn't particularly funny but I didn't care. Not even when her friend Lois approached me after school one day.

I saw her from a distance and figured she was waiting for Don so I didn't even try to duck her. As a matter of fact, I waved. She jumped out of the car and came running toward me.

"You have a minute, Geri?"

"Yeah, sure. What's up?"

"Can we go have a soda or something?"

"Huh?" It had been so long since anyone had suggested a soda to me. I felt like I was talking to someone from another planet.

"I'd like to talk to you," she said.

I panicked for a moment. "What's wrong? Has something happened?"

"No, no. I just want to talk, okay?"

I shrugged and followed her to her car. Naturally, the last thing I felt like doing was having a heart-to-heart with Lois. I mean, I liked her and everything, but it was far more important to me to get home and have a few while I played at doing my homework. Dave and I were meeting Marcelle and Bob at Yolanda's that night and if I didn't get home and pretend I'd spent the afternoon on school work my mother wouldn't let me go out. Also, I'd just had a couple of slugs of Scotch in the girls' room with Marcelle and hadn't wintergreened myself. That'd teach me. Never leave a drinking scene without shooting yourself full of mouth spray!

"Where do you want to go?" she asked.

"Go?"

"Well, I'd like to buy you a soda or a Coke or something."

"That isn't necessary," I said. If only I could have suggested that she buy me a beer.

"Well, *I'd* like something. We'll go to the luncheonette in Eastport, okay?"

"Perfect," I said. I waited for her to start talking but we drove about five miles and she said nothing. It made me very anxious. I tried to remember just how much Scotch I had left in the Jean Naté bottle I carried in my bag. I'd go to the ladies' room as soon as we got to the luncheonette and fortify myself. I hoped I hadn't used it all up. I couldn't remember. Anyway, I was going crazy from the silence. "What is it you want to talk about?" I asked.

"I'd rather wait until I'm seated," she said.

I didn't point out to her that she *was* seated. I stared at her out of the corner of my eye. Every red hair was in place, makeup perfect, her clothes neat and clean. There was nothing unusual about that but it made me realize just how far removed my mother was from that image. I hadn't noticed—or at least it hadn't really registered, until now—but my mother had let herself go. I wondered when she'd last done anything with her hair? She usually had it tinted. As a matter of fact, I wondered when she'd last washed it? And as for makeup, I couldn't remember the last time I'd seen her in any—which was terrific, as far as I was concerned, but very unlike her. Was it my mother Lois wanted to talk to me about? Of course. What else? Well, there was nothing I could tell her. My mother was leaving me alone and that's all that I cared about—that's all I wanted.

Finally, we got to the luncheonette. I went to the bathroom right away and discovered that my Jean Naté bottle was half full. I drank it down and sprayed my mouth before I went to the table. Now I was ready for whatever Lois had to say.

"What would you like?" she asked.

"A Coke is fine."

She ordered a Coke for me and coffee for herself.

"Now that I've got you here I don't know how to begin," she said, lighting a cigarette with a purple Cricket lighter.

I decided to help her out. "It's about my mother, isn't it?"

"Yes." She seemed relieved. "So you *are* aware of it."

"Sure."

"Well, what is it? What's wrong with her, Geri?"

"I dunno."

The coffee and Coke were set before us.

"Anything else?" the waitress asked.

"Not now," Lois answered. "Geri, I'm really worried about your mother."

I said nothing.

"She seems so . . . so out of touch."

"Well, she's always been out of touch with us," I said.

"Not with me. I can't seem to . . . to reach her anymore. She's lost interest in everything. When she does talk to me now it's always about her past."

"She's always done that with us."

"She has?"

"Sure. All about her terrific high school years and all-round popularity and that stuff."

"Yes, that's it. She's always telling me stories from high school. I mean, naturally we've told each other things out of our pasts before, I mean, you do, you know . . . when you're friends . . . but now it's all the time. I try to turn the conversation to the present . . .

talk about you and Jack or current events, but she always goes back to the past. I guess you think it's weird that I'm talking to you about this but I didn't know who else to talk to. Your mother's always told me how close you two are and—"

"She what?" I almost choked on my Coke.

Lois stared at me. "What's wrong?"

"My mother always told you how close we are?"

"Yes. Aren't you?"

Oh, wow! Did Ginger *really* think we were close or did she just want Lois to think so for some reason? I found it hard to believe that she knowingly lied to Lois because she had such a bug about lying. But it was equally hard to believe that she really thought we were close.

"Aren't you?" Lois asked again.

"Well, I wouldn't exactly call it close."

"Of course, I don't mean now . . . nobody could be close to her now. Anyway, I didn't know who else to talk to. Do you know what's wrong?"

All I wanted was to get home to the nice brand-new bottle of Scotch in my closet. There was nothing more secure-making than knowing you had a new bottle—unless maybe it was knowing you had two new bottles!

"I don't know," I said.

"Don't you care?" she asked, perhaps hearing the boredom in my reply.

There was a moment when I was tempted to say no, I didn't care, but I knew that would get us into a really big hassle and I didn't want this summit meeting to go on any longer than necessary.

"Sure I care, but there's nothing I can do about it."

"You kids," she mumbled.

"Well, what can *I* do?"

"What about your father?" she asked.

"What about him?"

"Doesn't he care?" She lit another cigarette.

"I don't know. He's hardly ever home anymore and when he is I don't talk to him." I finished my Coke and wished we could leave. "Listen, Lois, I have a lot of homework. . . ."

"And Jack? Doesn't he care?"

"He's hardly home either. He's always at Barbara's."

She took a long drag of her cigarette and said rapidly, "You know, Geri, you've gotten fat."

The words hit me like pellets from a shotgun. I knew I'd gained weight—in fact, I knew I'd gained twenty-five pounds since September—but nobody but Jack ever referred to it. It was a fact that I tried to ignore. I couldn't believe Lois had said it.

"Thanks," I said.

"What do you mean, thanks? You have. And you should do something about it. Obviously, your mother is in no condition to notice or help you with it so—"

"So you're going to take over? Well, don't bother," I said, sliding out of the booth.

"Where are you going?"

"Buzz off," I said and headed toward the door.

"Geri," she called after me, as ladylike as possible. She would do anything to avoid a scene.

I kept walking. When I was outside I hurried across the street to Grant's. I hung around in there for about twenty minutes until I saw that Lois' car was gone. Then I hitched a ride back to Goose Bay. As far as I was concerned, my mother had her problems and I had mine and that was that.

By the end of April I was definitely a daily drinker —no exceptions. I had gained another five pounds and I'd started smoking. There's something about drinking that makes you want to smoke. It was amazing that I'd held out as long as I had. I chose Vantage because I heard they weren't too bad for you. How ridiculous to worry about smoking being dangerous when I was doing such damaging things to my body with booze. But that never occurred to me then. Yes, there are two things that you can be pretty sure will accompany heavy drinking: smoking and sex.

I realize that I have said practically nothing so far about sex. I think that is because, in the deepest recesses of my soul, I am a Puritan! Although I grew up in the sixties and seventies the morality of the fifties was imparted to me by you-know-who. Anyway, no matter what your morals or values are, when you drink the way I drank it's inevitable that sex will become a part of your life. This is very difficult for me to talk about. Although, at this writing, I have been sober six months there are many other problems I haven't resolved and I guess sex is one of them. Most of the time, of course, Dave and I were much more interested in drinking than sex, but there were times when sex was very much present. Besides my Puritan streak, there's another reason I can't go into a lot of detail—I don't remember most of it.

A lot of the time we didn't do much except kiss and touch each other. That was mostly due to Dave. To put it bluntly, very often Dave just couldn't do it. I guess he was too drunk. But then there were other times when we managed. Did I like it? I don't really know. I guess I thought I did. I know that sounds funny but it's the truth. I never had sex with Dave when I was sober so how could I really know? We never planned it, so naturally neither of us ever took precautions. And when you're drunk like that you don't think about getting pregnant. It's just incredible that it never happened to me. (Linda's pregnancy, by the way, was a false alarm.) Anyway, I always felt terribly guilty about it the next day—when I remembered.

Let me go back to whether I liked it for a moment. I think it was my Puritan streak speaking when I answered that question before. I mean, maybe I wasn't being *completely* honest. It is true that I was dead drunk every time. And it is true that when you are dead drunk nothing is very real. But at sixteen, like every other sixteen-year-old girl, I *did* have sexual desires. I got turned on when I read sexual things in books or saw them in movies just like anybody else. And boys turned me on—Dave in particular. I loved Dave. I wanted him to touch me and I wanted to touch him. However, somewhere I felt it was wrong. To quote Ginger: "Nice girls don't sleep with boys until they are married." And even though I knew things had changed since her day, her morality was always there nagging me. When I was drunk *nothing* was wrong. When I was sober or hungover, *everything* was wrong. It was very confusing and upsetting.

By mid-May, I had gained another five pounds, bringing my weight up to one hundred and forty-five. This made me very depressed and I drank even more to pull myself out of the depression. To try and lose weight, I ate less. One day at Linda's I drank a little extra for lunch and passed up the cottage cheese, rationalizing that cottage cheese was fattening no matter what anyone said. I was a bit more smashed than usual and the kids said I shouldn't go back to school. But naturally, I knew better and said I could handle it—in fact, I could handle anything. So off I went in my blue and white serape (that's about all I could wear these days) weaving slightly.

My first class after lunch was shop with Potato Derrick and I tried to play it very cool as I came in. Since I never talked to anyone there, nothing was different in that respect. I had managed to make my art supply box during the first term and now I was working on a doghouse for Tansy and Max. The first thing I had to do was use the power saw. It didn't even occur to me how dangerous that was in my condition. Fortunately, though I didn't think so at the time, Potato came over just as I was about to turn it on.

"Hold it," he said.

I waited, looking away from him and stepping back so he couldn't smell my breath.

"If you think you're going to use the saw you're greatly, ahhh, mistaken. I don't know whether you're drunk or stoned or what, but you just get the hell out of this class. You think I want, aaaah, a lawsuit on my hands? You'd better go up to Mr. Stanton's office."

At that moment all the control I'd mustered up to come into class left me, as though Derrick had pushed an invisible button. All the hostility I had stored up for him, and probably everyone else in the world, came tumbling out. "Well, that's just too goddamn bad, you stupid cretin. My parents pay their taxes and I have a right to that saw." I reached for the switch and he grabbed my hand. "Let go, you ass."

His white face began turning red. "You get out of this class."

He was hurting my wrist. Everything had stopped and all the boys were staring at us. "What are you looking at, you bunch of stinking turds?"

Potato turned even redder. He began to drag me away from the saw. "You are going to Mr. Stanton right now."

"The hell I am," I screamed and with my free hand I swung at him, landing a fairly hard blow somewhere in that squishy face. He dropped my wrist and I ran toward the door.

"You can take your saw and shove it," I yelled and yanked open the door and ran down the hall. When I turned a corner I slowed down, trying to appear as normal as possible. I went straight to my locker, took a gulp from my thermos of Scotch and milk, got my coat and started toward the outside door. I had no idea where I'd go or what I'd do. I just knew I had to get out of that school. A monitor was sitting near the door.

"Can I see your pass, please?" she said as I approached.

"Up yours," I answered and kept walking.

"Hey, you can't leave without a pass," she called after me.

"Watch me," I said as I opened the door.

I spent about two hours hunched down in Dave's truck, sipping away at my Scotch and milk. When school let out and Dave appeared he knew all about what had happened. Since he had to go to work, he took me to Linda's where I drank some more. If only I'd pass out like other people—but I never did. I knew I'd have to go home eventually so when Dave came to get me at six I told him to take me there.

My mother was waiting for me. I expected it and I didn't give a damn.

"*Now* what have you done?" she screamed the moment I opened the door.

I said nothing. I was drunker than I'd been in a long time. I don't know how I stayed on my feet. My mind was racing and I felt crazy. I wondered if I *was* crazy.

"We've got to go to that school tomorrow . . . do you know that? We've got to go there," she screamed hysterically. I couldn't believe it, but she was twirling her hair on both sides with both hands. She looked like a devil with two horns and I began to laugh.

"What are you laughing at? What? What's funny? I can't go there . . . how can I go there?"

The more she screamed, the more furiously she twirled and the funnier it looked to me, the more I laughed. Suddenly, she slapped me hard across the face. My first instinct was to slap her back—and that's what I did. It shocked us both. We stood there staring at one another. Neither of us said anything for a moment or two and then she spoke in a strange voice.

"You're ruining my life, do you know that?"

"You ruined mine a long time ago," I answered.

"I tried to help you. I tried to make you what I . . ." She trailed off.

"You never let me be me," I cried. "You wanted me to be you . . . well, I'm not you. At least I wasn't. I couldn't help it if I was president of a lot of leftover people . . . that's all I knew how to be. But that wasn't good enough for you. . . ."

"Stop, stop," she yelled and started running toward the kitchen.

I ran after her. "No, I won't stop you, you son-of-a-bitch. You have to listen." I grabbed her and pushed her up against the refrigerator. My drunkenness gave me an incredible physical strength. My mother's eyes were wide and I could see that she was afraid of me. "You wanted me to have all-round popularity and I got it. Maybe not your way, but I got it just the same."

"You don't understand . . . you just don't understand," she mumbled. She began to cry and slid down the refrigerator onto the floor. "No one knows . . . no one . . . all alone . . . too much to carry . . . no one but me. . . ." She was in a heap, the tears running down her face, mumbling things I didn't understand and all I could feel was that I wanted to kick her. She made me sick. Drunk and angry as I was, I knew I could not—should not—kick her and I had to get away from her.

I went to my room, got my bottle from the closet and

took a long swallow. Then something snapped. I began to scream—not words, just screams. And before I knew what was happening I was smashing everything in sight. I tore pictures off the walls, knocked over furniture, ripped clothes and virtually destroyed everything that was destructible. I don't know how long it went on, but eventually I stopped because there was nothing left to smash. I fell on the floor in the midst of it all and began to cry.

I must have fallen asleep or maybe I did pass out. I don't know. It was light outside when my father woke me.

"What the hell happened here?" he was saying.

At first I didn't know what he was talking about and then I saw where I was lying and the mess around me and some of the pieces began to come back. I also realized I was lying in my own vomit.

"Are you all right?" he asked.

I nodded. My head felt as though someone had put it in a vise. That made me remember what had happened in shop. "What time is it?"

"Seven. We have to go to school with you at eight. What happened here?"

"I . . . I don't know." How could I explain?

I guess he decided not to push me at that moment.

"Get dressed," he said and left.

Amid the debris I found some clothes I hadn't ripped to shreds and took a shower, feeling as though I might faint at any moment. I thought about refusing to go with them but that was pointless. Unless I wanted to quit school, I'd have to go sometime. I vomited several times—bile mostly. I was shaking all over and the last bit of Scotch in my bottle seemed to help steady my nerves. I went downstairs to face my parents.

20

Only Jack and my father were at the breakfast table. I couldn't get down anything but a glass of milk.

"You'd better eat something," my father said.

"I can't."

"Mmmmm."

Jack finished his stomach-turning breakfast of fried eggs and bacon and left without a word.

My father sipped coffee and stared into space. I wondered why my mother wasn't down yet and if she was going to eat breakfast or if she already had? I looked at the daisy-shaped clock on the wall and saw we didn't have that much time. Daddy finished his coffee and stood up.

"We'd better go."

I rose, got my jacket and followed him out to the car. I started to get into the back seat.

"What are you doing? Get in the front."

Inwardly, I groaned. Once again I was going to have to sit in between them. I prayed my mother wouldn't be too heavy on the perfume this morning.

He started the car and began to back out of the driveway. It wasn't until he started down the street that I realized my mother wasn't coming.

"What about Mom?" I asked.

"She's sick this morning. She can't come."

I couldn't be sure whether that news relieved or hurt me. In one way I was very glad she wasn't coming because these days I never knew what she might say or do. On the other hand, it was as though she didn't give a damn about me. I knew very well she wasn't sick.

My father and I didn't speak on the ride to school. I stared out the window feeling queasy and shaky.

When we arrived at the main office my father identified himself to Ms. Moffat, Stanton's secretary. I sat silently on a wooden chair. After about five minutes Ms. Moffat said we could go into Stanton's office.

He was not alone. Derrick was there, a dark bruise on his cheek, and so was Ms. Laine. I had expected him but not her. What did she have to do with it?

Stanton rose from behind his huge desk, shook hands with my father, introduced him to Derrick and Laine and nodded to me. Then we all sat. Stanton said a few words about my general deterioration and then asked Potato to describe what had happened in his class.

Have you ever seen a potato salivate? No, of course you haven't. Well, believe me, as this potato told his story he was salivating. He loved every minute of it —especially quoting me, even though he looked rather embarrassed by some of the more raunchy words. The story seemed to take hours—but naturally it would, considering Derrick's rhythm. The whole time he was talking I kept trying to figure out what Laine was doing there. I couldn't understand the connection.

Derrick finally finished and Stanton explained. "You see, Mr. Peters, what we've decided is that your daughter has a definite drinking problem. Miss Laine came to me yesterday afternoon after hearing about Geri's episode in shop class. I might add that she came to me at great personal risk." He took a beat for dramatic effect, I suppose. "Without knowing how I would feel about it, Miss Laine admitted to me that she is a member of Alcoholics Anonymous and that, in her opinion, Geri is sick and needs help."

"Are you saying my daughter is an alcoholic?" my father asked.

"May I?" Laine said to Stanton.

He nodded.

I wondered why Laine had taken the risk. It couldn't be for my sake.

"Mr. Peters," Laine started, "it's not for me to say that anyone is an alcoholic but myself. However, everything I've seen and heard leads me to believe that Geri has a problem with alcohol.

My father was becoming increasingly uncomfortable. He kept crossing and uncrossing his legs. "I admit her behavior in your class was terrible, Mr. Derrick, but what makes you think she was drunk?"

"She smelled like a brewery," Derrick said.

"Well, even if she did have a drink or two I don't see why you're all leaping to the conclusion that my daughter is an alky."

"I didn't say that," Ms. Laine said. "I said she has a problem with alcohol."

"At least it's not pot," my father said. "It's not drugs."

"Alcohol is a liquid drug, Mr. Peters, and Geri uses it. She uses it a great deal. She's failing all her subjects and getting into trouble. And she's bloated . . . look at her face. That's not just fat . . . she's bloated from alcohol."

Suddenly, they were all staring at me and I felt like the fat lady in the circus.

Laine went on. "She has horrendous hangovers, she has blackouts, and she keeps liquor in her locker."

How did she know that? My father was still staring at me.

"Is that true, Geri?" he asked.

I didn't answer. It was as though my mouth was glued shut. What was going down here anyway? Just because a person drank a little didn't mean they were a skid row bum! Adults were always doing that. If kids blew a little pot adults immediately thought they were junkies. And they say *we* dramatize! I was beginning to feel really mad.

"Why don't you tell him the truth, Geri?" Laine said gently. "We don't want to punish you. We want to help you."

"Oh, yeah, sure you do," I mumbled.

"It's true," she said.

"Well, there's nothing to help . . . there's nothing wrong with me."

"Exactly what I aaah said," Derrick butted in. "Always coddling these rotten kids . . . making out like they've got a disease or something."

Laine took a deep breath and said calmly, "Mr. Derrick, if Geri is an alcoholic she *does* have a disease, a progressive disease that will only get worse if it goes untreated."

Derrick waved a fat white hand at her dismissively. "Come off it. Drunks just made that disease stuff up so they'll look better. They're . . . aaah weaklings, that's all."

"And the American Medical Association? Did they make it up so drunks would look better?" Laine asked.

"What? Make what up?"

"The AMA says alcoholism is a disease."

"They'd say aaah anything," Derrick said.

"Please, please," Stanton said in his prissy way. "We're not here to argue. We're here to help this child."

Derrick grunted. "So give her a couple of weeks of detention and aaah be done with it."

"It's not that simple," Laine said.

"Mr. Derrick," Stanton said, "I think you can go now. You've told us what you know . . . what happened in your class. I don't think we'll need your help any longer." He shifted some pencils around on his desk as though it was the most important thing he'd ever done.

"What about this?" Derrick asked, pointing to the bruise on his cheek.

"What about it?" Stanton asked, genuinely puzzled.

Derrick stared at him, then glared at me, at Laine, at my father and back to Stanton. "Well, what's going to be done about it?"

"I'm afraid," Stanton said, "I don't quite follow you."

"Is this kid going to get away with ahhh striking a teacher?"

"Oh, I see," Stanton said. "Well, what would you like?"

"An apology, ahhh something."

"Geri, will you apologize to Mr. Derrick for striking him?" Stanton asked.

By this time I was really at a bolling point. I could

have punched out all of them. And now I was supposed to apologize to that clown? Not on your life. "No," I said.

Derrick's face started turning pink and Stanton made some uncomfortable noises while my father looked at his feet and Laine looked at me.

Finally, Stanton said, "Mr. Derrick, I'll let you know what measures we take."

Derrick stood up and left the room bumping against several chairs on his way out. There was an awkward silence.

My father was the first to speak. "You should have apologized, Geri."

I said nothing but clenched my fists together.

"Well," Stanton said, "I guess we should wrap this thing up. I'm willing to let the matter drop if Geri will promise to let Miss Laine try and help her."

"What's that mean?" I asked, looking at the floor.

"I'd like to try to educate you about alcoholism," Laine said.

"What for?"

"Because I think it's possible that you have the disease and it would be best if you knew something about it."

"Are you sure that's necessary, Miss Laine?" my father said. It was the first time in years that I could remember agreeing with him. "I mean, aren't we making a mountain out of a molehill?"

"How do you mean, Mr. Peters?" Laine asked.

"Well, let's look at the facts. The girl got a little high, all the kids do it today it seems, and she got a little out of control. What's the big deal? I think what she did to Mr. Derrick was appalling ... hitting a teacher *is* serious. But Geri's never been in any trouble before. I think that's something that should be taken into consideration."

"I am taking that into consideration," Stanton said. "That's why I'm willing to let it go if Geri agrees to cooperate with Miss Laine."

"And just what does that cooperation entail, Miss Laine?"

"Just what I said, Mr. Peters. I'd like Geri to learn something about alcoholism."

"How?"

"Through talking, reading, perhaps going to some meetings."

"Meetings?" he asked. "You mean Alcoholic Anonymous meetings?"

"Yes."

"Oh, no. That's out," he said. "I don't want my daughter associating with those sort of people."

Laine smiled. "Mr. Peters, *I'm* those sort of people."

"Yes, well, I find that hard to believe, Miss Laine. I'm not a psychiatrist so I don't know why you've chosen to call yourself an alcoholic, but I'm sure there *is* an explanation."

"Maybe you should come and hear me speak sometime. Then you might understand."

"No thanks. Anyway, I don't want my child hanging around those places."

Something weird was happening inside me. I began to hate what my father was saying and the attitude he was taking. Something about it really rubbed me the wrong way.

"Why don't you just mete out a normal punishment for the girl and let's forget this other business, all right?" My father said to Stanton. He had risen and had his back to Laine.

"You mean, Mr. Peters, you don't want to consider Miss Laine's ideas on the matter?"

My father smiled a strange half-smile. "I think we all know that reformed alcoholics can be a bit . . . shall we say overzealous? I feel I know my own child, Mr. Stanton. If she had a drinking problem, I'd know it. I'm not blind, after all."

"No, of course not."

I couldn't understand why I was hating my father. After all, I wasn't an alcoholic and he was saying so. So why did I resent him for doing exactly what I wanted him to do? I was terribly confused.

"All right, Geri," Stanton was saying, "you'll apologize to Mr. Derrick and you'll spend an hour in detention hall every afternoon for the next two weeks."

How could I apologize to that rotten Potato? I'd rather be expelled. I was about to say that when I heard my father thanking Stanton. They shook hands and my father left, nodding to Laine.

"You'd better go to your homeroom, Geri. The bell's going to ring in a few minutes," Stanton said.

I started to leave, but Laine stopped me with a light touch on my sleeve.

"Geri," she said, "I'll always be there if you want to talk."

I felt as though I might burst into tears, but I just clenched my teeth and kept walking.

In the hall I ran to my locker. I really needed a drink. I opened the locker and reached inside for the thermos. My hands were shaking. The thermos wasn't there. I'd forgotten that the day before I had taken it with me. Fortunately, Marcelle was at her locker. I ran down the aisle and grabbed her.

"You got any booze?" I asked.

"Sure. Why?"

"Let me have some, will you? I'll give you some back later."

"You strung out or what?"

"Strung out isn't the word. I just came from Stanton's office."

Marcelle opened her locker and handed me her thermos. I unscrewed the top and, shakily, I poured some in the cup.

"It's vodka and orange juice," she said.

I nodded. Normally, I would have refused it but today I didn't give a damn what it was as long as it was booze. I would have drunk anything to get rid of that shaky, scary feeling inside me. I didn't think I could make it until lunch and I asked Marcelle if I could meet her back here after the first period. Suddenly I realized what I was saying. I couldn't make *what* until lunch? I couldn't get through without another drink is what I was saying. Maybe Laine was right. But that was crazy. Of course I could. And I would. I told Marcelle to forget it—I'd see her over at Linda's at lunch.

By third period I felt really sick. I was sweating and shaking and I thought I'd vomit if I moved the wrong way. By fourth period I was in the bathroom and I *was* vomiting. And then, at last, it was lunch and I could have a drink like everybody else.

The drinks at lunch helped get me through the rest of the day, although it was a long afternoon because of the extra hour of detention. Afterwards, I found Pete Stanzini and had him buy me a bottle. My mother was still in her room so I didn't have any trouble getting the bottle into the house and up to my closet.

I took a couple of drinks before I started cleaning up the mess. It was a long, slow job and I stopped every once in a while to fortify myself.

I heard my father drive in around six-thirty, just as I was finishing. Then I heard him on the stairs. He went into his own room and in a few minutes I heard their voices although I couldn't make out the words. Then the door slammed and mine was flung open. He stood in the doorway, the muscles in his cheeks jumping like crazy.

"I see you cleaned up the wreck you made," he said in an accusatory way.

I started to say that that was obvious but he went on.

"Okay, Geri, let's get this thing straight. I don't intend to go through anything like that crap I went through this morning ever again. I want you to shape up. There'll be no more drinking. Not out, not home. You can't handle the stuff, that's obvious. If you're too weak to know when to quit then you just shouldn't drink at all."

I was stunned. "But you said——"

"Never mind what I said. Did you expect me to go along with that sob sister? I thought I'd raised you to be a good kid. I thought you knew what was right and what was wrong but apparently you don't."

"You said everybody did it." I got that in fast.

"Forget what I said in front of those two. I was trying to save you from that Holy Roller. We'll handle this our own way. No more booze. Not beer or wine or anything. If I smell it on your breath I'll ground you for a month. Got it? I've got enough troubles in this house and I don't want you adding to them."

I knew he meant Mother but I wasn't interested enough to ask about her. All I cared about was me. If he was going to smell my breath every time I came into the house things were going to be really tough.

"If there's one thing I can't stand it's a weakling, Geri. If this booze thing has a hold on you then it's up to you to break it. You're not so weak that you *have* to drink. And I'll tell you something else. If you don't kick it now, you *will* end up with those bums in AA. It's all a matter of willpower. I know you have the stuff to do it, Geri. Don't disappoint me."

When he left I sat down on the floor and started crying. The thought of not drinking any more scared me and I knew I'd have to quit because he'd be sniffing me every minute. I didn't want to be grounded because then I couldn't see Dave. What the hell was I going to do? I'd have to give up drinking except when I could stay overnight at Linda's or Marcelle's or somebody else's. Well, okay—I'd just drink on the weekends. So if it was that simple, why was I still crying? I didn't know. All I knew was that I felt as though my life was coming to an end. But why should I? Daddy was right. It was just a matter of willpower. If I couldn't drink during the week, so what? Anyway, he'd let up after a while. I went to the closet and took my last week-time drink. I knew he wouldn't be smelling my breath tonight. Willpower, I thought. It was all a matter of willpower—well, I had plenty of that.

I thought I would die during the next two days. I didn't go to Linda's for lunch, telling the kids I had extra work to do. I sat by myself in the cafeteria, my head in a book. But I didn't see the words. All I saw was a drink. And that was all I thought about, too. Physically, by the second day, I was feeling pretty good —I mean, it was the first time in a long, long time that I didn't have a hangover. But what was going on in my head was not to be believed.

If it was all a matter of willpower, why did I feel so crazy? Why couldn't I think of anything except drinking? Could Laine have been right?

One thing I did know was that my father's new

rules were making me feel worse than I'd ever felt. And I also knew that I'd never hated him as much as I did now. I remembered the feeling I'd had in Stanton's office when he was putting Laine down. Why had I disliked him for that?

At the end of the second day, after doing my hour in detention hall, I found myself staring through the glass in the door of Laine's room. She was sitting at her desk going over some papers. I guess she felt me staring because she finally looked up. Our eyes held for a moment and then she motioned me in. I didn't want to go in and yet I knew I had to. I mean, something other than myself seemed to make me open the door.

"Hi," she said.

"Hi." I started to cry.

She got up and came over to me.

"Oh, Ms. Laine," I said, sobbing now.

"Kate," she said, putting an arm around me and stroking my hair.

After a few minutes, I said, "Will you help me, Kate?"

"I thought you'd never ask," she said and we both laughed.

I will always remember that day. Although a great deal happened afterwards that was horrible, that day remains a wonderful one in my memory because it was the first step of my recovery. It was the first step toward really living.

21

Kate took me back to her house. I called my mother and told her I wouldn't be home for supper. She didn't even ask where I was or why I wouldn't be home. I was glad because I knew Kate didn't want me to lie and yet I also knew my father wouldn't like me being with her. I'd have to deal with him later. At least I wouldn't be coming home with liquor on my breath.

I sat on her couch feeling as though I would shake apart.

"Have you eaten anything today?" she asked.

"No."

"That's no good, Geri. It's very important that you eat."

She disappeared into the kitchen. In a minute or so I heard a blender whirring. Soon she stood in front of me with what looked like a chocolate malt.

"It's called Tiger's Milk," she said. "It's very healthy for you. Lots of protein. It'll help."

I took it and then I heard myself saying, "I'd rather have Scotch." I don't know why I said it. I really would've rather had Scotch, but I knew I wasn't about to get any here so why say it?

"Drink this first," she said.

"First? You mean you'll give me a drink?"

"If you really need one . . . of course. But you probably don't. When did you have your last drink?"

"The day we were in Stanton's office."

"Then you probably don't *need* one, Geri. At least not physically. The alcohol should be out of your system. Of course it's likely that mentally you still have the desire . . . the compulsion."

"I'll say." I drank some of the Tiger's Milk. "This is good. It tastes like a milk shake."

"I'm glad you like it. Listen, Geri, you have the desire and the compulsion, but you don't want to drink. Why?"

"What makes you think I don't want to?"

"You wouldn't be here if you wanted to."

She was right, of course. I told her about what had happened with my father.

"So what you're telling me is that the only reason you don't want to drink is because if you do, and your father finds out, then he'll ground you and you won't be able to see your boyfriend? Is that right?"

"Yes," I said. But I wasn't sure that was the only reason.

"And that what's what you meant when you asked me to help you?"

"Yes . . . is that awful?"

"No, it's not awful."

"See, I don't think I'm an alcoholic."

"Then why do you need help?"

"What do you mean?"

"Well, it seems to me that if someone is told they'll be grounded if they drink, and being grounded means not being able to do something they want to do, then it's very simple. The person just doesn't drink. Unless, of course, they *can't* stop."

"I can. I have. I just don't want to. I mean, look, all the kids drink."

"Not all."

"Well, most of them. The fun ones do anyway. But not everybody gets in the kind of trouble I do. If I could just drink like my friend Linda."

Kate began to smile. "Oh, I get it," she said. "You'd like me to teach you how to drink normally, is that it?"

I hadn't really thought it through, but maybe that was part of it. "Yeah, I guess."

"Well, Geri, you've certainly come to the wrong person. If I could drink like a social drinker I wouldn't be in the program, would I?"

"Program?"

"AA."

"Oh." I hadn't realized it but learning to drink socially was exactly what I wanted. "My father says it's all a matter of willpower. If that's true then I should be able to drink like other people."

"That's right. *If* it's true. I don't happen to believe it *is* true. Not if you're an alcoholic."

"Am I?" I was terrified of the answer.

"I don't know. Only you can know that."

I felt angry. "Well, how the hell can I tell? You know a whole lot about the subject and if you don't know, how am I going to know?"

"Maybe this will help you," she said, picking up a small yellow booklet. "This is a meeting book . . . it tells where the meetings are in this area. It also has a questionnaire on the front entitled *Are You an Alcoholic?* There are ten questions. Are you game?"

I was scared, but I didn't want Kate to know it. "Sure."

"Good. Number one. Do you lose time from work due to drinking? In your case it would be school."

"No," I said quickly.

"Really? You've never stayed home with a hangover? And what about Thursday?"

She was right. And, of course, I had stayed home with hangovers. "Yes."

"Two. Is drinking making your home life unhappy?"

Was it? I thought of Sophie. I thought of my mother on the floor by the refrigerator. I thought of my father looking at my wrecked room. "I guess so. Yes."

"Three. Is drinking affecting your reputation?"

"That depends on whose point of view it is." I thought of B.J. and Carolyn. "The kids I hang around with all drink, so how could it?"

"What about your reputation with your teachers, for instance?"

I couldn't deal with that question. "Can we skip that one?"

"Sure. Four. Have you felt remorse after drinking?"

"Not because I drank," I said.

"Then what?"

"Because of what I *did* when I drank."

"You're equivocating, Geri."

"Okay . . . yes . . . plenty."

"Five. Do you crave a drink at a definite time daily?"

"You mean like cocktail hour or something?"

She nodded.

"No. There's never a set time."

"Six. Do you want a drink the next morning?"

Easy. "Yes."

"Seven. Do you drink alone?"

I was beginning to feel uncomfortable. "Yes," I sighed.

"Eight. Have you ever had a complete loss of memory as a result of drinking?" She smiled.

"I guess you know better than anyone the answer to that. Next."

"Is drinking jeopardizing your job or business? For you, education."

Since I was failing all my subjects I guess I qualified. "Yes."

"Ten. Have you ever been to a hospital or institution on account of drinking."

What a relief. "No," I practically yelled.

"If you have answered yes to three or more of these questions, you have a definite problem with alcohol," she read.

I had answered yes to seven! I felt frightened and angry. "Well, who made up those questions anyway?" I asked.

"They were developed by doctors at Johns Hopkins Hospital."

Well, what the hell do they know—that was my first thought. But I didn't say it. Even I realized how stupid that was.

If three yes answers meant you had a problem with alcohol, what did seven mean? I asked her.

"Why don't you come to a meeting with me tonight and see if you hear anything that helps you figure that out?"

I thought about what my father had said. *A bunch of bums.* And I remembered what Dave had said about the women who'd come from AA to help his mother.

Some blue-haired old ladies. Bums and blue-haired old ladies certainly didn't seem to go together. And then there was Kate herself. She didn't fit into either category. I didn't know what to think. I said the first thing that came into my head.

"How long are these meetings and when do they start?"

"The one I'm going to tonight starts at eight-thirty and it lasts an hour and a half."

"That means I wouldn't get home until after ten . . . I dunno."

She smiled. "Pretty late for you, hmmm?" she asked with a touch of sarcasm.

Of course, her implication was right. I'd been getting home between ten and eleven on week nights all year. "What do you do at the meeting?"

"Well, this happens to be a closed meeting . . . that means only alcoholics, or people with a drinking problem, can attend. Anyone can go to an open meeting. Usually, in closed meetings, there's a speaker who tells his or her story and then there's a discussion."

"What do you mean, discussion?"

"The speaker picks a topic and everyone who wants to discusses it. You don't have to say anything if you don't want to. There's nothing you *have* to do. Sometimes it's boring, sometimes it's interesting, but almost always I hear at least one thing that makes me think."

It sounded deadly. I wouldn't go. Now I know I was afraid to go, but I couldn't admit that to myself at the time. "Well, I don't think my father would like it if I went."

"Suppose I take the responsibility for that?" she asked.

"How?"

"I'll talk to him about it. I'll call him and tell him we're going."

"No, that's okay. I don't think I'll go tonight. Maybe we could just talk some more."

"All right. We'll talk some more and then we'll have dinner and then I'm going to a meeting. I'll take you home."

I nodded. But I felt angry. She didn't care if I went or not. She only cared about herself. I wanted to hurt her.

"I think you're a crummy liar," I said.

She looked at me, bewildered. "Why do you say that?"

"You told me on the way over here that you didn't miss drinking."

"That's right."

"Well, how come, if you don't miss drinking, you still have to go to those lousy meetings?"

"I go for several reasons. Alcoholism is a mental disease as well as a physical one. Sometimes my thinking can get very screwed up and I need meetings to straighten me out. Another reason is because there's much more to AA than simply not drinking. It's a whole new way of life. It helps me to keep growing and to live comfortably."

"That sounds like a crock."

She shrugged. "I can't prove it to you. You'd have to see for yourself. Shall we start dinner?"

While she cut up stuff for a salad I peeled some carrots. She told me about her years of drinking and how she'd stopped and what her life had been like since she had. She drank for seven years before she hit what she called her "bottom." She explained that alcohol seemed to move much more rapidly in teenagers than in adults. She also said that everyone was different. Two adult alcoholics could drink exactly the same amount and one might go on for twenty or twenty-five years, while the other might hit bottom in five or ten. Then she said it was possible I hadn't hit bottom yet and that maybe I had years of drinking ahead of me. After all, I'd never been jailed or institutionalized. The only sure things she knew about alcoholic drinking were that there were only two ways it could end—insanity or death—and that the only way to arrest the disease was to stop drinking.

"Do you think I should go to the meeting?" I asked.

"Should?"

"Well, you know what I mean."

"Should isn't part of my vocabulary anymore . . . at least I try to live without it. You do what you'd like to do."

"What if what I'd like to do is drink?" I asked, testing her.

"If you really want to drink, you will. If you want to try not to, I can try to help."

I felt mad again. "Don't you even care if I drink?"

"Of course I care. But there's nothing I can do unless you're willing. Try to remember one thing: chances are you wouldn't have just one drink or even two. Chances are you'd have lots of drinks and end up drunk doing God knows what. Is that what you want?"

I didn't know. But did drink always mean drunk? And did drunk always mean trouble? So far it hadn't *always* meant that, but it did happen often enough. And the thing was I couldn't predict it. Drink almost always meant drunk and I never, never knew if drunk would mean trouble. If only I could control it. But I couldn't—that was the problem. I just seemed to be going around in circles. I didn't know what to do.

During dinner I asked Kate a question that had been nagging me for days. "When we first talked about all this before Christmas, you told me it was a secret because people didn't understand. How come you told Mr. Stanton? I mean how come you took that risk?"

"Well, Geri, I thought you were worth it."

"Oh, come on," I said. "There must be some other reason."

"Why?"

"Why what?" I asked.

"Why must there be some other reason? Aren't you a good enough reason?"

I didn't say anything. I just went back to eating. I couldn't understand it. Well, I thought, that does it. If she could do that for me, I could certainly go to the meeting for her!

I felt marvelous—like a saint. I was doing something for someone else and it felt good. I didn't know at the time that going to meetings for someone else or not drinking for someone else was absolutely no way to get sober. Still, on that particular occasion, it didn't really matter if I thought I was The Great Giver. At least it got me to my first AA meeting—and oh, how I hated it!

22

The meeting was held in a church basement, as most AA meetings are, I discovered. Kate had warned me I would be the youngest and indeed I was. I felt like I'd walked into a geriatric ward! Not that anyone looked sickly or anything. In fact, most of them looked quite healthy. They just looked old. Kate seemed to be the person closest to my age—and she was about thirty.

Then I got a real surprise. Standing near a window, talking to a woman, was Harvey Rosner, the postmaster! I never knew he was a—and was that really? Yes, it was. Justine Doyle, the librarian! Well, she had blue hair, but how could she possibly be a—drunk? I looked around the room for more familiar faces. Oh no! But oh, yes! Cliff. One of Goose Bay's finest! Just then I felt a tap on my shoulder and I turned.

"Hiya, kid. Thought ya might turn up here someday. Get my drift?"

"Yolanda! But . . . you. . . ." I was sputtering.

"I what? I run a bar? So what? I sell the rotten stuff, I don't drink it . . . anymore. Glad to see ya here, kid. Maybe ya can get that lousy boyfriend of yours ta join ya sometime. Keep comin'." She gave me a funny little salute and walked toward another group of people.

"I don't believe it," I said to Kate.

"Why not? Alcoholism doesn't have any favorites."

"But Yolanda! I just don't get it. If she's an alcoholic

and knows it's a disease and all that stuff, then how come she sells to minors?"

"Well, her attitude is that kids are going to drink anyway so it might as well be in her place where she can keep an eye on them. It's a logic I'm not sure I agree with, but that's how she feels."

"I just can't get over it. I never thought I'd see anyone here that I knew. And Yolanda isn't the only one."

"I'm sure she's not. Now let me introduce you to some other people."

The people Kate introduced me to were very nice. They shook my hand, welcomed me and said things like "Glad to see you here." "Keep coming." "You're in the right place." Things like that. And I hated all of them. I didn't feel like I was in the right place at all. What could I possibly have in common with these old people? They were all drinking coffee and laughing with each other and all I wanted to do was get the hell out of there. Why had I come? I had never wanted a drink more than I did then.

There were tables set up like a T with the speaker and secretary at the top of the T. The rest of the jerks sat around the stem of the T or behind it. Kate led me to a seat at a table.

After a few minutes the secretary—that's what they call the person in charge—banged on the table with an ashtray and everyone stopped talking. She read what is known as the preamble. I'd read the beginning of it months ago in the pamphlet Kate gave me. The rest went like this:

"The only requirement for membership is a desire to stop drinking. There are no dues or fees for AA membership; we are self-supporting through our own contributions.

"AA is not allied with any sect, denomination, politics, organization or institution; does not wish to engage in any controversy; neither endorses nor opposes any causes.

"Our primary purpose is to stay sober and help other alcoholics to achieve sobriety."

After that the secretary read a bunch of announcements that made no sense to me and then she introduced the speaker. He was an old man about fifty or sixty named Red. I guess his hair had been red once but now it was mostly gray.

"My name is Red and I'm an alcoholic." That was the way he began.

Then he told about his drinking life. He kept talking about gin mills—that's what a lot of the old people called bars—and spending time in jails and in hospitals. And then he talked a lot about God and I hated him. When he was finished everybody clapped and they took a coffee break.

Kate looked at me. "So, do you hate it a lot?" she asked.

"More than a lot," I said.

She laughed. "Not everybody in AA is like Red. Everybody is different."

"Yeah, well, it doesn't look like anybody is like me."

"They may not be your age, but I'm sure some of them have had the same experiences as you."

I doubted that.

"All of these people have had blackouts and hangovers and have done things they'd never have done sober."

"What kind of things?"

"Stick around and you'll find out."

I looked around the room. Near the far end of the table sat a small white-haired old lady with glasses. "How about her?" I asked, nodding in her direction.

"Harriet? The one with the glasses?"

"Yes. Don't tell me she ever got drunk or did anything crazy."

"I'm surprised at you, Geri . . . judging someone by her appearance. As a matter of fact, during one of Harriet's last drunks, which took place after her son's wedding, Harriet ended up with her dress over her face in the middle of the buffet table. Her head, if I remember correctly, was lying dead center in the wedding cake."

"You're kidding."

"Nope."

I started laughing. "Actually, that's kind of funny." I imagined drawing that.

"Lots of drunk stories are funny . . . lots of them aren't."

The secretary rapped the table. She passed around a wicker basket and everybody put some money in. I dropped in a quarter I found in my pocket. Red said the discussion topic would be "A Higher Power." Inwardly, I groaned. That, I knew, meant God. And for a lot of people that's exactly what it did mean. My mind wandered while they raved on. Then I heard a woman say she didn't believe in God and I came to attention.

"I have never believed in God and I doubt that I ever will. As most of you know, I've been sober almost ten years and I've changed a lot in that time. But on the subject of a higher power, meaning God, I haven't changed a bit. For me, my higher power has been the power of the group. Gathered here in this room is probably a total of over a hundred years of sobriety and that's far greater than I am. So that's my higher power."

I wasn't sure I understood what she said, but at least she wasn't a God-believer and that was something. There were others who didn't believe in God and Kate was one of them. When it came to me I felt panicky and just shook my head.

During the meeting there was lots of laughter and even an argument about something. I couldn't follow it nor did I want to. All I wanted was for the meeting to be over. It seemed like it had been going on for days. I kept feeling more and more angry and yet every time someone said my name is so and so and I'm an alcoholic I felt like I was going to cry.

Finally, the horrible thing was over. Everyone stood and said the Lord's Prayer. You didn't have to. I didn't and Kate didn't and I suppose there were others.

"How do you feel?" Kate asked, as she drove me home.

"Furious," I said.

"Why?"

"I don't know."

"Well, don't worry about it. I remember feeling that way."

"How often do you go to those things?" I asked.

"Now I go about twice a week . . . sometimes more if I feel I need it. In the beginning I went every night."

"Every night? How could you stand it?"

"Sometimes I couldn't but I wanted to stay sober and it was the only way I knew how."

"You mean if I want to stay sober I have to go to one of those boring things every night?"

"You don't *have* to do anything. It's suggested in the beginning that you make ninety meetings in ninety days. *Suggested*. I told you that sometimes it's boring. I couldn't identify with Red either except that he drank, got drunk and got into trouble. Didn't anyone say anything that you could identify with?"

"No."

"Well, maybe another time you'll listen differently and be able to hear something."

"What do you mean, another time? Who said I was going to go again?"

"I'm sorry. You're right . . . I'm making an assumption. I guess it's wishful thinking." She stopped the car. We were in front of my house. "Geri, if you should want AA it may be harder for you because you're so young . . . I'm aware of that, believe me. In the city they have young people's groups but we don't out here . . . not that we don't have the need . . . but not everybody is as courageous as you."

"Courageous?"

"Yes. It takes courage to admit you have a problem with anything. It takes courage to ask for help."

"I haven't admitted anything," I said quickly.

"But you *did* ask for my help," she said gently.

I must have been crazy, I thought. But I didn't say it. What would you have said under those circumstances? I said, "Yeah . . . right."

"Would you like me to come in with you and talk to your father?"

"No, that's okay. I can handle it. Well, thanks for everything."

"There's a meeting in Eastport tomorrow night. I'll

be going and if you'd like to go I'll be glad to give you a lift. Just let me know."

"Okay, I'll let you know." I don't know why I couldn't tell her right there and then that I wouldn't be going but I couldn't.

We said good night and I went into the house. My father was sitting in the living room reading one of his mysteries.

"Where've you been?" he asked.

I saw no reason to tell him the truth and get into a big hassle over it since it was never going to happen again so I said that I'd had dinner at my friend Ceil's and we'd done our homework together. He motioned me over to him. I knew what was coming.

"Lean down."

"Oh, Daddy, this is so ridiculous."

"Lean down," he said in a firmer voice.

I leaned down close to him and gave him a big whiff of my breath. "Okay?" I asked.

He nodded.

"Are we going to have this sniff test every night?"

"Yes. Until you can be trusted again."

"When will that be?"

"When I decide."

"What a drag," I said.

"Drag or no drag, that's the way it's going to be." He stared at the pages of his book.

I heard the sound of the television coming from the den and assumed my mother must have been watching. Since the refrigerator thing, I'd only seen her at dinners and then we hadn't spoken to each other except to ask for something to be passed. I thought about going in to talk to her now, but then I realized that I had nothing to say to her. What would we talk about? Besides, she was probably in the midst of looking at one of her dumb movies and I'd just be in the way.

"Well," I said to my father, "I guess I'll go to bed."

"Good night," he said without looking up.

"Good night."

After I got undressed I went to the closet and got out my bottle of Scotch. I got in bed and started to review the last seven hours. When I had gone to Kate's room at school I'd been very mixed up. Now I was still mixed up but in a different way. I knew a few things I hadn't known before, but I wasn't sure I believed all of them. Was alcoholism really a disease like Kate said? Or was it something alcoholics made up so they'd feel better, like Potato Derrick said? How could I believe anything he said? And why was I the one in my crowd who got into trouble? Everyone drank just as much as I did—some of them more, like Dave and Marcelle. How come they could keep drinking and get away with it? I'd asked Kate about that and she'd said what made me think that they were getting away with anything? For all I knew they were suffering terribly. Well, I couldn't be sure about Marcelle, but Dave didn't seem to be suffering about anything. As for the others in my group—well, Kate said that not everybody was alcoholic no matter how much they drank. Some people drank to be part of the crowd, not because they needed it or even liked it. I guessed that was Linda. I'd never felt that she really liked drinking. Ceil Nardone drank a lot too, but in a different way than I did. She never did anything really crazy. She never had what Kate called a "personality change."

It was all terribly confusing. The only thing I was sure of was that I was much too young to never be able to drink again. After all, I had at least four years of college to go through. How could you possibly go through college and never take a drink? That was half of what college was about, wasn't it? Maybe I *could* learn to drink properly. Why not? Who said I couldn't have a drink and quit? I'd never tried. Well, I'd do it right now. I opened my bottle and poured the first drink I'd had in days—and oh, God, it tasted good. I turned on my radio and turned out my light. There was nothing I liked better than sipping a Scotch, listening to WABC and smoking a cigarette. That was really living. I thought about all those jokers at the meeting and it made me laugh. How could anybody think I was like them? I mean, it was obvious that we had nothing, and I mean *nothing* in common. Just because they couldn't learn to hold their liquor didn't mean that I couldn't. Because Kate couldn't learn to have just one drink, did it mean that I couldn't learn? I thought about that as I looked at my empty glass. Well, nobody had just *one* drink, did they? I mean, what would be the point? So two drinks. I poured myself another. Two drinks. There was nothing wrong with having just two drinks. I thought about the quiz Kate had given me. I had a definite problem with alcohol. That's what the questionnaire said and I could accept that. You have a problem, you solve it. That's what I would do. Somehow I would solve it—myself. I didn't have to go to some crummy meetings with a bunch of alcoholics to do that.

I could do very nicely on my own, thank you very much. I had it all worked out. I would only have two drinks at lunch and by the time Daddy got home from work he wouldn't be able to smell it on my breath. I wouldn't drink when I went out with Dave after supper. I mean, I didn't *need* to drink to be with him. When I got home I'd have my two drinks before bed if I felt like it. And on the weekends I'd stay over at one of my friend's and have a ball. Weekends were different, weren't they? Everyone got fired up on weekends. But during the week I'd definitely stick to my two-drink regime. I poured myself another drink. It was going to be simple. What was so hard about having just two drinks? Nothing. It'd be easy and I'd be happy to do it—starting tomorrow.

23

I won't say it was easy sticking to my new plan because it wasn't. Not that I would have admitted that at the time. Instead, I told myself it was a snap. But if there was any snap anywhere it was about to happen inside me. I stuck to my plan and told the kids I was only having two drinks at lunch time because I wanted to lose weight. I was pushing one-fifty and about the only thing I could wear was an old piano shawl I'd found in the attic. Really. I cut a hole in the center and wore it over the clothes that my hugeness was stretching to their limits. After a few days I discovered that keeping myself to two drinks was too hard. It was easier to skip them altogether. So, I told the kids and myself that I could use the lunch hour to catch up on my school work or I'd never make it to my senior year.

The next thing I discovered was that it was the same thing at night. If I had my drinks at night, before I went to bed, I wanted more than two. The first week I stuck to two, but then I couldn't sleep. So the second week I upped it—not to three or four, but as much as I wanted. Naturally, that led to a hangover and the morning drink which set me off for the day. By noon I was a wreck and wanting very much to go to Linda's but I didn't dare. So, by the end of the second week, I quit the bedtime drinks altogether. Now I was just a weekend drinker. Very normal, yes? Very normal, no!

I also decided after that first AA meeting that as long as I was going to watch the drinking and try to buckle down to some school work, I might as well clear up whatever else I could. The first thing I did was to apologize to Potato. I could have puked doing it. He was so righteous and disgusting I felt like telling him off all over again, but I kept myself in check and did a number on him. The next thing I did was talk to Laine. I didn't want her bugging me about AA and I knew I couldn't avoid her so I figured the best thing to do was to set her straight right away.

"How do you feel today?"

"Terrific." Of course I didn't because I had a hangover.

"Do you want me to pick you up tonight?" she asked.

"That's why I came in. I've done a lot of thinking and I appreciate your interest and help, but I've decided to do it on my own."

"I thought you'd already tried that."

"Yeah, well, this'll be different." I wanted to get the hell out of there.

"You're going to control your drinking, right?"

How the hell did she know everything? She made me sick. "I don't know what you mean," I said, kicking at the corner of a chair.

"So many drinks a day or drinking just on weekends . . . some kind of control or restriction."

"So what?"

"So nothing. I wish you luck."

"You don't think I can do it, do you?"

"I don't know. If you're an alcoholic, I doubt it. Oh, maybe you can for a while, but eventually you won't be able to."

"Well, I'll tell you this, if being an alcoholic is being like those jokers I saw at that meeting last night, then I'm not."

"Fine. As I said, I wish you luck. If you change your mind you know where to reach me."

"Go screw," I said and slammed out.

I don't know why she made me so mad. She was just trying to be nice. But I hated her. Thank God school was almost over and I wouldn't have to see her rotten face for three months.

So back to the weekends. Almost every weekend I

stayed overnight at Linda's or Ceil's or sometimes
Dave's. When Bunny was off on a drunk Dave's father
was rarely around either, so no one knew I was there.
Of course, I always had a cover. If my mother or father
called Linda's to talk to me, Linda would say I
was in the bathroom and then call me at Dave's. It
hadn't happened yet, but I was sure if it did they'd
never catch on.

Friday nights were really hard because even my
mother and father wouldn't let me stay out two nights
in a row. I say *even* my mother and father because,
aside from the breath sniffing from my father, which
was erratic, no one really paid too much attention to
me. My mother was deeper into her own world than
ever. It was like a morgue in our house—except for one
night when I heard my parents arguing. It was the most
I'd heard my mother speak in a long time.

"I want you to see a doctor, Ginger," my father said.

"What for?"

"Because you're not acting normally. Do you have
pains or what?"

"No."

"Then why are you acting like this?"

"Like what?"

"You never come out of your room except to eat.
You don't comb your hair or put on makeup. And do
you know how long it's been since we've slept together?"

That was a shock. I was embarrassed to have heard
it, but at the same time I was fascinated—real confirma-
tion that they did it other than two times in their lives.

"Do you?" he went on.

"Leave me alone, George. You don't understand."

"Then, for God's sake, help me to understand."

I wished they'd get back to the sex part.

"I can't. I can't."

"And I can't go on like this, Ginger."

"So leave."

Hey, wait a minute. As bad as it was I didn't want
that. Or did I? If he left there wouldn't be any more
sniffing.

"Is that what you want?" he asked, a little more softly.

"I don't care."

"Christ."

A long silence.

He finally spoke. "So what are you going to do?"

"About what?"

"About yourself, dammit."

"Leave me alone, George."

"You're goddamned right I'll leave you alone."

Slam! Door. Steps. Slam! Front door. Car. Crying.

After that he moved into the guest room. So typical. Couldn't they ever do anything original?

Back to the weekends again. Friday nights I usually went to the movies with Dave and then he dropped me off and he went out drinking. At first I tried going with him, but it was too hard. Saturdays I got out as early as possible and stayed out until dinner on Sunday night. Since I came home early on Sundays my father never bothered sniffing me. I guess he thought drinking only took place after sundown or something—like sex. Have you ever noticed about parents? They insist you be home by a certain hour because supposedly you won't do any sex before midnight or something. I think that's so dumb. Anyway, my heavy drinking was confined to Saturday nights and then I really made up for the dry week. And I really paid for it on Sunday. My hangovers were getting worse, if that was possible. Possible or not, they *were* worse. I could barely move on Sundays. When it was time for me to go home I could just about make it. Even drinks didn't help much. And it was Tuesday or Wednesday before I felt okay again.

So that's the way it went and somehow at the end of June I finished my junior year. A minor miracle. Dave was not so lucky. He'd have to go to summer school and make up history and English or repeat his junior year. He said he didn't give a damn and wasn't about to screw up his summer with school. We didn't talk about what would happen in the fall. It seemed a long way off.

Jack was valedictorian of his class and I was forced

to attend the boring graduation exercises with my parents. Somehow my mother managed to pull herself together and go. I wondered if she would have done that for me. I sincerely doubted it.

The summer job I got was in a shop called The Country Store in Eastport. It carried kitchen stuff and gourmet foods and things like that and was run by a very big Swedish woman who was always saying things like "Gollygee whiskers." It was an okay job when she wasn't around but I almost went nuts when she was. Not only was Bibi very particular and fussy about her stock being dusted and in place, she was insulting to her customers and she drank like a fish. Naturally, she never offered me any because she thought I was too young. I made two dollars an hour and that gave me plenty of booze money, enough to buy people drinks in the V.S. (I was reinstated by now), which I adored doing. Nothing gave me greater pleasure than picking up the check or saying, "Drinks for everybody, Johnny." Of course, my pleasure the next morning when I found only a dollar left out of my paycheck wasn't quite as great as it had been the night before.

I was convinced now that I definitely was not an alcoholic. If I was an alcoholic, I told myself, I could never confine my drinking to Saturday nights. I didn't know then that many alcoholics go through periods of what's known as "controlled drinking" for that very reason: to prove that they're not alcoholic. What I was doing was very typical—very unoriginal! Had I known that I'm sure I would have tried something else. After all, the Great Me did not like doing things everybody else did.

On July sixteenth I turned seventeen. It was a Saturday and Bibi gave me the day off. I'd asked her when she was quite high, telling her it was very important to me that I be able to go to the County Center and get my driving permit. Feeling benevolent, she'd said yes. Saturdays were very busy and I was sure she'd regret it when she sobered up.

By ten in the morning Dave and I had gotten my permit and he was giving me my first driving lesson.

We were in the truck and it was no mean trick learning to shift those sticky gears. By eleven we both decided maybe it would be better for me to learn on my father's car. I would ask him at dinner.

Dinner was a laugh. I would have much perferred having dinner—the hell with dinner—drinks with my friends. But because it was my birthday my father insisted I eat at home. Jack was forced to stay home too. Ginger suggested I invite Dave, but I made up an excuse. My father tried to make conversation, but nobody was particularly interested. I did ask him if I could learn to drive on his car, and he said he'd be happy to teach me. I asked if it would be all right if Dave taught me, and he said no, he'd start the next day. I knew that would never work. Maybe Linda would let Dave and me use her car.

My parents gave me a whole lot of art supplies. They were terrific things—brushes, acrylics, canvas, chalks, pens—but I couldn't have cared less. I had no interest in drawing or painting anymore. I pretended I loved them. Jack gave me some book about Gestalt Therapy which was what he was into now. The inscription he wrote said: "Dear Geri, Getting to know yourself can be fun. Love, Jack." I felt like throwing it in his face but instead I thanked him and said I'd read it soon. What a joke. I couldn't remember when I'd read a book last.

After dinner my mother brought out this cake and they all sang "Happy Birthday" like they were under water. We ate the cake in silence except to say how good it was—mocha, my favorite, baked by a local.

Finally I escaped, saying I was staying at Linda's and I'd be home around six the next day.

Well, we really celebrated that night. Dave wanted to go to Yolanda's, but I begged off and, since it was my birthday, I won. I think he wanted to go to see if there was any news of his mother who'd been gone for almost a week this time. But we hit all the other bars we could get served in without trouble. Naturally, I didn't spend a cent. Everybody was buying me drinks. And the presents! Every single one of the kids gave me something. I'd never had such a terrific birthday. They were really great friends. I remembered my sixteenth. What a difference. I had spent it with Carolyn and B.J. We'd watched a Joan Crawford movie on TV and had two chocolate sodas apiece. Whoopee! Dave gave me a gold square on a chain. The square had my initials engraved on the front and on the back it had the date. I was a little disappointed it didn't have his initials on the back but he explained that this way, if I ever got tired of him, I could still keep wearing it. Though the square was gold the chain wasn't because when it got very hot my neck turned green!

So it was a great night and by the time we got back to Dave's house we were really smashed. I don't remember what happened next. I just remember walking through the front door and the next thing I was conscious of was daylight and Mr. Townsend standing over the bed staring down at us. His face was white, as though it had been drained of blood, and he was shaking. For a second I wondered if he was going to beat us up. He'd never found us there together before. But then I realized that if he'd noticed I was there he didn't care. He was staring at Dave and his mouth was moving but no words came out.

"What is it, Dad?" Dave asked sleepily.

His mouth moved again. Still nothing.

Dave leaned up on his elbows, pulling the covers slightly off me. I grabbed for them since we were both naked.

"Dad?" he asked again.

Finally, the words came. "She's out there . . . Bunny . . . out there . . . dead . . . Bunny's dead . . . out there." He pointed through the bedroom door. The gesture could have meant anywhere, but I was pretty sure it meant somewhere in the house.

"Oh, shit," Dave said.

I closed my eyes. The bed heaved as Dave got up and they both left the room. I wasn't sure what I was supposed to do. What would you have done? I pulled the sheet over my head and turned my back to the door.

Amorette "Bunny" Townsend died lying on her living room floor by choking on her own vomit. When Dave told me that I couldn't help thinking of myself. I'd awakened twice in the last few months lying in my own vomit. Bunny had been on a drunken rampage for almost a week and somehow had found her way home. Mr. Townsend had been out all night looking for her and when he came in at six, there she was. I found out later it wasn't uncommon for drunks to die that way. When Dave told me how she died something inside me was scared—but only for a few minutes. After all, Bunny was a hard-core alcoholic who was almost forty years old. We had nothing in common so why should I be afraid?

The funeral was two days later. There was no church service or anything because Dave and his father didn't believe in that. Only four of us, besides the funeral director and three gravediggers, were at the cemetery: Dave, his father, Yolanda and me. The funeral director said the Twenty-third Psalm and that was it.

Dave and I walked off down the path. His father stayed behind. We stopped to light cigarettes and I felt a tap on my back. I turned and looked down at Yolanda.

Her John Wayne voice echoed throughout the quiet cemetery. "Do you get the drift now, kid?"

"What drift?" I asked.

"That could be you about to push up daisies," she said, motioning with her head in the direction of Bunny's grave.

"Buzz off, Yolanda," Dave said.

"And you too . . . I mean you, too, Mr. Smartass."

"Shove it," he said and grabbed my arm and started walking.

I didn't like him talking to her that way, but I knew he was upset.

Yolanda boomed after us, "Bunny was a good kid. She was sick and she couldn't get helped. It don't have ta be like that with you. She couldn't make it. Some can't . . . but you can, I know."

"Pay no attention to her," Dave said to me.

"Two bigshots," she growled. "Two dumb bigshots." We got to the truck.

"I'd like to belt her one," Dave said, pulling off his tie.

He started up the truck and we roared away. When I looked back Yolanda was standing there looking smaller than ever, shaking her head. I felt horrible. She was like a conscience or something. I'd never told Dave about my brief AA experience so he didn't know that Yolanda was AA or that I knew her except from her place.

"I'm never drinking in her joint again," he mumbled. "Jesus. She could've at least said she was sorry."

"That's what she *was* saying."

"What are you talking about?"

"Nothing."

Dave drove faster than I'd ever seen him drive and directly to the V.S. It was ten-thirty in the morning. We started with beer and ended with vodkas at about five. We sat in a booth and took turns crying.

By the time Dave dropped me at home I was smashed in a way I had never felt before. But I still had certain wits about me. My parents knew about Dave's mother's death and that I'd taken off from work to be with him. So when I came in, a Kleenex practically covering my face, and ran directly to my room, no one questioned me. I knew there would be no sniffing my breath. A few minutes later Jack knocked on my door and asked me if I wanted anything to eat. I said no and no one bothered me again for the rest of the night.

But I bothered plenty of people. I called Linda, Marcelle, my grandparents, Ceil and Kate. Those are the ones I remembered. The death of Amorette became my tragedy as I gulped my Scotch and wept booze tears all over the phone. According to me, Bunny had been: (1) My best friend. (2) Closer to me than my own mother. (3) The only person I'd ever loved. (4) The most positive influence I'd ever had. (5) A courageous and wonderful woman who had a tragic life because no one understood her except me. (6) And finally, she was, though it was a secret, my *real* mother who had

had to give me up at birth! This to Kate Laine, of all people. Of course, it didn't occur to me until the next day that that made my relationship with Dave incestuous!

Well, I ended that night of borrowed tragedy, my head in the toilet, puking up my guts and crying at the same time. And when the knock came on my door to wake me for work, I found myself wedged between the toilet and the sink, smelling of vomit and urine. Just another pretty teenage girl after a real fun night!

And did I go do it again and again?

You betcha!

24

Nothing much happened for about a month. I kept getting real messed up on weekends. During the week it was getting harder not to drink, but I forced myself to keep away from it. In the middle of August my mother went into her room and refused to come out. She also refused to speak—at all. My father begged, bargained and threatened, but nothing did any good. Finally, near the end of August she refused to eat and something had to be done.

My father had an old friend, Dr. Meaker, who worked in a private hospital called Cummings. He called her and she came to see my mother. After an hour with her, Dr. Meaker told my father that Mother should go into the hospital. Fortunately, no men with white coats came. Two days later my father took my mother to Cummings, which was two and a half hours away. He said he'd stay overnight in New York and see Jack and me the next day. It was a Thursday. A weekday. He was gone. She was gone. I could drink. Besides, who could blame me? My mother had been taken off to the bins so who had a better right? No one I knew.

I met Dave after work and we started to really tie one on. We hit a lot of bars, ate some fried chicken from a takeout place, hit some more bars, and then around midnight we got into a fight. It was about our mothers. He said his mother had gone to the bins because she was a drunk, but my mother was really nuts. Then I said maybe my mother was nuts, but his mother was a whore. And it went on like that. This took place driving in the truck. He stopped about half a mile from my house and told me to get the hell out. I said gladly. He drove off. I stood there with my half empty Scotch bottle in my hand. Who needed him when I had that?

The rest of the night was spent in and out of blackouts. Naturally, I can only tell about the parts out of the blackouts, so I'll try and do it just that way.

I take a long swig of my Scotch. I start walking toward home.

Black black black.

I am standing in front of my house on the lawn. It occurs to me I should howl like a wolf. I reject this idea. There is a light on downstairs. Jack's car is in the driveway. My mother's car is in the garage. Dave has been teaching me to drive on Linda's car which is something like my mother's.

Black black black.

I am driving my mother's car down our street. I don't have a license. So what? I drive with one hand and hold the Scotch bottle to my mouth with the other. I keep driving. Out to the main road. I head west. Through one town. Through another town.

Black black black.

The radio is on and I am singing. I am on the expressway. I will go to New York City!

Black black black.

I am driving on the dividing grass. Fear. I stop. I wait. I drink. I start the car again. Carefully, I drive back onto the road, still heading toward New York.

Black black black.

I am driving on the grass on the right side of the road. Fear. I get back on the road. I take the next exit off the expressway. Fear. Where am I? I see a bar. My bottle is empty. I park, no, stop the car. I get out. A man is coming out of the bar. He comes toward me.

Black black black.

I am riding in the passenger seat of a small car. There is a beer can in my hand. It is almost full. I feel happy and drink some. I look at the driver. It is a man. I have seen him before. Yes, the man who came out of the bar. What bar? He drinks from a beer can. He hands me a lit cigarette. I smoke.

He says, "You're real cool, Geri."

I say, "How do you know my name?"

He laughs, showing empty spaces where teeth should be and says: "Don't try and put me on, baby. Old Pete knows the score."

Old Pete, I say to myself. This man with no teeth and gray hair is Old Pete. I drink my beer.

Black black black.

I am sitting on a couch. No, a bed. Dirty madras spread. Peeling paint on walls. A man is coming toward me. He hands me a can of beer. It's Old Pete. He grins at me. I drink. He sits next to me. His arm comes around my shoulder.

Black black black.

I am lying down. There are no lights except those from outside. Something is on top of me. A body. I see a head. Old Pete. I am naked. I scream. Something slams me across the face—hard. I taste blood. I scream. I am hit again, harder.

Black black black.

I am on the floor. What floor? I am naked. It is getting light outside. Fear. Slowly, I sit up. I look around. Peeling paint. Bed. Dirty madras spread. Naked man on bed. Old Pete. My face hurts. My body aches. I look for my clothes. They are scattered everywhere. I quietly get dressed. I find my wallet, check for money. Three dollars and change. As I tiptoe toward the door I pass a dirty mirror. Who is that? Fear. It is me. My nose is swollen, my mouth cut and bruised and my right eye is purple and yellow. Fear. I think of Bunny. Tears come. I must get out of here. Carefully I open the door. I get out.

Outside it is quiet. It must be early. I look at my watch. It is gone. I must have left it up there. Then I realize that my ring and the pendant Dave gave me are gone, too. All with Old Pete. But I can't go back.

Where am I? What town? What state? The car. Where's the car? I begin to cry. Big tears. Help me. Who will help me? I see a phone booth. I go in and pick up phone. Who should I call? Kate. Kate will help me. I put the phone back and open my wallet. I open the zipper part. There is her number. Thank God I carried it there almost as though I'd known. I get out my change. Forty-five cents. I put in a dime and dial Kate's number.

The operator comes on. "What number are you calling, please?"

I tell her.

"What area code is that?"

What area code? Fear? What state am I in? I am afraid to ask. I give her the area code.

"That will be seventy-five cents for the first three minutes, please."

I am a long way from home and I do not have seventy-five cents in change. I ask her to make it a collect call. I hear Kate answer, sleepily. There is a slight pause when she hears my name from the operator and then she accepts the call.

"Hello," she says. "Geri? What's wrong?"

I start to cry.

"Geri? What is it?"

"Help me," I say through my tears. There are no jokes this time.

"Yes, yes. What is it? Where are you?"

"I don't know."

"Are you alone?"

"Yes."

"Look, Geri, I want to help you . . . I'll come get you wherever you are, but I have to know where. What town are you in?"

"I don't know." I was still crying.

"Click for the operator."

I did.

"May I help you?"

"Yes, operator," Kate said. "Can you tell me what town this call is coming from?"

"It is coming from Littlewood in Baldwin County, New York."

That's why the area code business. I lived in Hoover County.

"Thank you, operator. Geri, are you in a house or what?"

"A phone booth."

"Do you know the name of the street?"

I look out of the phone booth. Fortunately it's on a corner and there's a street sign.

"I'm at the corner of Sixth Street and Robinson."

"Okay. I'll get there as soon as I can. It'll take me about an hour."

"An hour?" I'll never live that long.

But I did. I waited in the phone booth, terrified. I was afraid Old Pete would find me and I was afraid I'd faint or vomit. And I was afraid someone would come along and see me looking the way I did. But only a few people passed and they didn't even seem to notice me.

I think that hour was the longest in my life and when Kate pulled up I was ready to jump off the Empire State Building if she asked me to.

"My God," she said when I was seated next to her and she got a good look at me. "My God, you poor baby."

And that opened the floodgates. I cried for the entire hour ride back to her house.

She fixed my cuts, ran a bath for me and put me in bed after feeding me some Tiger's Milk. I slept on and off until about two in the afternoon.

When I got up I was very shaky and I threw up the Tiger's Milk I'd had earlier. I knew the only thing that would make me feel better was a drink and I told her.

"If that's what you really want I'll give it to you, Geri, but it'll just start the cycle all over again. Try and get through this without it. It's not going to be easy and you'll feel like hell, but it'll get better. I promise you that. It will get better."

I started crying again.

About an hour later I was able to get down some tea and keep it down. Then Kate told me that she'd called my father and told him where I was. She said he was very upset, not just about me, but that I was with her. She said we'd have to be patient with him and try to teach him that alcoholism is a disease.

My first reaction was a feeling of anger. I never said I was an alcoholic! Well, then, what the hell was I doing there? I remembered the first of the twelve steps of AA. *We admitted we were powerless over alcohol— that our lives had become unmanageable.*

Well, my life certainly was unmanageable. Powerless over alcohol? I wasn't sure.

When Kate took me home and we walked through the front door, my father began to cry when he saw me. Then I began to cry. And then—and I could hardly believe this—Jack began to cry. We all stood in the middle of the living room holding each other and crying. When the crying was over we sat down and Kate tried to explain to my father and Jack.

"Do you think you're an alcoholic?" my father asked me.

I didn't know what to say. "I don't know."

"Do you drink because you're so unhappy at home?" he asked.

I shook my head. "I liked the way it made me feel. But now . . . it's different now. Oh, Daddy . . . I don't know what to do."

"Do you want Kate to help you?"

"I . . . I guess I do."

"The most important thing," Kate said, "is do you want to stop drinking?"

This time I didn't hesitate. I knew the answer to that. "Yes. Yes, I can't stand it anymore."

"Are you willing to help, Mr. Peters?" she asked.

"George. To help Geri? Of course."

"Jack?"

"Well, yeah. I'm leaving for college day after tomorrow but, sure, I'll help."

"Then tonight there is an Alanon meeting in Eastport that both you and Jack can go to. Alanon is for the families of alcoholics. It will help you understand Geri and yourselves in relation to her. And, Geri, you and I can go to a meeting right here in Goose Bay."

Meetings again. I hated it. "Isn't there some other way?" I asked.

Kate smiled. "Well, you tried it on your own and that didn't work. You could try therapy but its success rate with alcoholics isn't very high. You could take antabuse. . . ."

"What's that?"

"It's a pill. You take it every day and if you drink while it's in your system you get very sick. You can even die."

"But you could just stop taking the pill any time, right?" Jack said.

"Right."

"Are you saying," my father asked, "that AA is the only way?"

"It's the only way *I* know," Kate said. "I tried it on my own and flunked out."

"You mean once a person goes to AA they never drink again?" asked Jack.

"No. It's not that simple. First of all, you have to really want sobriety. And you have to be willing to go to any length to get it. It has to be the most important thing in your life. Going to meetings is part of it. Often, when people in AA drink again, it's because they've drifted away, stopped going to meetings."

"I can't stand the idea of going to those things for the rest of my life."

"One of the first things you have to learn, Geri, is not to think in terms of the rest of your life. You have to learn to live within the moment. Now. Today. Remember . . . one day at a time."

"Who can live like that? You have to plan."

"Sure. I mean, you can plan a vacation or save money for the future or pick a college you want to go to —things like that. But you don't have to think about going to a party next week without drinking. It may never even happen—the party might be canceled or you might be sick or you might not feel like going or any number of things. All you have to worry about is today. You can't really do anything about next week today, can you? And when next week comes and the party is still on and you still want to go and you're still worried about how you'll get through it without drinking, there's plenty of time to deal with it then."

That made sense. But it seemed almost impossible. "Isn't it hard to live like that?"

"Very hard at first. But it gets easier. It's a habit like anything else. Of course, once in a while I forget and start projecting all kinds of things . . . things I can't do anything about that day. Then I get nervous and irritable and sometimes I think about drinking."

"So what do you do?"

"I go to an AA meeting." She laughed. "I know that's not the answer you wanted to hear. But it's the truth."

"Well, how can I go looking like this?"

"Geri, an AA meeting is probably the one place in this town that you *can* go looking like that. There's not a person there who won't understand."

So I went. And my father and Jack went to Alanon.

This meeting was in a different town from the other one I'd gone to although some of the same people were there.

Kate had been right. No one looked at my bruised, horrible face and snickered or whispered. They came up and took my hand and some who'd seen me before said they were glad to see me again—glad I was back and hoped they could help. Yolanda was there. She put her arm around me, hugged me and for once said nothing. Everything she needed to say was in that hug.

I heard a lot of things that night. As much as I thought I didn't want to be there, a big part of me must have wanted to be. Some of the things I heard were "Stay away from people, places and things that make you think about drinking." "It's not how much you drink, it's what happens to you when you drink." "Don't get too tired, too hungry or too lonely." "It's the first drink that gets you drunk." "Alcohol is cunning, baffling, powerful." "Be good to yourself." "Alcoholism is a twofold disease: a physical allergy coupled with a mental obsession." "The only requirement for membership is a desire to stop drinking." "Alcoholism is one of the few reversible diseases." "Everyone has their own Bowery."

There were also some slogans hung on the walls. THINK. LIVE AND LET LIVE. EASY DOES IT. FIRST THINGS FIRST. Corny? You said it. Just looking at them embarrassed me so I stopped looking. Months later they began to make sense and mean something to me.

Feeling as sick and awful as I did that night kept me from reacting with too much hostility. But there was still a part of me that wasn't convinced and Kate knew it.

"It takes time with some people, Geri. Be patient. Alcohol can be very patient . . . it'll always be there waiting for you. There's plenty of time to go back to it if this doesn't work for you. Give it a try, okay?"

I said I would.

Jack and my father got home a few minutes after I did.

"We'll do anything we can to help you," my father said.

I felt like snapping at him that he'd obviously gotten a good brainwashing but I was too tired so I just thanked him.

After I'd gotten into bed, Jack knocked on my door.

"I just wanted you to know," he said, "that I'm sorry I haven't been more understanding and more helpful."

I shrugged. "How could you know?"

"Yeah, I guess. The police called a few minutes ago. They found Mom's car. Dad and I'll get it tomorrow."

I felt too guilty to answer.

"Well, if you want to rap or anything. . . ."

"Thanks."

He started to leave then stopped and looked at me. "It's funny, you know."

"What is?"

"That you're the one who ended up with a disease!"

I smiled. "You'll get one one of these days, Jack. Don't give up."

We both laughed and then he did an extraordinary thing. He walked over to the bed and he kissed me on the cheek. What would you have done at that moment? I kissed him back.

After he left I curled up with Tansy and Max and turned out my light. How could he have kissed me? I was so disgusting. I was fat and ugly and I'd spent the night with some awful man I didn't even know. Then I heard Kate's words: *You're not a bad person, Geri . . . you're a sick person.* Okay, so I was sick. I had a disease. But why me? Why me? I kept saying it over and over in my head. A man at the meeting had said he felt lucky to be an alcoholic. He must be crazy. How could he feel lucky? I knew I'd never feel like that. I'd go through life feeling horrible and empty, never having any fun, never having any friends. Who would my friends be? Those old fogies in AA? I wouldn't be able to hang out with Linda and the kids and not drink. And what about Dave?

We'd had that fight but who knew if he'd even remembered. Of course, he hadn't called me—well, maybe he had and no one was home. Then I remembered. If we did make up maybe it would be all right because Dave was going to be eighteen in September. In three weeks, in fact. And he was going to quit drinking when he was eighteen, wasn't he? But what if he didn't? What if he couldn't? What would happen to our relationship then? Wait a minute—hold it. I remembered Kate's words. I didn't have to solve any of this *now*. Maybe I was depressed and maybe the future seemed bleak but at least I wasn't drunk. I was in my own bed and though I had a battered face and an aching body I was safe. For now. And that's all there was. Now. It didn't matter what had happened in the past and I couldn't do anything about tomorrow. Now. That's all I had. That's all anyone ever had. I fell asleep.

25

The next few weeks held few smiles for me. Jack had gone to school and it was just Daddy and me in the house. Though he was still going to Alanon meetings and trying to be helpful and talk with me I knew he was very distracted by my mother's illness. I couldn't think about her. Kate said that was understandable and that when I could I would. She said AA was a selfish program. For now I had to do what made me most comfortable and stay away from things that would upset me until I was ready to handle them.

I went to meetings every night. Kate usually took me, but a few times I rode with Dean and Aileen, a husband and wife team. They were very nice, but I couldn't ever think of anything to say to them. Sometimes I even went alone and my father drove me and picked me up.

The worst problem was Dave. The day after everything happened I stayed home from work, but I went in the next day. At five o'clock when I left Dave was parked outside.

"Jesus, what happened to you?" he asked, accompanying it with a long, low whistle.

"It's a long story. Listen, Dave, I want to talk to you."

"About the other night," he said, "we both were bombed, right?"

"Right."

"So we can just forget it, okay?"

"Sure," I said. "But I want to talk to you."

"We're talking," he said, giving me a smile that made

me want to forget everything I knew I had to say to him.

"Can we go someplace?" I asked.

He started up the truck. "The V.S.?"

"No. No bar, please."

"You afraid to let them see you like that?"

"I'd rather not."

"Well, people saw you all day at work, didn't they?"

"Yes. I'd just rather not go there, okay?"

"Okay." Then he rattled off the names of some other bars.

"I'd prefer not going to any bar."

He looked at me a moment then swung the truck up toward the water.

When we got to the beach, we parked and walked a bit before we sat down in the sand. It was the same spot we'd gone that very first night. How long ago that seemed. He opened his thermos and offered it to me. I said no.

"Why not?" he asked.

"I'm allergic," I said.

"Since when?"

"Since always, I guess."

He took a long swig from the thermos. "I think you're flipping out."

"I was. Not now." I knew I was being cryptic and I knew it unfair to him but I just couldn't bring myself to explain. How could I tell him? What could I say? Then I thought of Bunny. "I'm like Bunny was," I said.

"What are you talking about?"

I took a deep breath and started talking. I told him everything I could remember about what had happened. He didn't say anything. He didn't try to interrupt me. He just listened and drank. When I was finished he looked at me.

"Are you trying to tell me you're an alcoholic?"

"Yes," I said, and realized that was the first time I'd actually admitted it.

"That's a crock. If you are, then I am."

I shrugged.

"Well, I'm not," he said angrily. "I could stop any time and it wouldn't bother me a bit."

"So, why don't you?"

"Because I don't want to. I told you . . . I'll stop when I'm eighteen."

I nodded. "That's only three weeks away."

Dave stood up and walked toward the water. He skimmed a few rocks along the surface. He was angry. Why? I waited for him to come back and finally he did.

"Are you telling me that you're not going to drink anymore?"

"Yes." I couldn't believe I'd said it.

"Well, what *are* you going to do?"

"What do you mean?"

"For fun?"

"I don't know. I just know I'm not going to drink . . . today."

"Today? You mean you might drink tomorrow?"

"I don't know about tomorrow. I only know about today."

"Oh, don't hand me that crap, Geri. I'll tell you this . . . I'm not hanging around with any goody-goody . . . I don't intend to be bored to death."

He couldn't have said anything worse to me. My greatest fear was that sober, I'd be boring. After all, hadn't I been boring before I started to drink? I must have been. Nobody paid any attention to me except B.J. and Carolyn and I knew what the kids thought of them. Even my mother thought I had B.P.

The thing was that I thought sober I was boring and drunk I was Great. Drunk I could talk to anyone. I was funny and bright. I could dance. I could—well, there wasn't anything I couldn't do. But sober? Sober, I was a drag. Boring. So who'd want to be boring if they could be Great? Yet the price I had to pay for being Great was too high—shakes and vomiting and madness and maybe death. It wasn't worth it.

"I'm sorry you feel that way," I said to Dave. "But what about you? When you quit on your birthday will *you* be boring?"

He didn't answer me. He just said, "C'mon, I'm taking you home."

We drove to my house in silence. As I was getting out

of the truck he said, "If you ever want to be a real person again, let me know . . . maybe I'll still be around . . . maybe I won't."

For a moment I wanted to tell him to forget everything I'd said. I wanted to tell him to take me to the V.S. But something stopped me. I got out of the truck and went inside my house without looking back. Kate explained later that Dave was probably threatened by my decision. If he had a problem with alcohol, my not drinking was a constant reminder.

My life for the next few weeks was very lonely even though school had begun. I went to school, came home immediately afterwards, did my homework, cleaned up or shopped for food and prepared dinner. At night I went to a meeting. I hated the meetings. I hated school. I hated my life. I couldn't remember ever having been so miserable. If this was the way life was going to be, I couldn't see the point. I missed the Great Me and everything that went with it. And every day was a battle against the desire to drink. Kate said that was because I hadn't really surrendered. She said I hadn't completely given up. I didn't know what she was talking about.

I hadn't told Linda or any of the other kids about my decision. I didn't have to. Dave did it for me. Some of them, like Marcelle, made snide remarks to me but Linda said nothing. Then, about three and a half weeks after I'd stopped drinking, we bumped into each other one day in the john.

"Geri," she said, "all the kids are coming over this afternoon. Why don't you come, too? We miss you. I don't care if you don't drink."

And I knew she didn't. Drinking wasn't really that important to her. I wanted very much to go, but I didn't know if I could handle it. I thought of what I'd heard at meetings: *People, Places and Things.* Stay away from people, places and things that make you think about drinking.

"I'll think about it," I said.

She told me to meet her at her locker if I decided to go. I thought about it all afternoon. I thought of asking Kate what to do, but I was pretty sure she'd tell me not to go. Right before the last bell I decided that if sobriety was going to mean that I'd live the rest of my life the way I had been living the last three and a half weeks, it just wasn't worth it. That kind of thinking —thinking about the rest of my life—was, of course, my first mistake. I met Linda at the lockers.

There's no point in going into a lot of detail. I'm sure you've guessed what happened anyway. But briefly, this is what took place. For the first half hour I drank Coke and said very little. I couldn't think of anything to say. Then I decided that a Scotch or two wouldn't hurt me—it would just take the edge off things and relax me a little. That, of course, was the beginning of the end. By five-thirty I was dead drunk and puking. Somehow in my drunkenness I managed to call Kate. She came and got me and took me to her house where I puked some more. By seven-thirty I had the most horrendous hangover of my life.

I hadn't really drunk that much. I mean, in the past I had drunk a lot more than that in the same amount of time. But the most important thing was that while I *was* drinking, I didn't really enjoy it. It didn't even make me talkative. It just made me feel guilty. I sat in a corner by myself hating everyone. Kate said that AA was bound to ruin anyone's drinking even if it did nothing else. I agreed with that one hundred percent. She also reminded me that alcoholism was a progressive illness. It advances in your body even when you're not drinking. That sounded pretty far out to me but judging by my performance that afternoon, I suppose it was possible.

As sick and horrible as I felt, I went to a meeting that night. I don't know if it was because I was hungover and feeling very vulnerable or what, but that meeting was a turning point for me. I cried through the whole thing. For the first time I didn't feel angry sitting there and for the first time I didn't wish I was somewhere else. I even felt the people weren't my enemies anymore. I knew they understood me, and more important, I knew they cared. That was near the end of September. The beginning of the beginning.

26

After that experience I went back to school knowing that the Great Me was dead—the Late Great Me. Now I was just Me. And that was enough.

Dave had not come back to school and was working full time for Mr. Bless. His birthday had come and gone and he was still drinking. He was also going with Marcelle. Losing him was terribly hard, but I knew that as long as he was drinking and putting me down for not drinking I couldn't afford him.

In October I heard someone at a meeting say that she realized she wasn't *giving up* something when she stopped drinking, she was *getting rid* of something. I thought about that a lot. I had a disease that was activated by alcohol—it made sense to get rid of the thing that made me sick. If eating lobster gave me hives I wouldn't do it, would I? I began to feel less deprived and that made life a lot easier.

Another thing that happened in October was that I made up with B.J. and Carolyn. I came into homeroom one morning and purposely joined their table. I smiled at my two old friends and slowly Carolyn smiled back at me.

"I've missed you," I said. "I wish we could be friends again."

First they looked at me, then at each other, then back at me.

"We do not drink, you know," B.J. said.

"Neither do I."

"I'd heard that," Carolyn said.

"It's true. I haven't had a drink since the end of September."

"So," B.J. said, "now that your drinking buddies don't want you around you think we're good enough, is that it?"

"I don't want them," I said.

"You think we should forgive and forget, just like that?" B.J. snapped her fingers. "Hmmm?"

"No. Not necessarily. I know I was awful to you and I regret every minute of it. I know it would be very hard for you just to forget it all. But I'd like to try and explain."

Carolyn said, "My uncle is an alcoholic, Geri."

"You know then," I said.

"I'd heard . . . you know what a small town this is," Carolyn said. "My uncle is in AA. Are you?"

"Yes."

She smiled and seemed relieved. "Well, then I guess you're really doing something about it."

B.J. still looked angry, her face screwed up in a million furrows. "How do we know," she said, "that you won't drink again?"

"You don't. I don't. I only know that I won't drink today—hopefully."

"That doesn't sound very secure to me."

"Well, today is all I've got," I said. "It's secure enough for me."

The bell rang for the first class and the three of us walked into the hall.

"You know, Geri, you think you can do anything you please any time you want," B.J. said. "Well, it's not that easy. You're a really selfish person. I know it, you know it and God knows it." She walked away.

Carolyn squeezed my shoulder. "She'll come around . . . she's just stubborn."

I nodded.

"Want to have lunch?" Carolyn asked.

"Yes, very much."

"See you then," she said.

Eventually, B.J. did come around, but we were never as close as we once had been. I guess sometimes there are things you can't put right no matter how hard you try or how much you want them. That was one of the most difficult things I had to learn. I couldn't have everything my way. And I also had to learn to accept the things I could not change. That was a line from a prayer that was used in AA, the Serenity Prayer. It's a favorite of mine. This is the way it goes: "God, grant me the serenity to accept the things I cannot change, the courage to change the things I can, and the wisdom to know the difference." I always left out the God when I said it.

But Carolyn and B.J. were not my only friends. I got to know some other kids by making an effort. And I guess my new attitude showed because kids seemed to seek me out. Don't misunderstand. I didn't suddenly become the hit of my senior class or anything, but I didn't want to be that either. I was happy to have five or six friends and if by the school's standards we were all freaks, I didn't care. I liked them and they liked me and that was all that was important. And, of course, I had my AA friends. Sure, they were much older than I was but, eventually, that didn't matter. What did matter was our common problem. There was always someone I could call if I needed to talk, not just about the desire to drink—that cropped up now and then—but anything.

I don't want to give the impression that life without drinking was a cinch. It wasn't. Drinking was everywhere. Unlike drug taking, drinking is socially acceptable. No—it's more than that. You are considered strange by many people if you don't drink. So it wasn't easy. There was booze at dances—I'd begun to date a few boys, none of whom I liked as much as Dave—and at parties and lots of other places. And when other people got drunk it was boring for me. So it was hard.

But it seemed like something new happened every month. In November I started to draw again. Also a new thought clicked into place. Drinking was no longer a viable alternative for me. That sounds so simple and it is, once you get it. But getting it can be really hard.

Near the end of December, right before Christmas I'd been sober ninety days. Three months! I had learned there were no *musts* in AA so when Aileen asked me if I would tell my story at a meeting I used that. I *must* not speak, you *must* not ask me! I was terrified. Then she reminded me that though there were no musts, there *was* the suggestion that one should not say no to anything in AA. She had me there so I agreed.

I'd spoken often during discussions at meetings and I always said, "My name is Geri and I'm an alcoholic." I was convinced, however, that when I led the meeting I would say, "My name is alcoholic and I'm a Geri." But I didn't. Even though I thought I'd have a heart attack and my whole body was shaking. I told my story. When it was over, I felt wonderful. Geri Peters had spoken to a group of people without the aid of alcohol. Yes, I had been nervous. But so what? I was finding out, daily, that I could do things I *wanted* to do sober.

Another very important thing happened in December. I went to see my mother. My father had been going every weekend, but she didn't begin talking again until early December. Dr. Meaker had felt I shouldn't see my mother until she was speaking.

I was very, very nervous as we drove to Cummings. I hadn't really missed her that much because I'd been so involved in my own life. I'd been completely absorbed in getting well myself. But now that I was about to see her, I missed her. Maybe that doesn't make sense but that's how it was.

I had finally talked about my mother with Kate and I'd expressed very angry feelings about her. Kate said it was all right to feel angry as long as I didn't keep it inside. She said that when my mother was better we would probably both be able to express our anger toward each other but to ask mother's doctor about that. I didn't have to. She brought it up.

"Geri," she said, "your mother is going to tell you some things that will probably make you very angry."

"Like what?"

"I think it's important for her to tell you herself. I'm

warning you about it because I want you to know that if you do feel angry it's all right to express it. Your mother can take it."

Maybe she could take it, but could I?

Dr. Meaker felt it would be best if I saw my mother alone. She showed me to her room and squeezed my hand before she left. I stood in front of the door for what seemed like a very long time. Then I knocked.

"Come in." My mother's voice sounded so small.

She was sitting in a chair near the window and the sun was shining in on her, making her hair sparkle. I thought she looked terrific even though she'd lost a lot of weight.

"Hello, Mother," I said.

At first I was afraid she didn't know who I was, but then she smiled, stood up and stretched out her hand. I crossed the room and took it. It was sweaty and so was mine. I guess we were both nervous. That was something else I had learned—I wasn't unique. I was an individual, but I wasn't unique.

"You look lovely," she said.

I'd lost a great deal of weight by then and my father had bought me a new pantsuit for the occasion. "Thank you," I said. "So do you."

"Thanks. Let's sit down, okay?"

We sat down opposite each other.

"Is it okay if I smoke?"

"If you mean are you allowed, yes. But it isn't okay."

I felt my stomach go into a knot. I guess she sensed it.

"I only mean, Geri, that I wish you didn't smoke. It's not good for you."

"I know. I'll get rid of it when I can." I lit up.

A long heavy silence fell between us as I smoked and she looked at her nails. Finally, she spoke.

"Well, I guess I'd better just plunge in."

"Dr. Meaker told me you had something to tell me and that it might make me mad, if that helps," I said.

"I know she did. Thanks. It's about . . . it's about my past."

I wanted to say that I thought we'd heard enough about that to last a lifetime, but I knew that was being arrogant (part of my disease) so I said nothing.

She smiled. "I guess you probably think you've heard all that, don't you?"

I smiled and nodded.

"Well, as Mr. Jolson would say . . . you ain't heard nothin' yet!"

I laughed. It was a long time since I'd heard my mother make a joke.

"Geri, this isn't easy . . . in fact, I feel like it's the hardest thing I've ever had to do."

"What could be so bad? I've been through a pretty horrible time myself, you know . . . I don't think anything could shock me anymore."

She smiled again. "I know you have, dear, and I want you to tell me all about it if you like."

"After you," I said.

"Got me! Okay, okay . . . no use putting it off. Just say it, Ginger. I did not miss being voted Most Popular by two votes. I missed it by three hundred and twenty-two."

I didn't get it. "Huh?"

"There were three hundred and twenty-two in my graduating class."

"But what about Bill and. . . ."

"It was a lie. Everything I told you was a lie. I wasn't even president of the leftover people. Even *they* thought I was strange."

"But your yearbook?" I didn't want to believe what she was telling me. "All the kids wrote stuff to you. You and Myra had all that fun in typing and the boys. . . ."

"I wrote every one of those myself," she said.

"You couldn't have."

Softly she answered, "But I did, Geri. I used different pens and wrote and printed different ways. Maybe even then I knew that someday I'd be making up a life for other people. Maybe I just needed to see the inscriptions myself. I'm not sure. But I'm sorry. I'm so, so sorry."

I could feel the anger starting up inside me. I lit another cigarette and blew the smoke in her direction. "And that's why the photographs are missing . . . the ones from your teenage years, right? They weren't lost, were they?"

She shook her head. "The few I had, of me alone or with my parents, I threw away. I thought I was doing something good for you, Geri. Of course, it started with George. I didn't want him to know what an outcast I'd been. Then it just grew and grew. I couldn't stop myself."

"Why the hell did you have to say *anything?* If you didn't want me to know you were a creep then you didn't have to say *anything.*"

"I'm sorry, Geri," she said and reached out to touch me.

I pulled away and walked to the other side of the room, my back to her. "Did Daddy know the truth?"

"Not until a few weeks ago."

"What'd he say?"

"He cried."

"He would," I said angrily. I didn't mean that. I don't know why I lashed out that way. I just felt so— so betrayed.

"He said he loved me for me when we met and not because of the person I said I was in the past."

I said nothing.

"Geri, I didn't think I was hurting anyone. I certainly didn't *want* to hurt you. But then when you lied to me about the dance I began to realize what I'd done. Then when all the drinking started—"

"Don't flatter yourself." I spat it at her. "I didn't drink because of you. I mean, well, I guess you did put a little extra pressure on me . . . but I'm an alcoholic and it would have happened eventually anyway."

"Yes, I know. I've been reading about alcoholism. but I didn't know then. I thought it was *all* my fault."

I just stared at her.

"I don't blame you if you hate me, Geri . . . I know I did a dreadful thing to you . . . and to myself," she added.

"Why'd you stop talking altogether?"

"It's complicated, but I'll try and make it simple.

Because of my complete isolation as a girl . . . I was
always so afraid of other people . . . so shy . . . I made
up this whole life. And then it backfired. When I saw
that you were lying and drinking I started to get dis-
oriented. I didn't know what the truth was. I didn't
know what was real and what wasn't. I stopped talking
because I didn't want to lie anymore and I couldn't
face telling the truth."

I didn't know what to say.

"I'm trying to understand your illness, Geri. Won't
you try and understand mine?"

Something happened when she said that. Maybe it
was her acceptance of me. I don't know. But I realized
that all of what she'd told me was in the past and there
was nothing I could do about it. I had to accept something I could not change. She was better *now*. That
was the important thing.

"I'll try," I said.

Slowly we moved closer to each other and then we
were hugging. My God, hugging is good! We hugged for
a long time. When we sat down, I told her everything
that had happened to me and much of what I'd learned
in AA. She showed me the books she was reading and
said that when she came home she was planning to go
to Alanon with Daddy.

When Dr. Meaker returned and said it was time for
my mother to rest, we hugged again and I said I would
come back the following week. Just before I left she
stroked my cheek with the back of her fingers and
kissed me on the forehead. Then she said, "Geri . . . I
want you to know something."

"What?" I asked.

"I want you to know that I . . . I like you. Just the
way you are."

"I like you, too. Just the way *you* are." And I did.

Now it is the end of March and Mother has been
home a little over a month. She's a very different person
and it will take time to get used to her this way. I do
like her much better than the Ginger she used to be
and so, it seems, does my father. They are trying to get
to know each other all over again and they're finding

out that they do have some mutual interests besides their children. My father's home a lot more now and though we all still have our problems with each other there is a certain kind of peace in the house. Jack will be home at Easter. And we have a new cat named Gilda, who spends all her time lying on her back posing.

One thing hasn't changed. In fact, it's going on right now. My mother still plays her music. She says she really likes it and Dr. Meaker says there's nothing wrong with that. So, at this writing, I hear strains of something called "Mule Train" by Frankie Laine drifting up to my room.

I've been sober six months now. I weigh one hundred and ten again and I really like me. I keep learning new things about myself all the time. And about other people, too. I've been doing a lot of drawing and painting and I've decided that next year I'll go to the School of Visual Arts in New York, if they'll have me. My parents say it's all right with them. They'd rather see me go to a regular college, but we've all learned to respect each other's right to do with our lives as we wish.

Today a wonderful thing happened. Marcelle called me and said she wanted to stop drinking. So tonight I am going to take her to her first meeting. Who would ever have thought that Marcelle would do that? Who would ever have thought that Geri Peters could help someone else stop drinking? I know it might not work. Maybe Marcelle won't take to it. Maybe she'll drink again—but at least I can try. After all, trying is what it's all about, isn't it? What do you say to that? I say, yes!

ABOUT THE AUTHOR

SANDRA SCOPPETTONE, a novelist, screenwriter and playwright, has had her work produced on television and film, as well as on the stage. In 1972 she received a Eugene O'Neill Memorial Theatre Award and the following year was given a grant by the Ludwig Vogelstein Foundation. Her novel *Trying Hard to Hear You* was selected by the American Library Association as one of the best young adult books of 1974. She now lives in Greenport, New York.